WHERE ARE YOU LEOPOLD?

THE INVISIBILITY GAME

BY SCHMITT & CAUT

BiG

Michel-Yves Schmitt
Writer

Vincent Caut
Artist

•

Miceal Beausang-O'Griafa
Translator

•

Fabrice Sapolsky
US Edition Editor

Amanda Lucido
Assistant Editor

Vincent Henry
Original Edition Editor

Jerry Frissen
Senior Art Director

Fabrice Giger
Publisher

Rights and Licensing – licensing@humanoids.com
Press and Social Media – pr@humanoids.com

WHERE ARE YOU, LEOPOLD?, BOOK 1: THE INVISIBILITY GAME. This title is a publication of Humanoids, Inc.
8033 Sunset Blvd. #628, Los Angeles, CA 90046. Copyright © 2020 Humanoids, Inc., Los Angeles (USA).
All rights reserved. Humanoids and its logos are ® and © 2020 Humanoids, Inc.
Library of Congress Control Number: 2019920399

 is an imprint of Humanoids, Inc.

First published in France under the title "*Où es-tu Léopold ?*" Copyright © 2013 La Boîte à Bulles & Michel-Yves Schmitt, Vincent Caut.
All rights reserved. All characters, the distinctive likenesses thereof and all related indicia are trademarks
of La Boîte à Bulles Sarl and / or of Michel-Yves Schmitt, Vincent Caut.

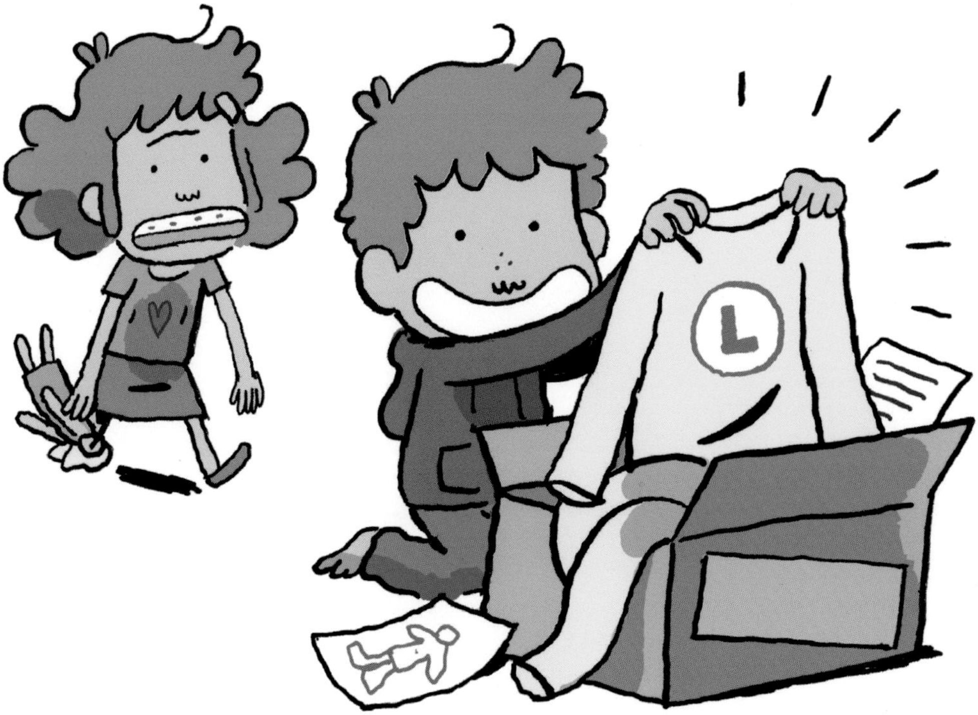
L

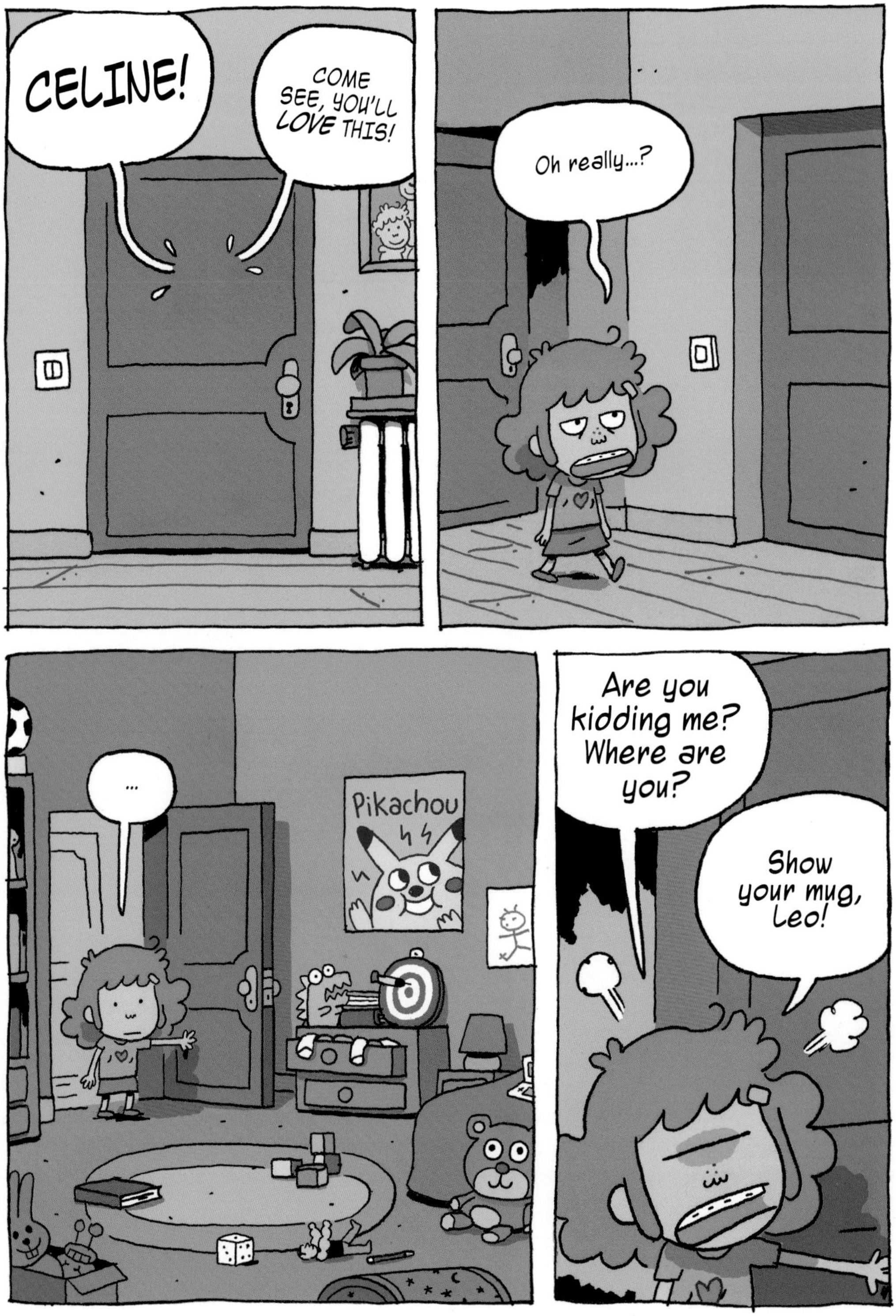
CELINE!
COME SEE, YOU'LL LOVE THIS!
Oh really...?
...
Pikachou
Are you kidding me? Where are you?
Show your mug, Leo!

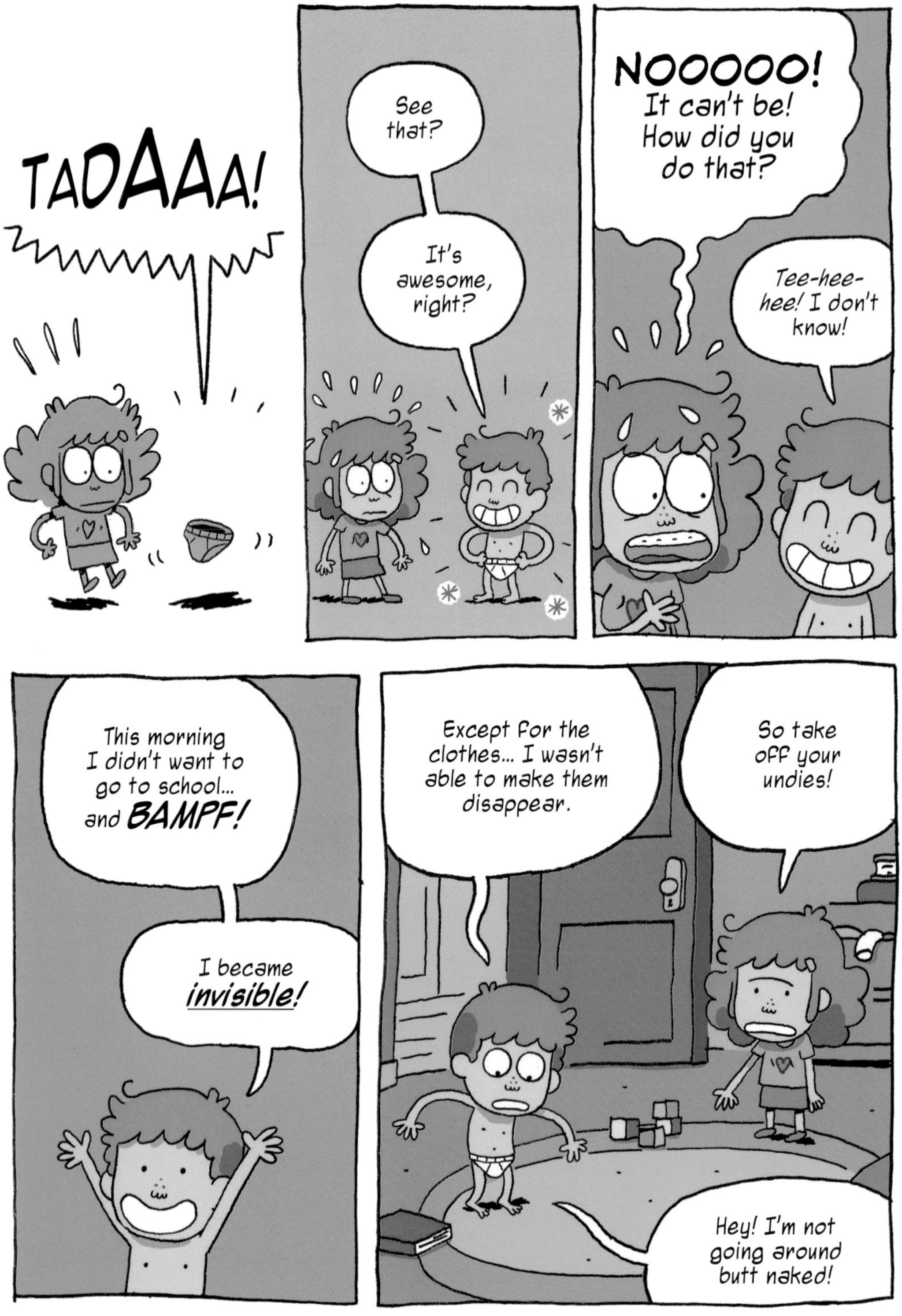
TADAAA!
See that?
It's awesome, right?
NOOOOO! It can't be! How did you do that?
Tee-hee-hee! I don't know!
This morning I didn't want to go to school... and BAMPF!
I became invisible!
Except for the clothes... I wasn't able to make them disappear.
So take off your undies!
Hey! I'm not going around butt naked!

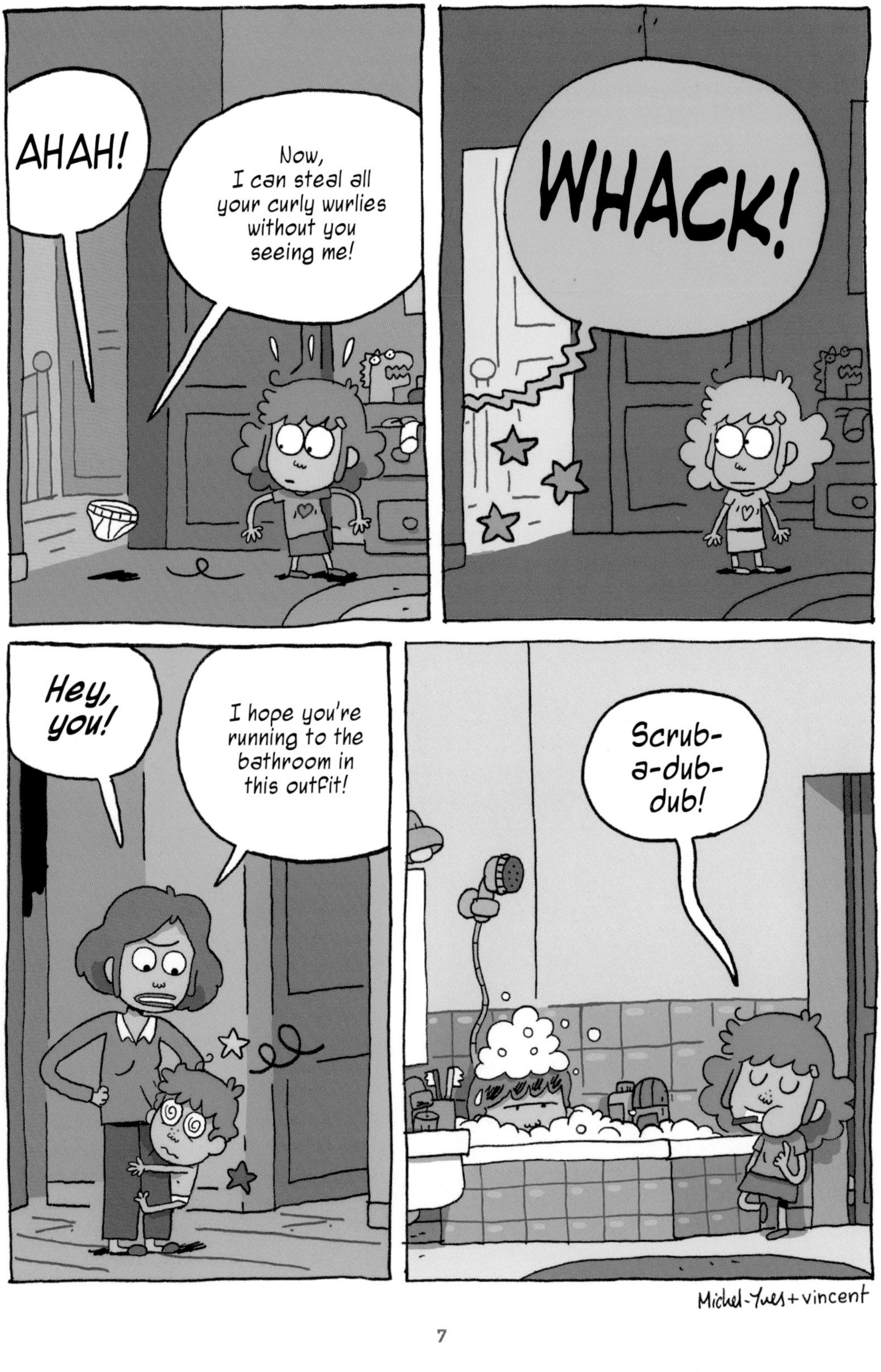
AHAH!
Now, I can steal all your curly wurlies without you seeing me!
WHACK!
Hey, you!
I hope you're running to the bathroom in this outfit!
Scrub-a-dub-dub!
Michel-Yves + vincent

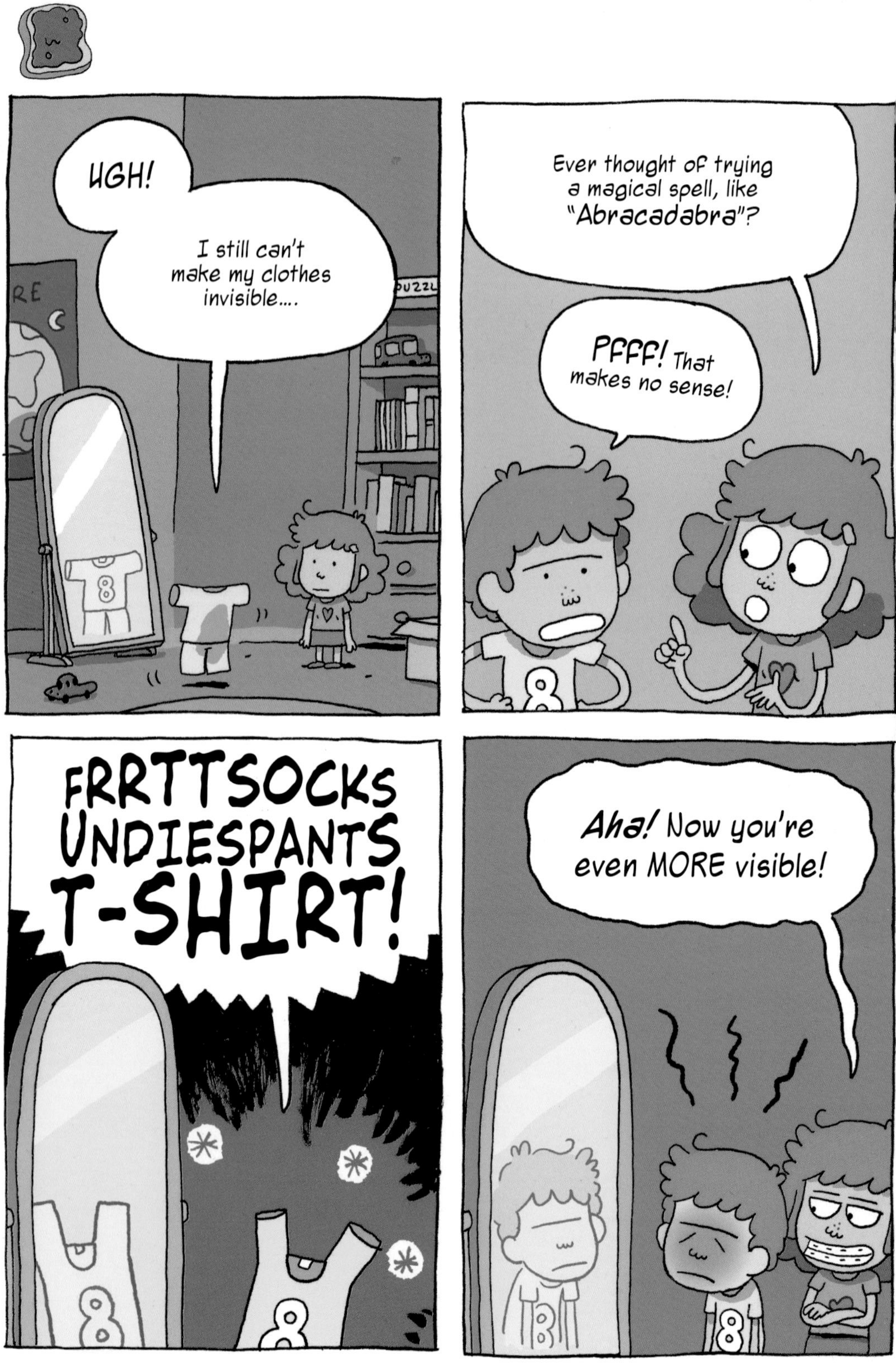
UGH!
I still can't make my clothes invisible....
Ever thought of trying a magical spell, like "Abracadabra"?
PFFF! That makes no sense!
FRRTTSOCKS UNDIESPANTS T-SHIRT!
Aha! Now you're even MORE visible!

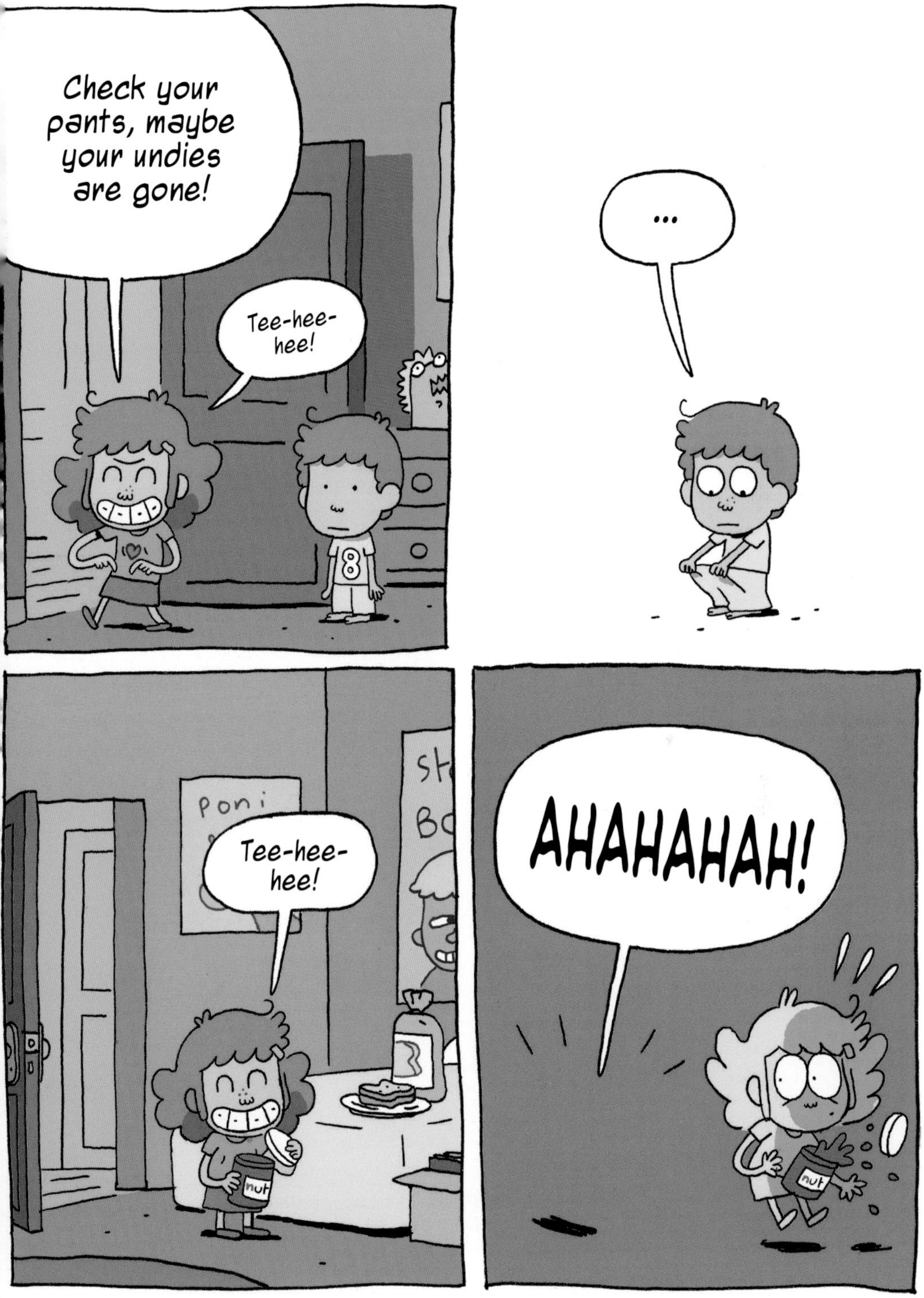
Check your pants, maybe your undies are gone!
Tee-hee-hee!
...
poni
Tee-hee-hee!
nut
AHAHAHAH!
nut

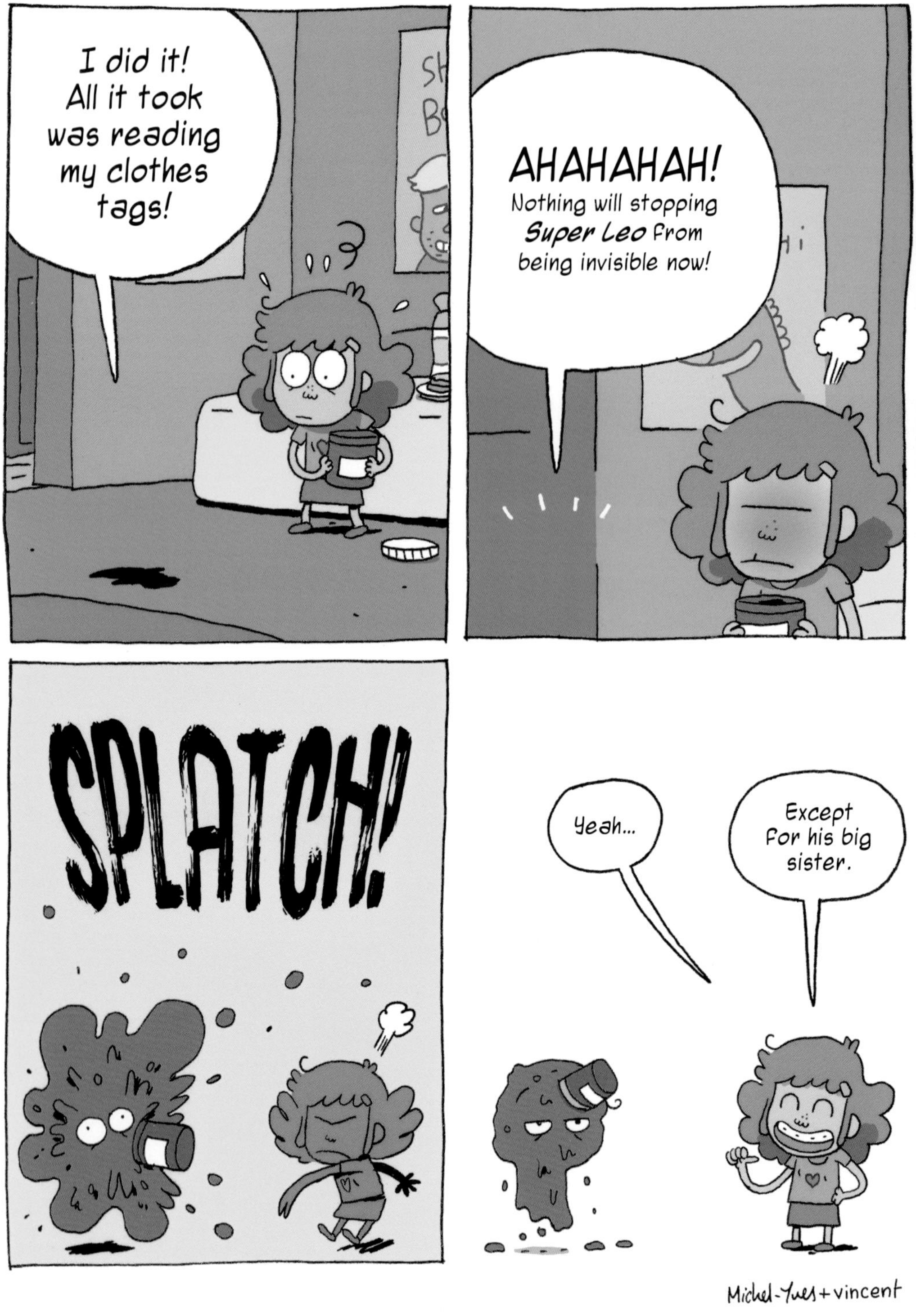
I did it! All it took was reading my clothes tags!
AHAHAHAH! Nothing will stopping Super Leo from being invisible now!
SPLATCH!
Yeah...
Except for his big sister.
Michel-Yves + vincent

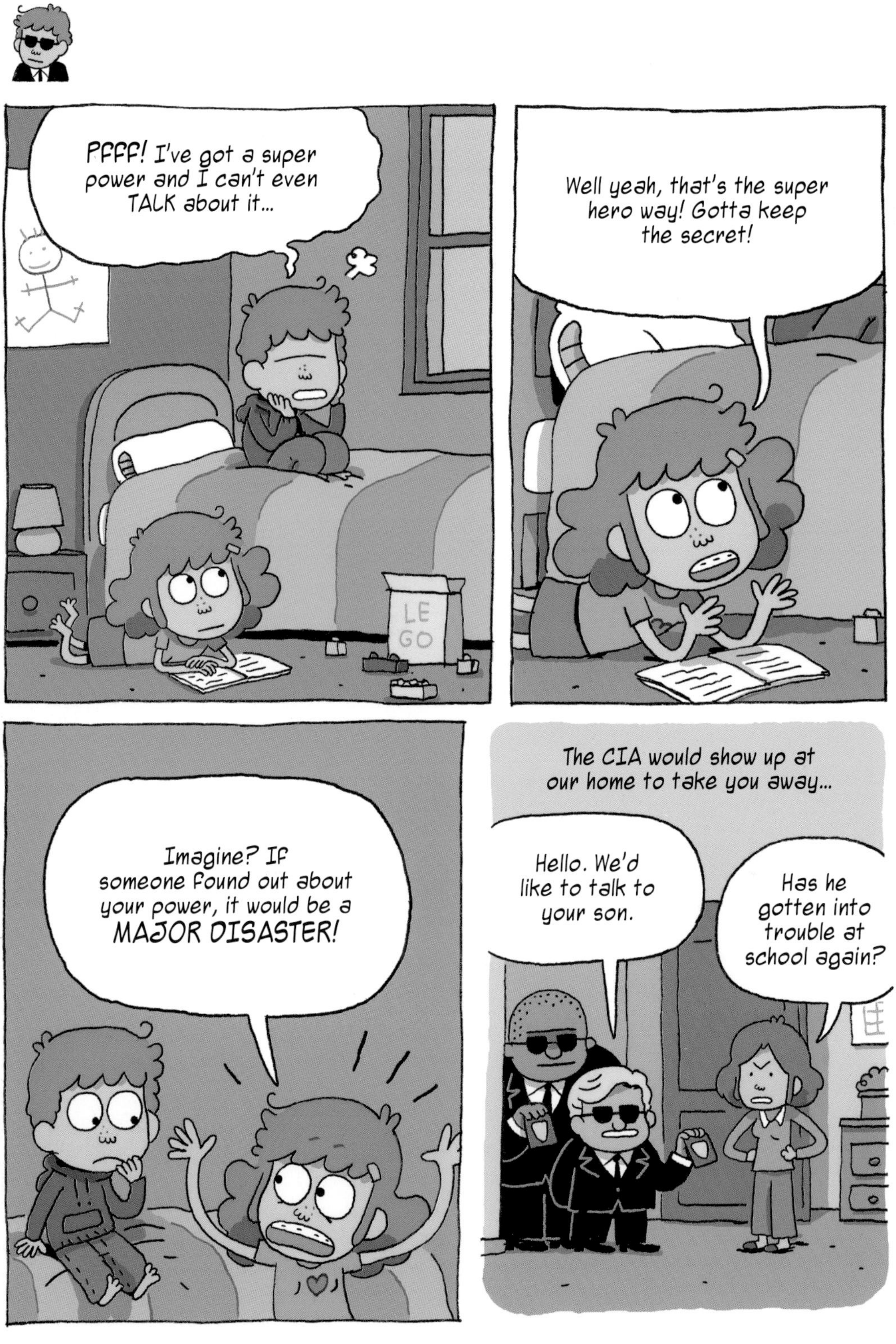
PFFF! I've got a super power and I can't even TALK about it...
LE GO
Well yeah, that's the super hero way! Gotta keep the secret!
Imagine? If someone found out about your power, it would be a MAJOR DISASTER!
The CIA would show up at our home to take you away...
Hello. We'd like to talk to your son.
Has he gotten into trouble at school again?

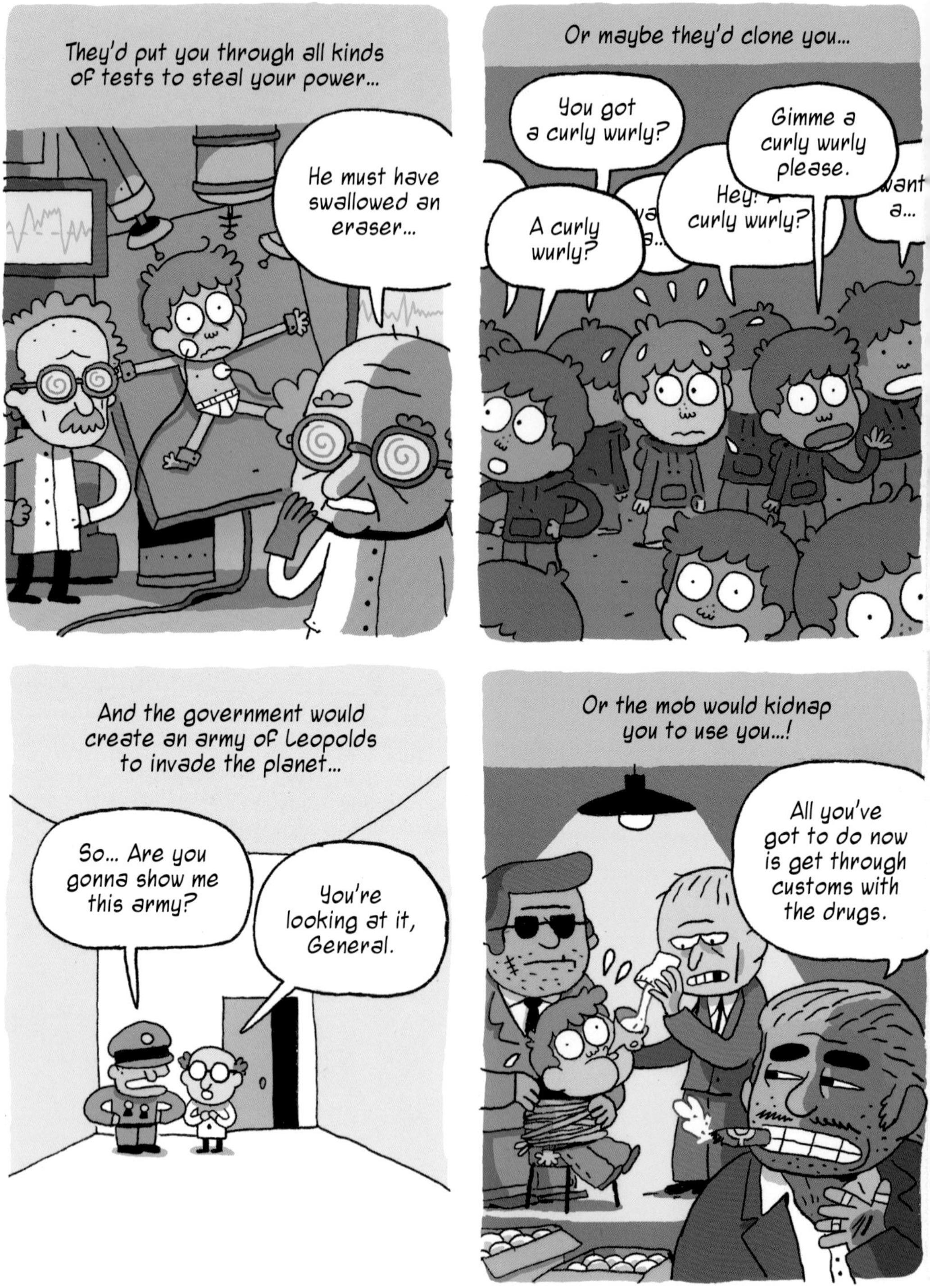
They'd put you through all kinds of tests to steal your power...
He must have swallowed an eraser...
Or maybe they'd clone you...
You got a curly wurly?
A curly wurly?
Hey! A curly wurly?
Gimme a curly wurly please.
And the government would create an army of Leopolds to invade the planet...
So... Are you gonna show me this army?
You're looking at it, General.
Or the mob would kidnap you to use you...!
All you've got to do now is get through customs with the drugs.

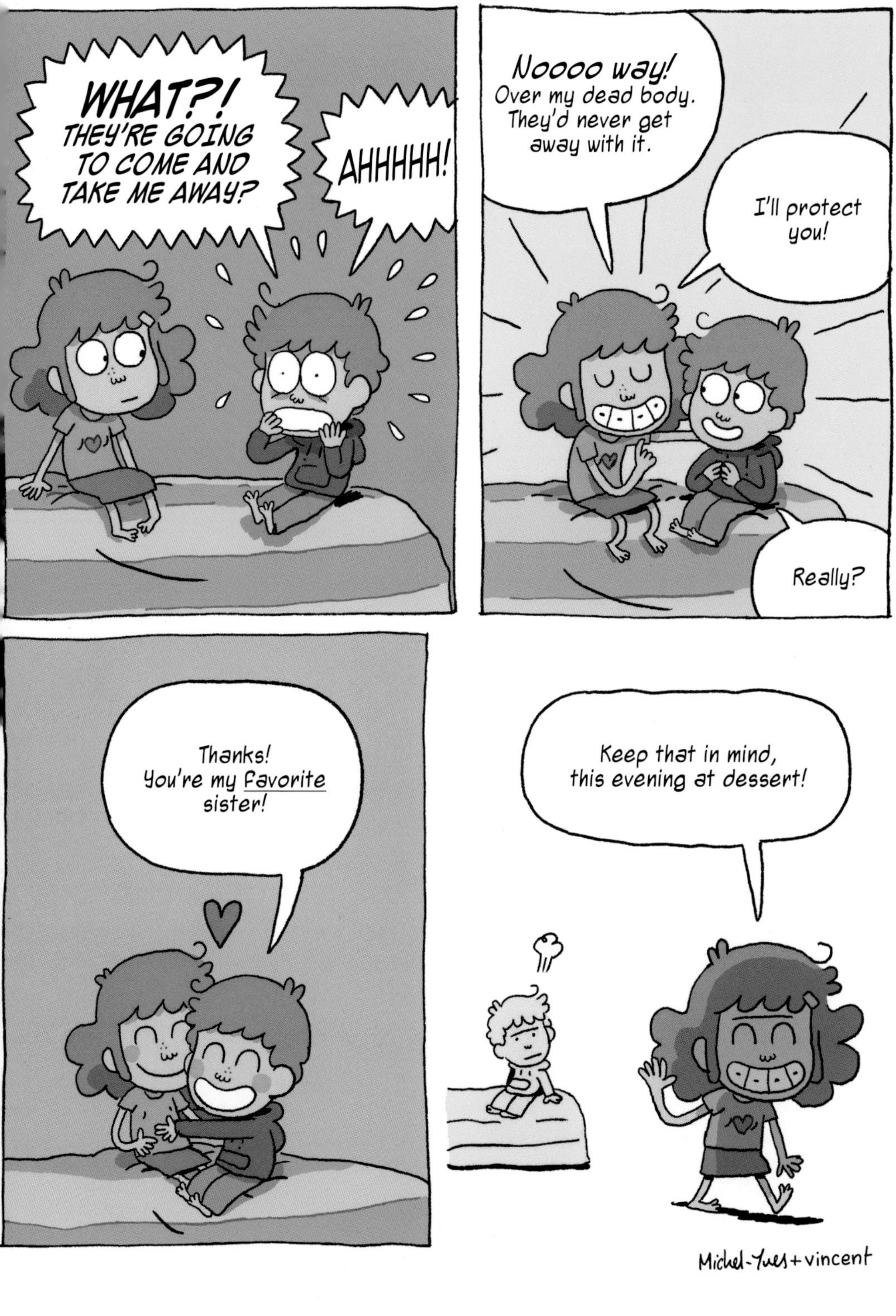
WHAT?! THEY'RE GOING TO COME AND TAKE ME AWAY?
AHHHHH!
Noooo way! Over my dead body. They'd never get away with it.
I'll protect you!
Really?
Thanks! You're my favorite sister!
Keep that in mind, this evening at dessert!
Michel-Yves + vincent

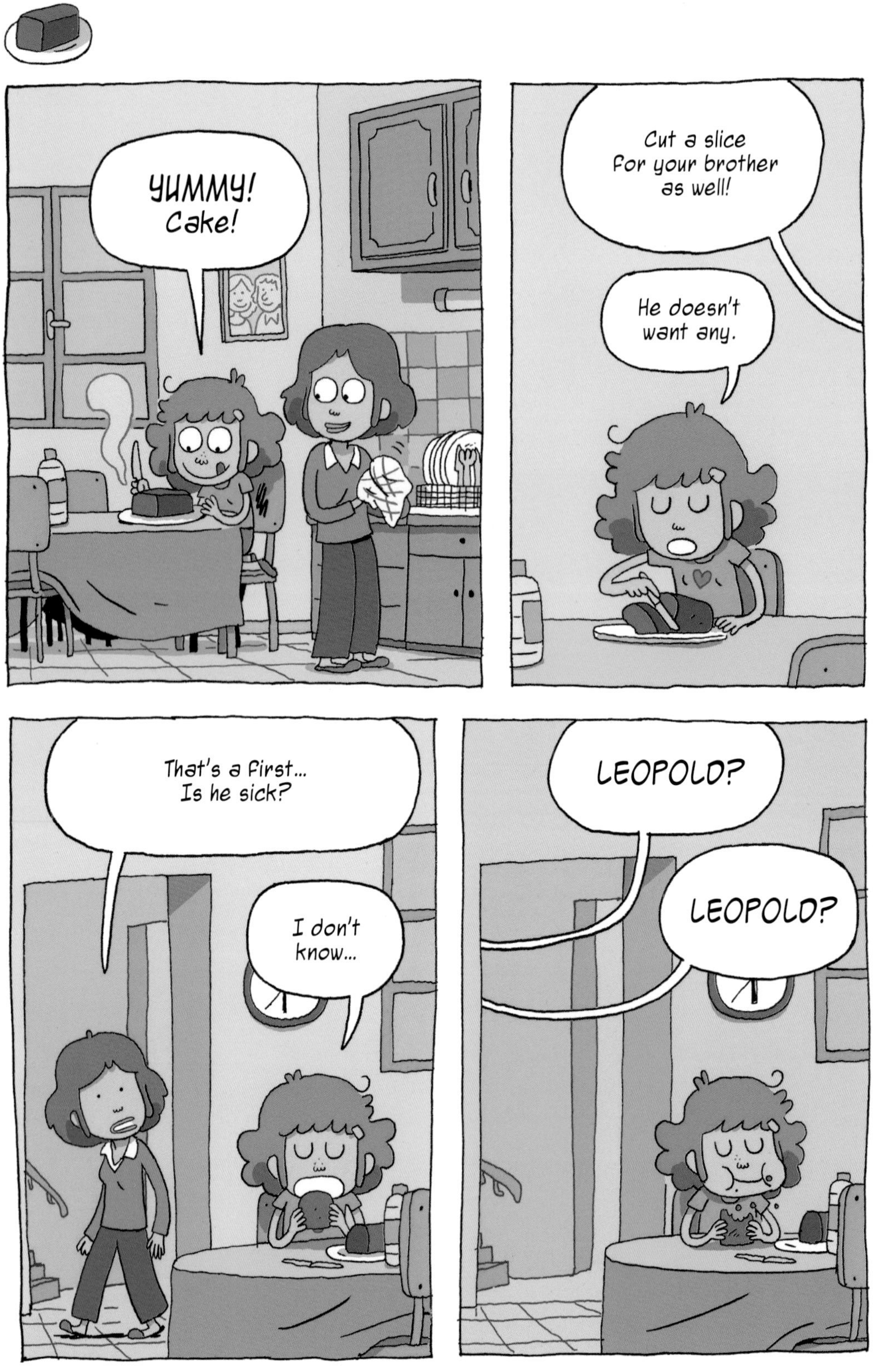
YUMMY!
Cake!
Cut a slice for your brother as well!
He doesn't want any.
That's a first... Is he sick?
I don't know...
LEOPOLD?
LEOPOLD?

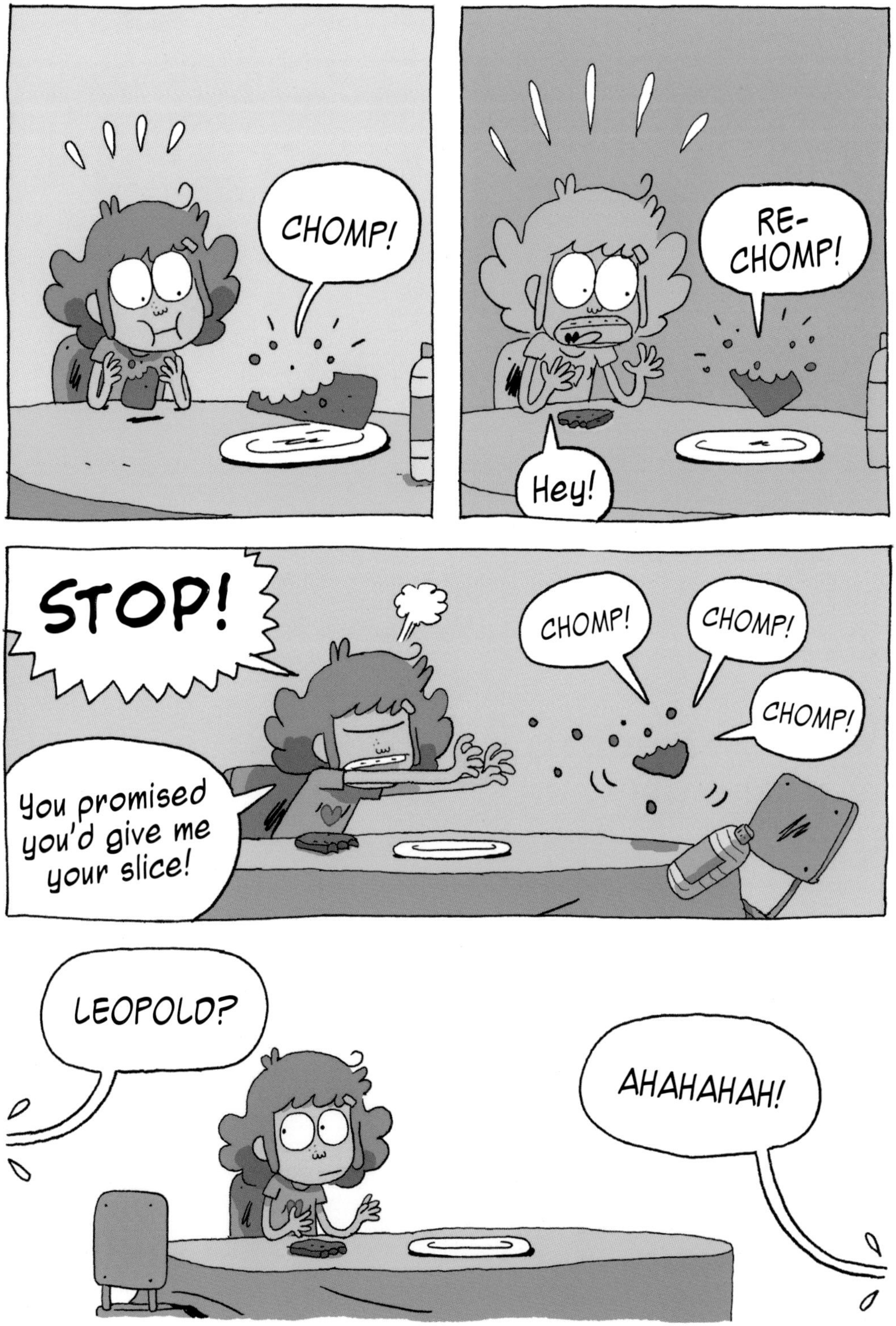
CHOMP!
RE-CHOMP!
Hey!
STOP!
You promised you'd give me your slice!
CHOMP!
CHOMP!
CHOMP!
LEOPOLD?
AHAHAHAH!

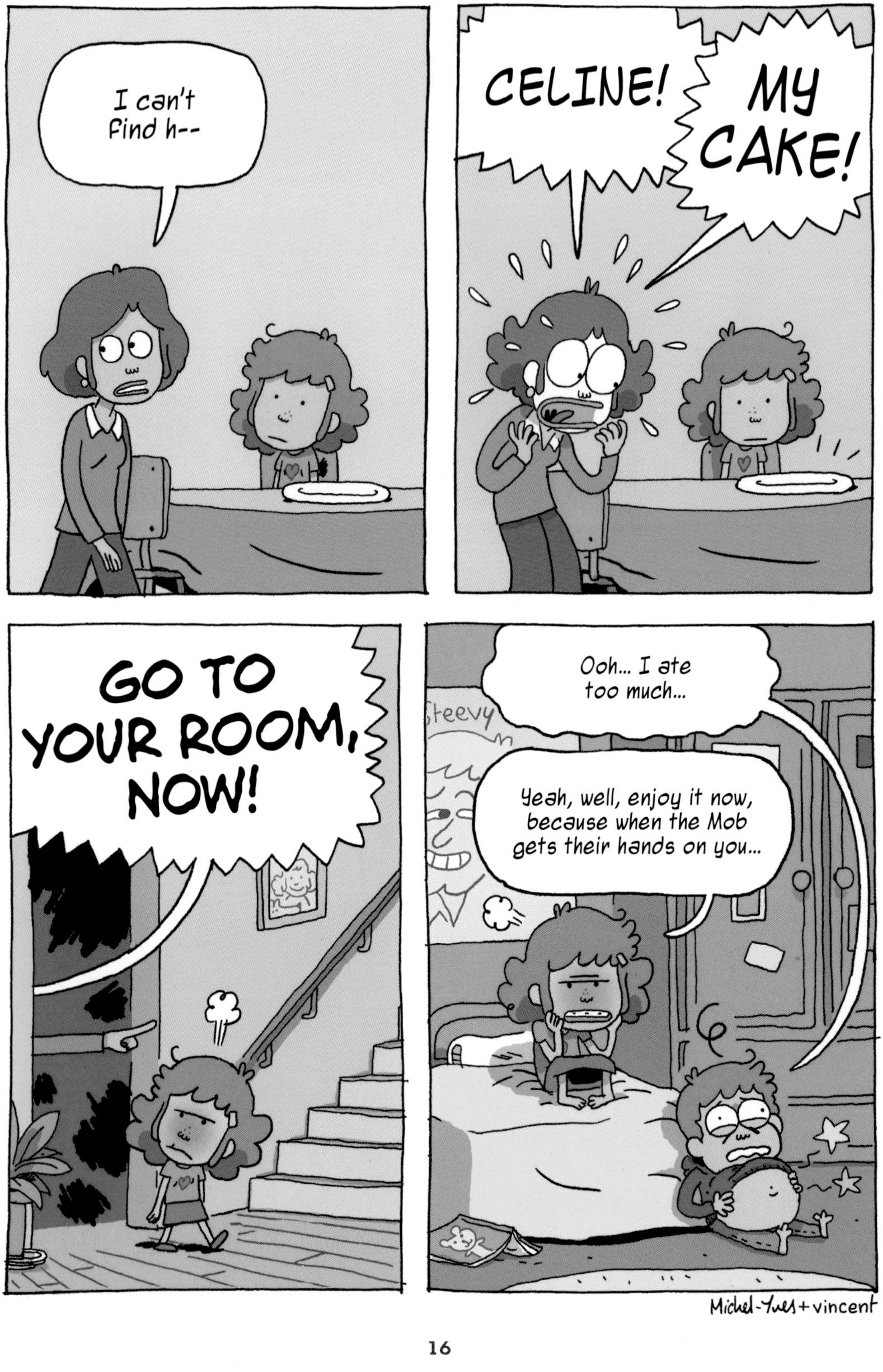

I can't find h--
CELINE!
MY CAKE!
GO TO YOUR ROOM, NOW!
Steevy
Ooh... I ate too much...
Yeah, well, enjoy it now, because when the Mob gets their hands on you...
Michel-Yves + vincent

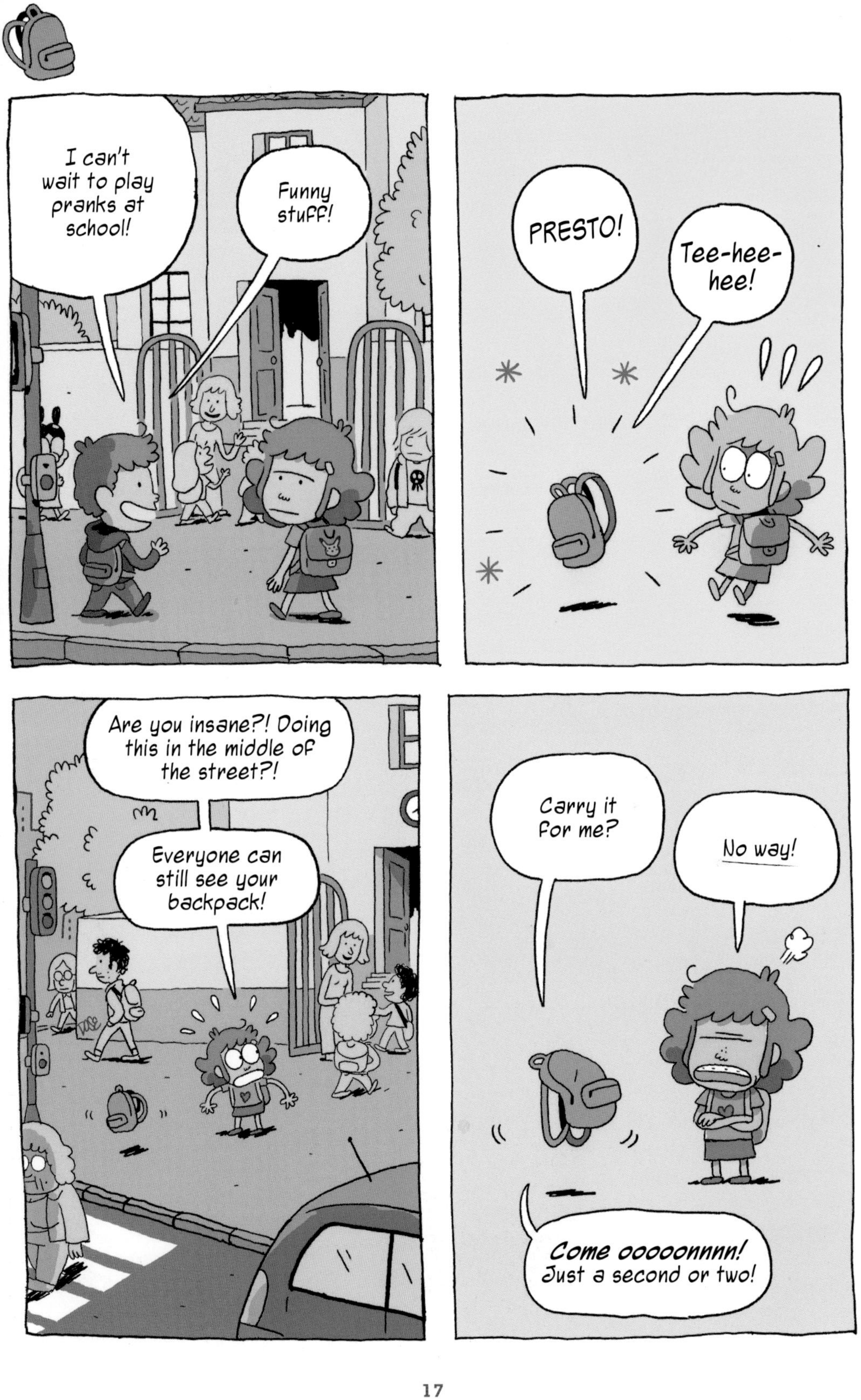
I can't wait to play pranks at school!
Funny stuff!
PRESTO!
Tee-hee-hee!
Are you insane?! Doing this in the middle of the street?!
Everyone can still see your backpack!
Carry it for me?
No way!
Come oooonnnn! Just a second or two!

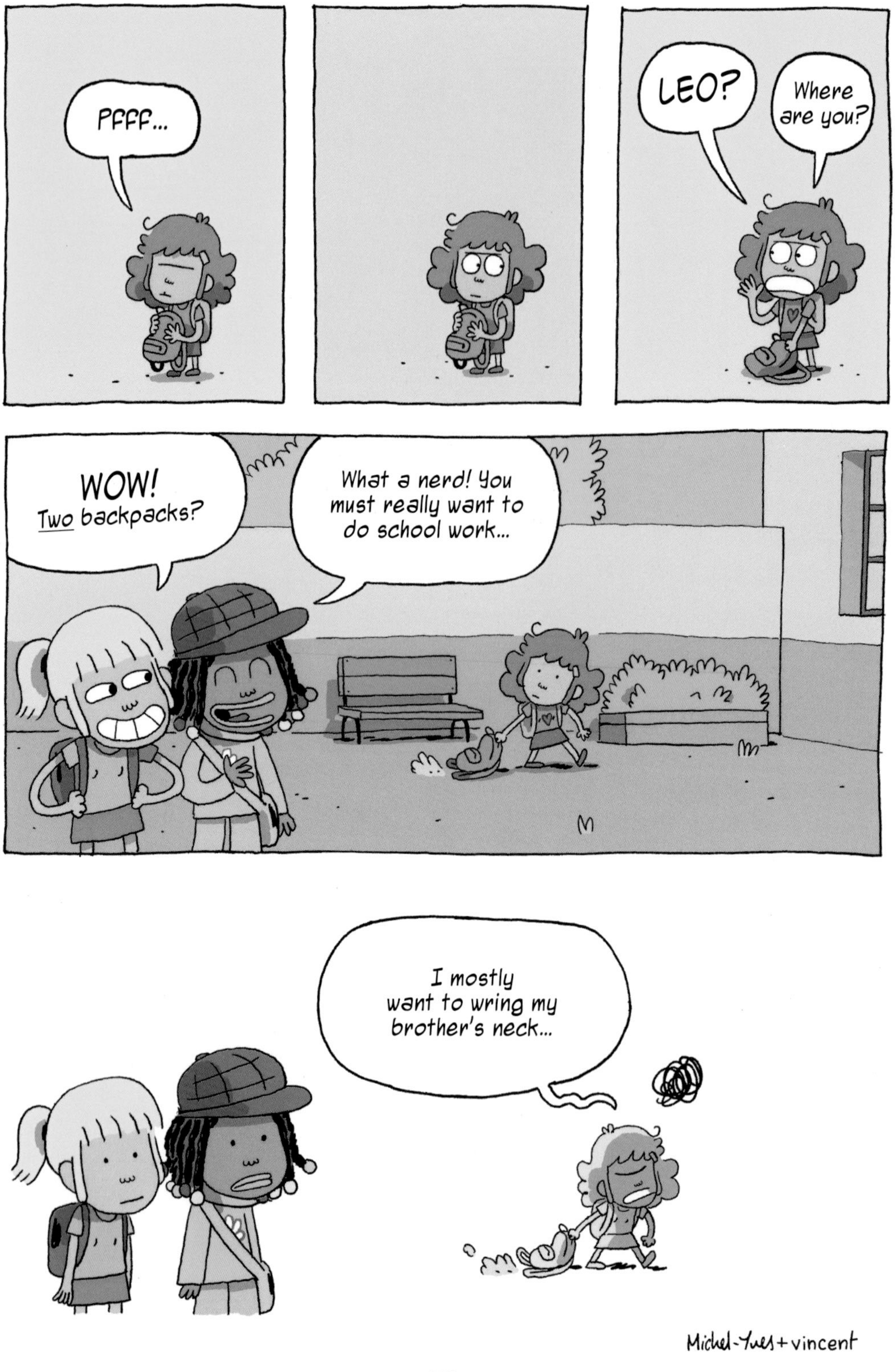
PFFF...
LEO?
Where are you?
WOW!
Two backpacks?
What a nerd! You must really want to do school work...
I mostly want to wring my brother's neck...
Michel-Yves+vincent

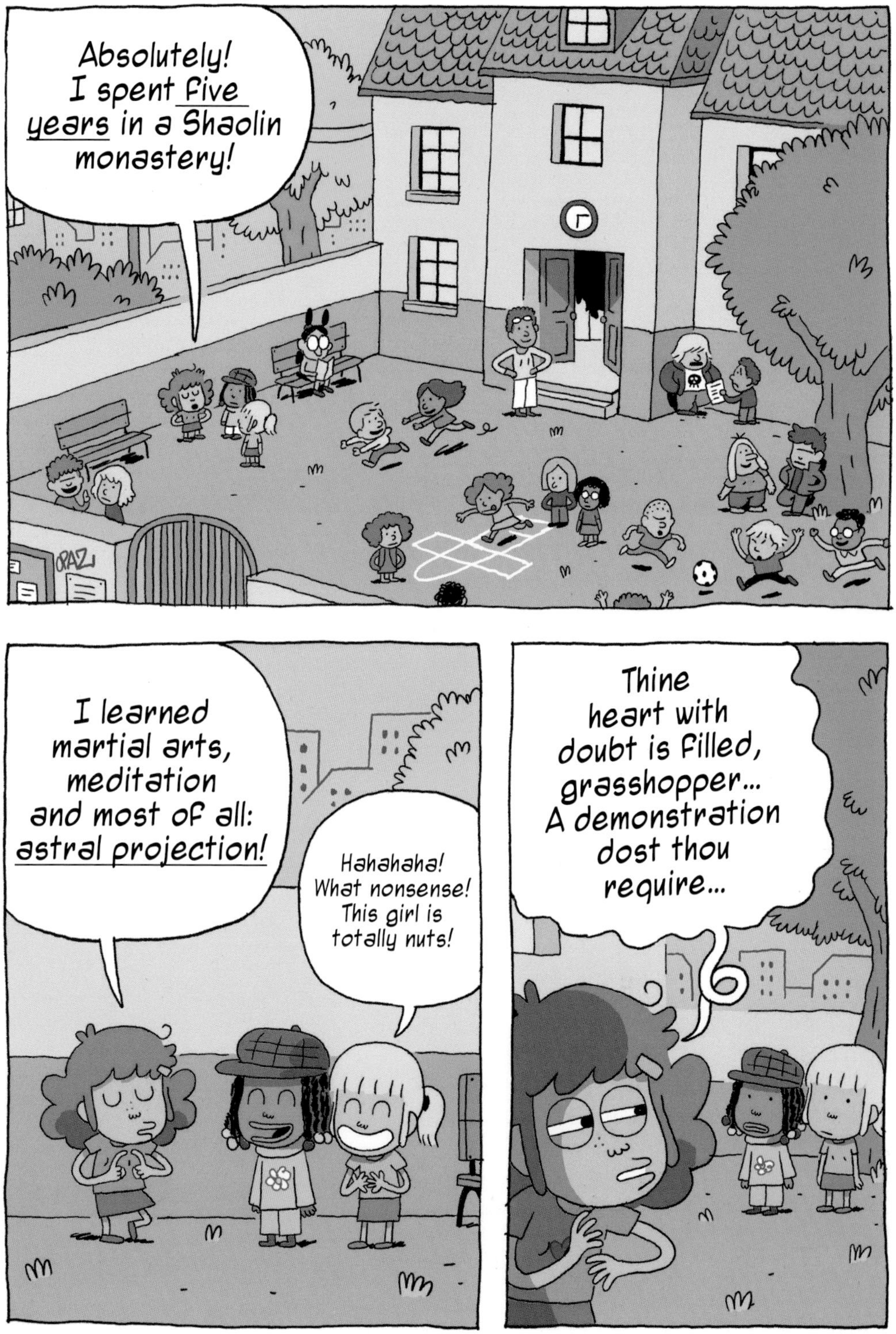
Absolutely! I spent five years in a Shaolin monastery!
I learned martial arts, meditation and most of all: astral projection!
Hahahaha! What nonsense! This girl is totally nuts!
Thine heart with doubt is filled, grasshopper... A demonstration dost thou require...

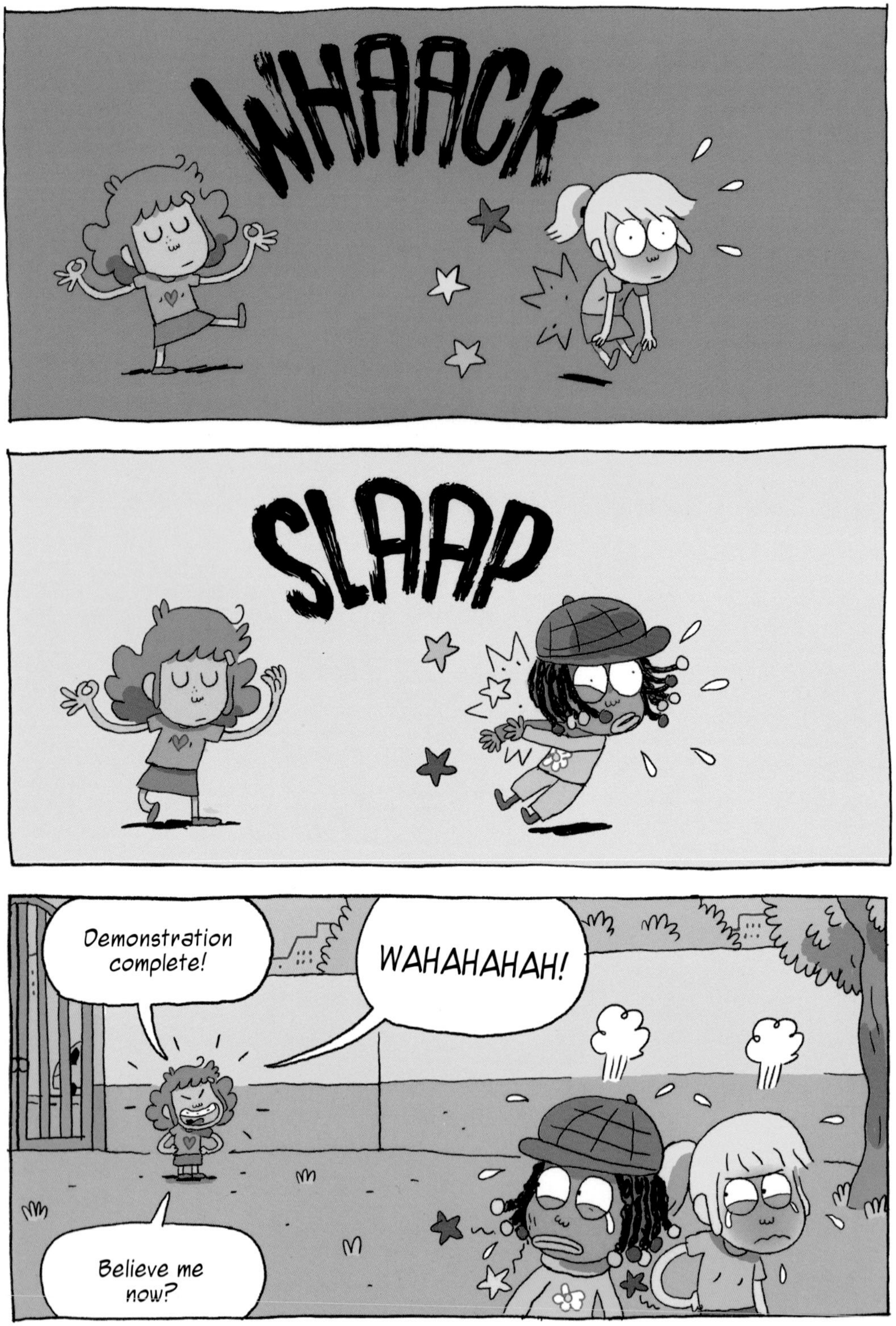
WHAACK
SLAAP
Demonstration complete!
WAHAHAHAH!
Believe me now?

All clear Leo, they're gone!

Here, a curly wurly as promised.

Hey! We agreed on __TWO!__

Sorry, it's all I've got left...

Wrong answer!

AAAAAAAAAH!

Totally nuts, told you so...

Michel-Yves + vincent

21

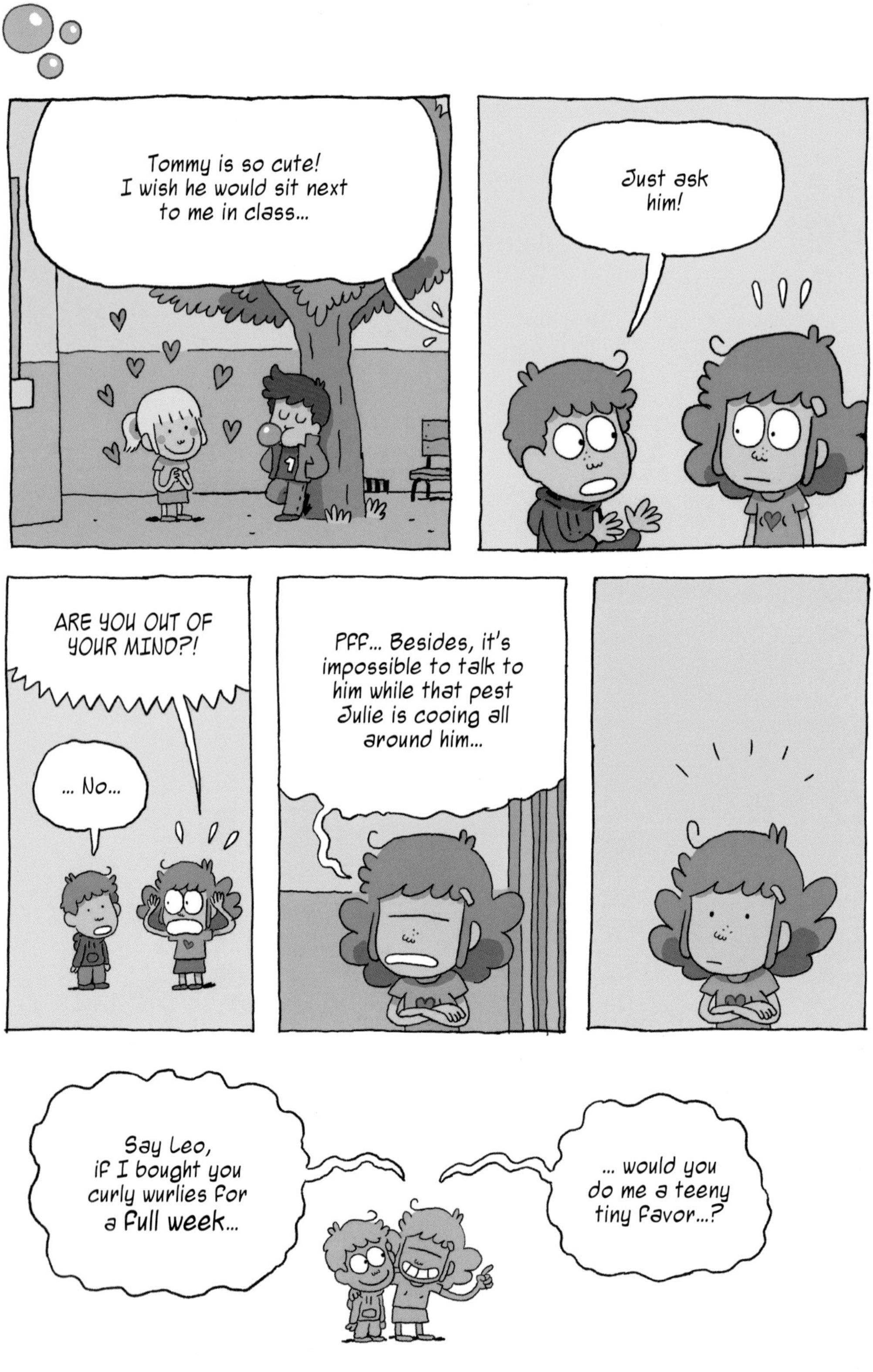
Tommy is so cute! I wish he would sit next to me in class...
Just ask him!
ARE YOU OUT OF YOUR MIND?!
... No...
PFF... Besides, it's impossible to talk to him while that pest Julie is cooing all around him...
Say Leo, if I bought you curly wurlies for a full week...
... would you do me a teeny tiny favor...?

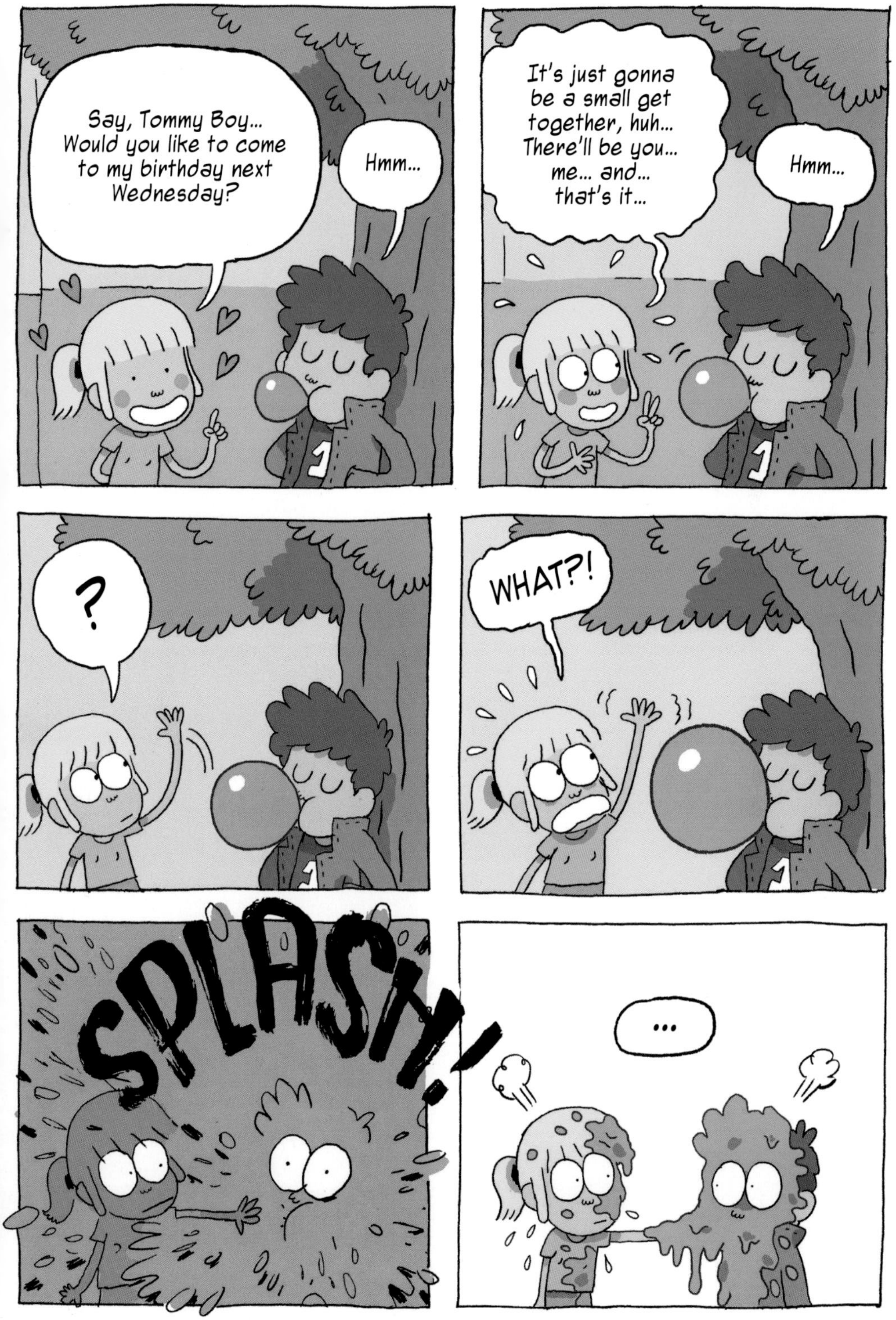
Say, Tommy Boy... Would you like to come to my birthday next Wednesday?
Hmm...
It's just gonna be a small get together, huh... There'll be you... me... and... that's it...
Hmm...
?
WHAT?!
SPLASH!
...

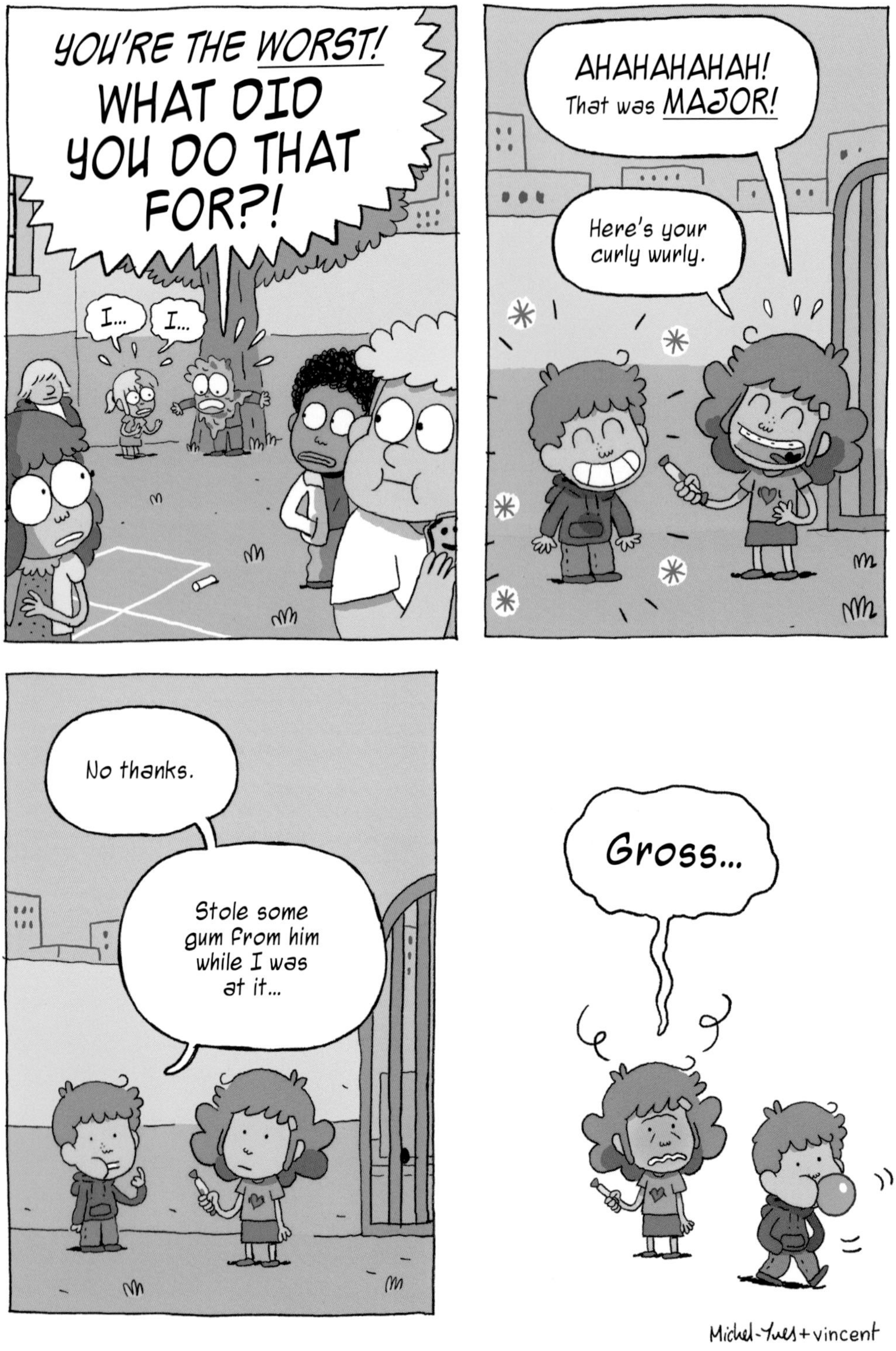
YOU'RE THE WORST! WHAT DID YOU DO THAT FOR?!
I...
I...
AHAHAHAHAH! That was MAJOR!
Here's your curly wurly.
No thanks.
Stole some gum from him while I was at it...
Gross...
Michel-Yves + vincent

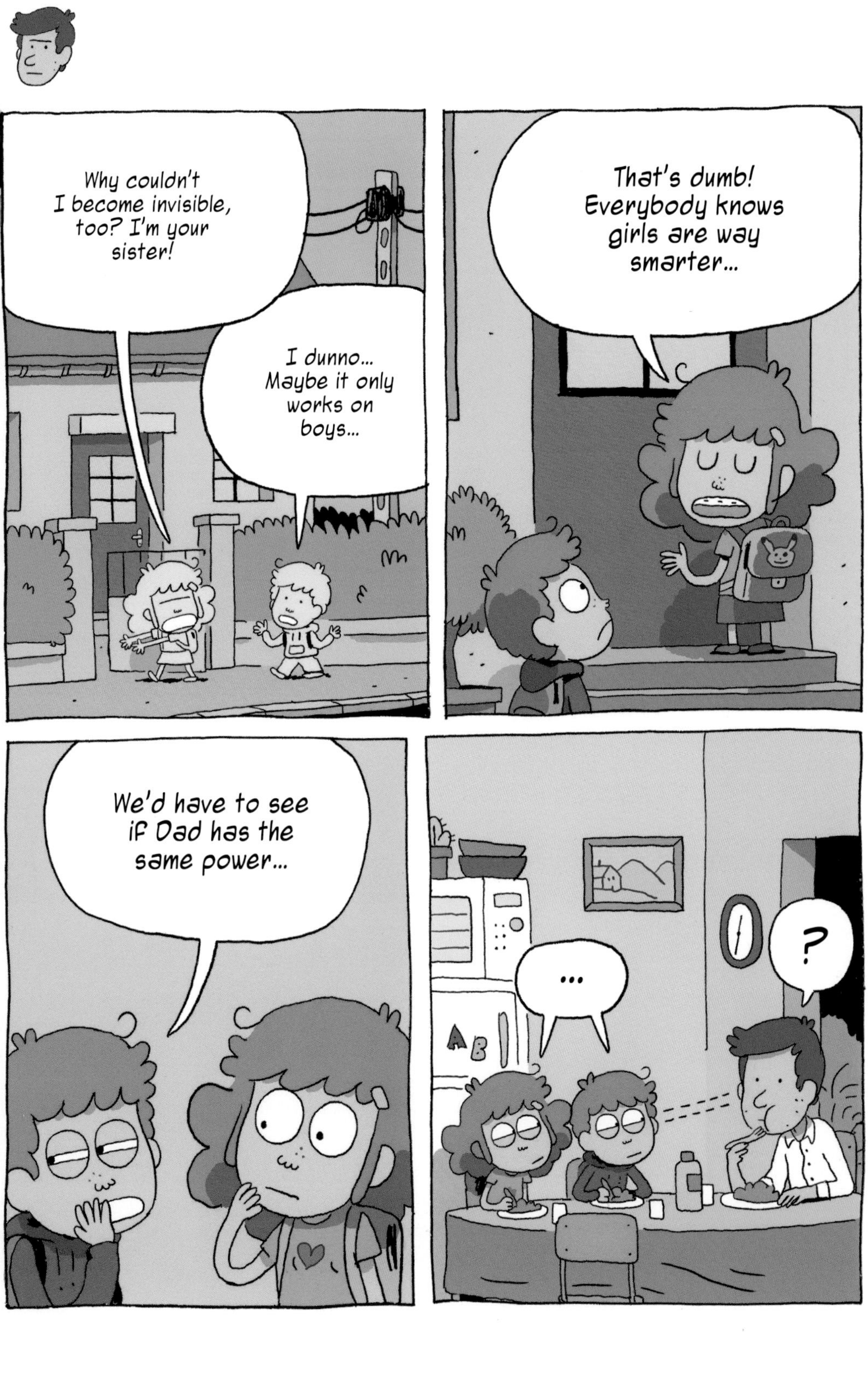
Why couldn't I become invisible, too? I'm your sister!
I dunno... Maybe it only works on boys...
That's dumb! Everybody knows girls are way smarter...
We'd have to see if Dad has the same power...
...
?
A B

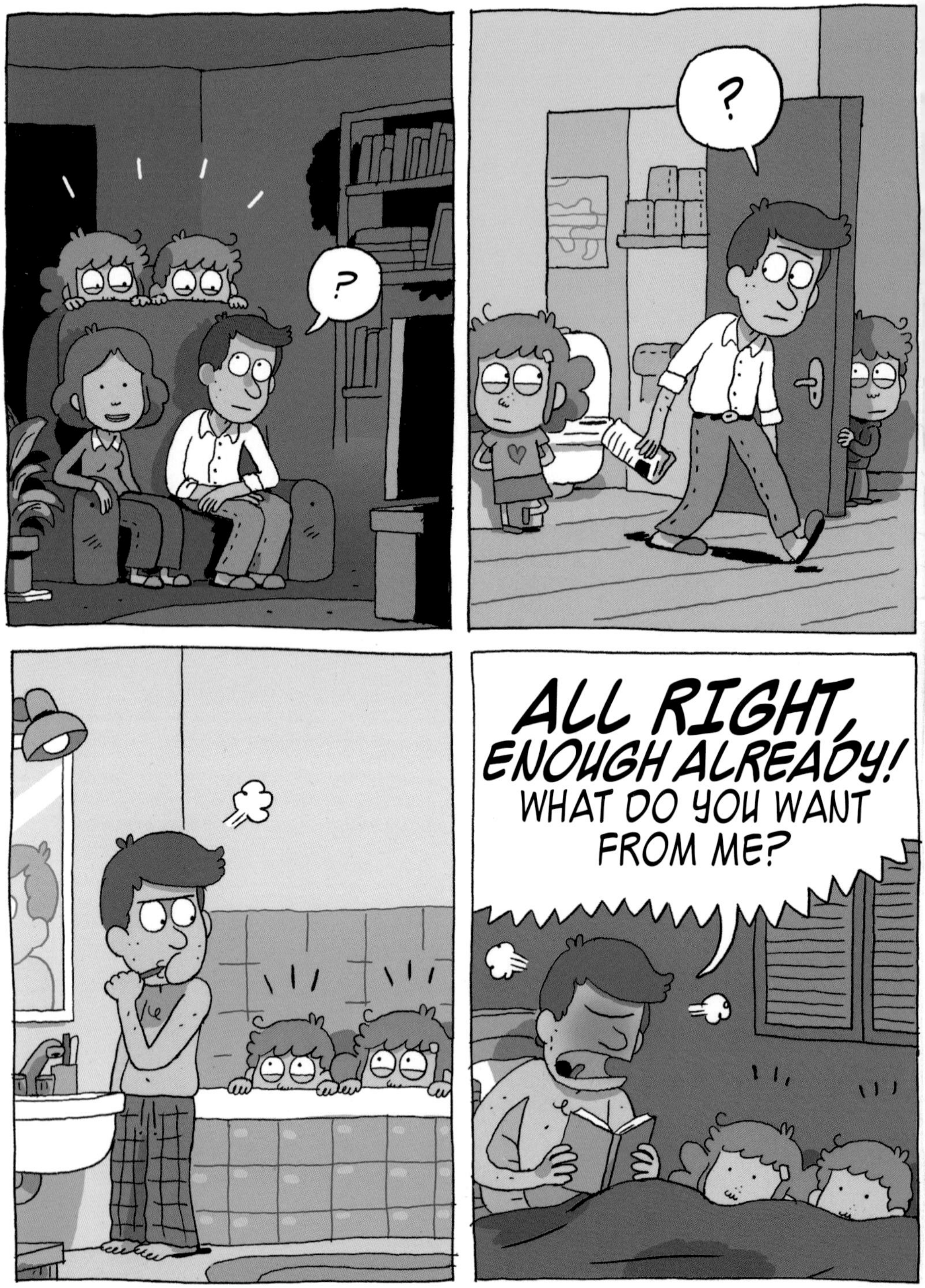
?
?
ALL RIGHT, ENOUGH ALREADY!
WHAT DO YOU WANT FROM ME?

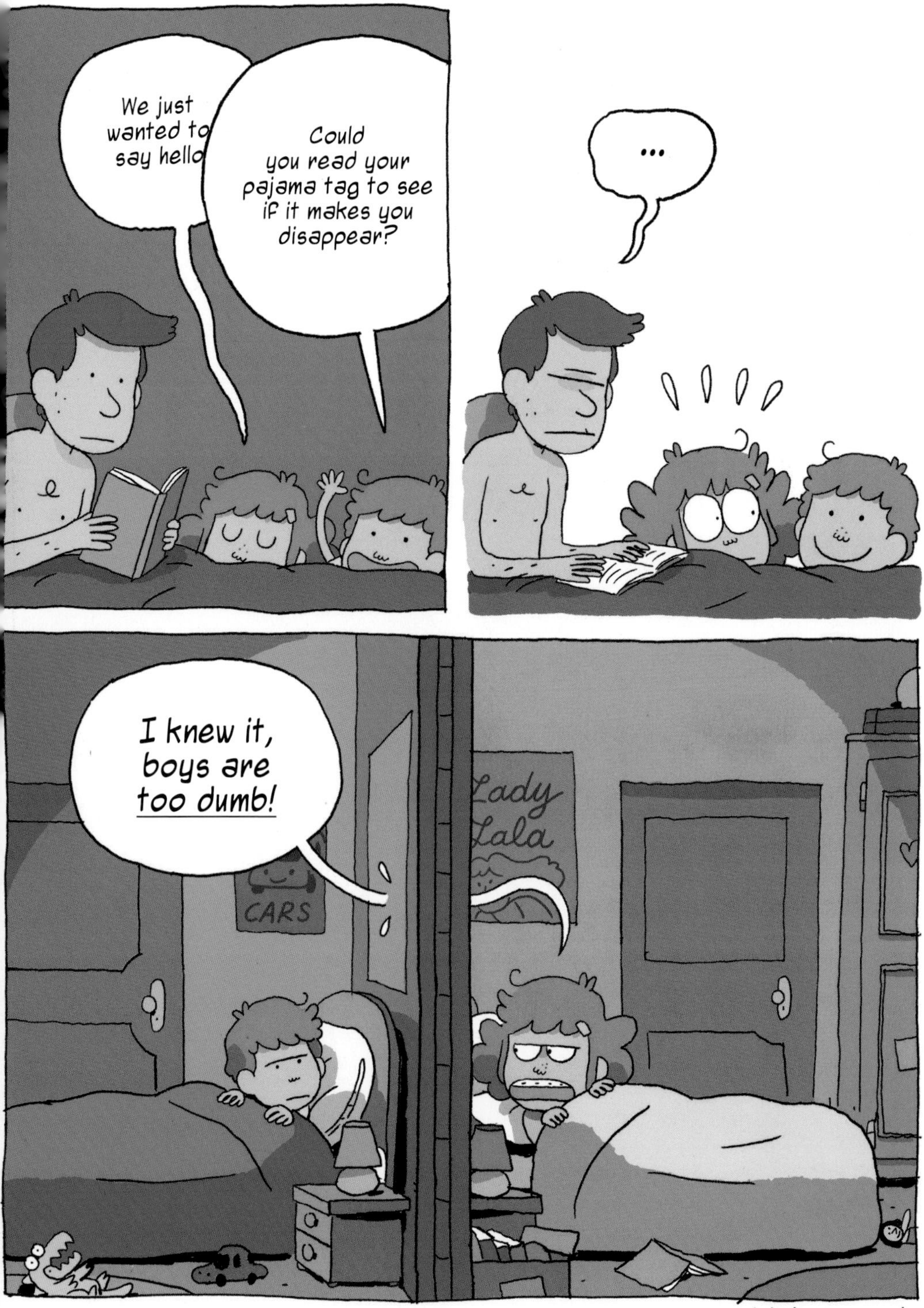
We just wanted to say hello
Could you read your pajama tag to see if it makes you disappear?
...
I knew it, boys are too dumb!
CARS
Lady Lala

Michel-Yves + vincent

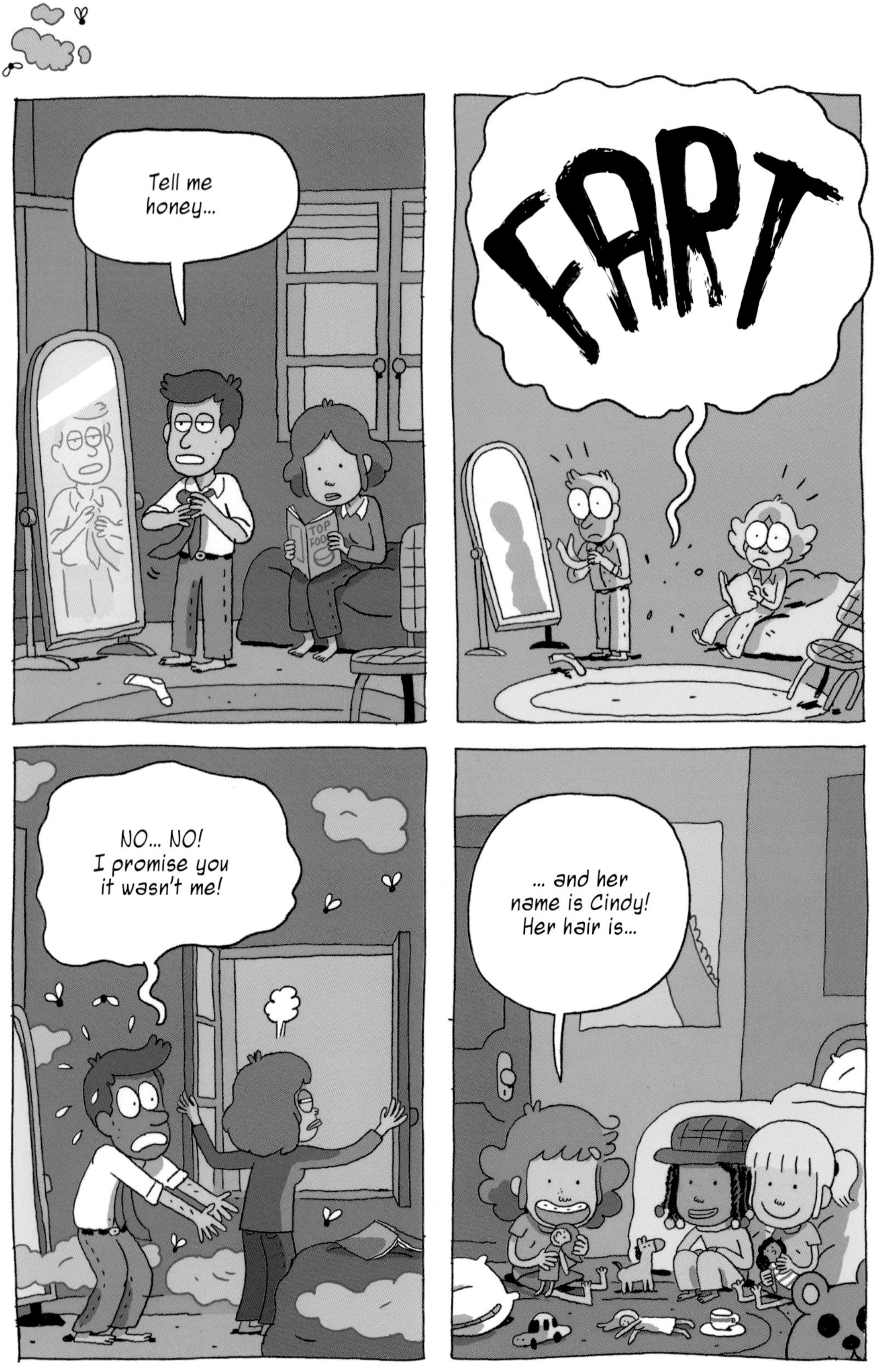
Tell me honey...
TOP FOOD
FART
NO... NO! I promise you it wasn't me!
... and her name is Cindy! Her hair is...

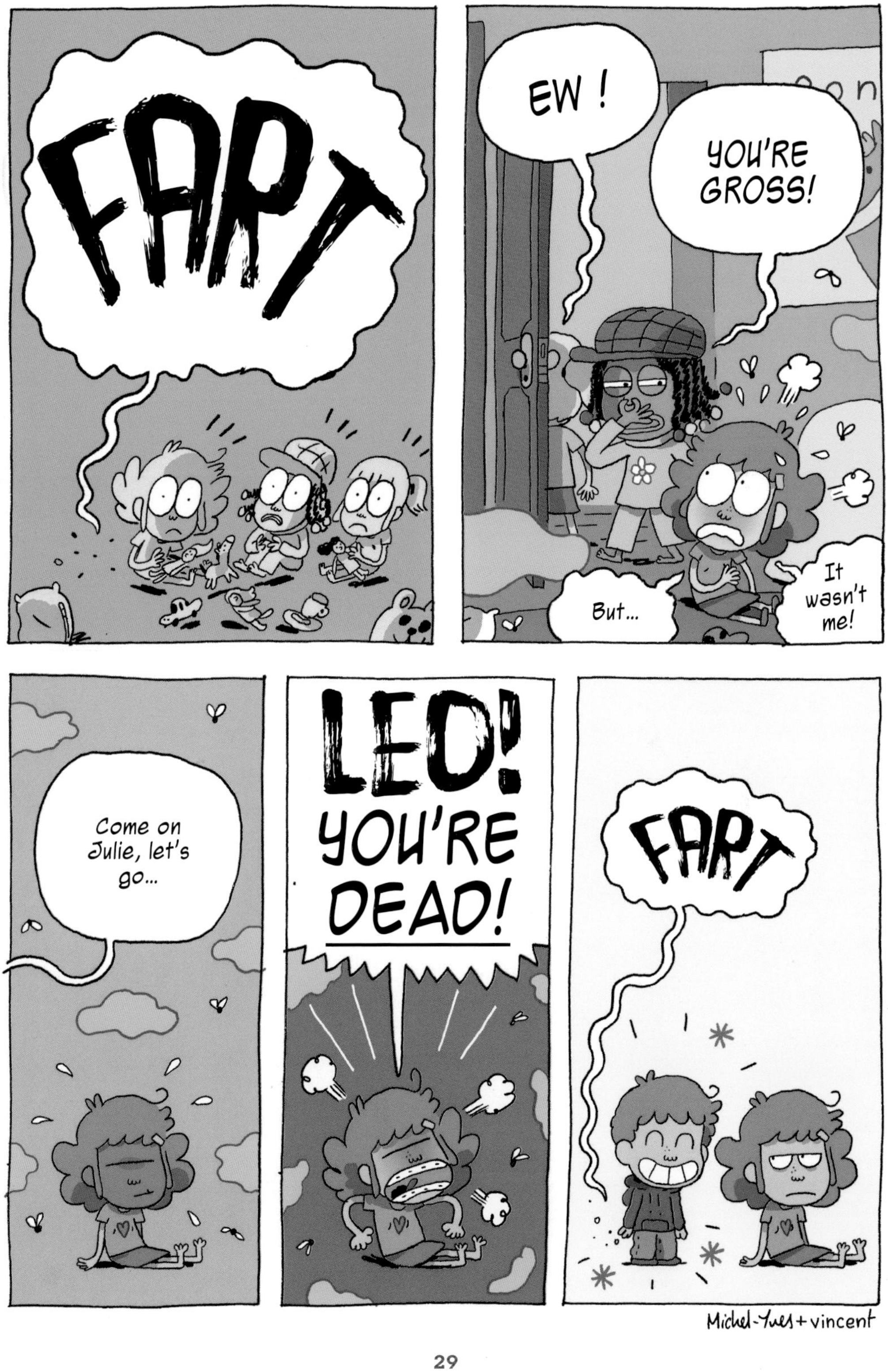
FART
EW !
YOU'RE GROSS!
But...
It wasn't me!
Come on Julie, let's go...
LEO! YOU'RE DEAD!
FART
Michel-Yves + vincent

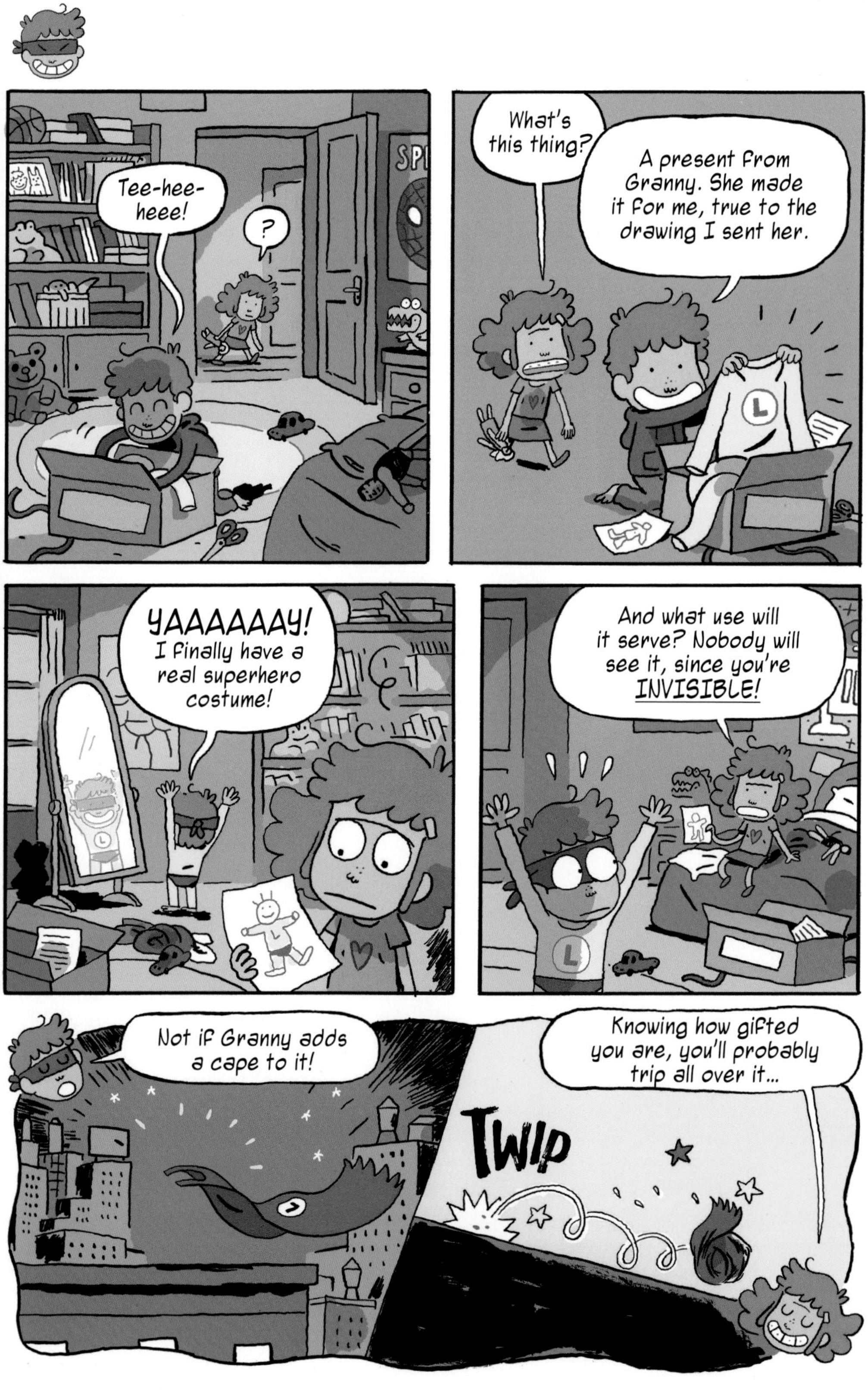
Tee-hee-heee!
?
What's this thing?
A present from Granny. She made it for me, true to the drawing I sent her.
YAAAAAAY! I finally have a real superhero costume!
And what use will it serve? Nobody will see it, since you're INVISIBLE!
Not if Granny adds a cape to it!
Knowing how gifted you are, you'll probably trip all over it...
TWIP

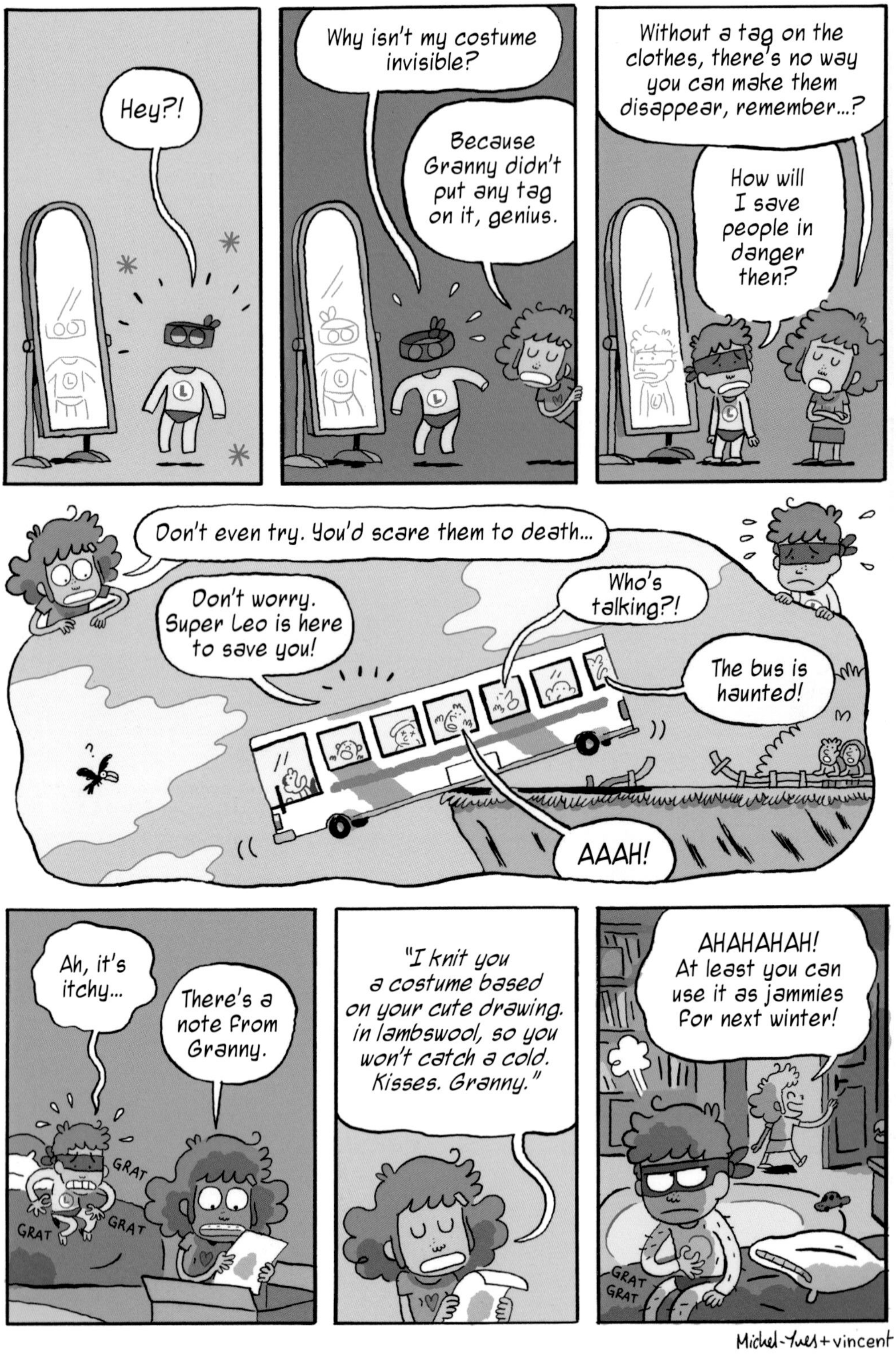
Hey?!
Why isn't my costume invisible?
Because Granny didn't put any tag on it, genius.
Without a tag on the clothes, there's no way you can make them disappear, remember...?
How will I save people in danger then?
Don't even try. You'd scare them to death...
Don't worry. Super Leo is here to save you!
Who's talking?!
The bus is haunted!
AAAH!
Ah, it's itchy...
There's a note from Granny.
GRAT
GRAT
GRAT
"I knit you a costume based on your cute drawing. in lambswool, so you won't catch a cold. Kisses. Granny."
AHAHAHAH! At least you can use it as jammies for next winter!
GRAT
GRAT

Michel-Yves + vincent

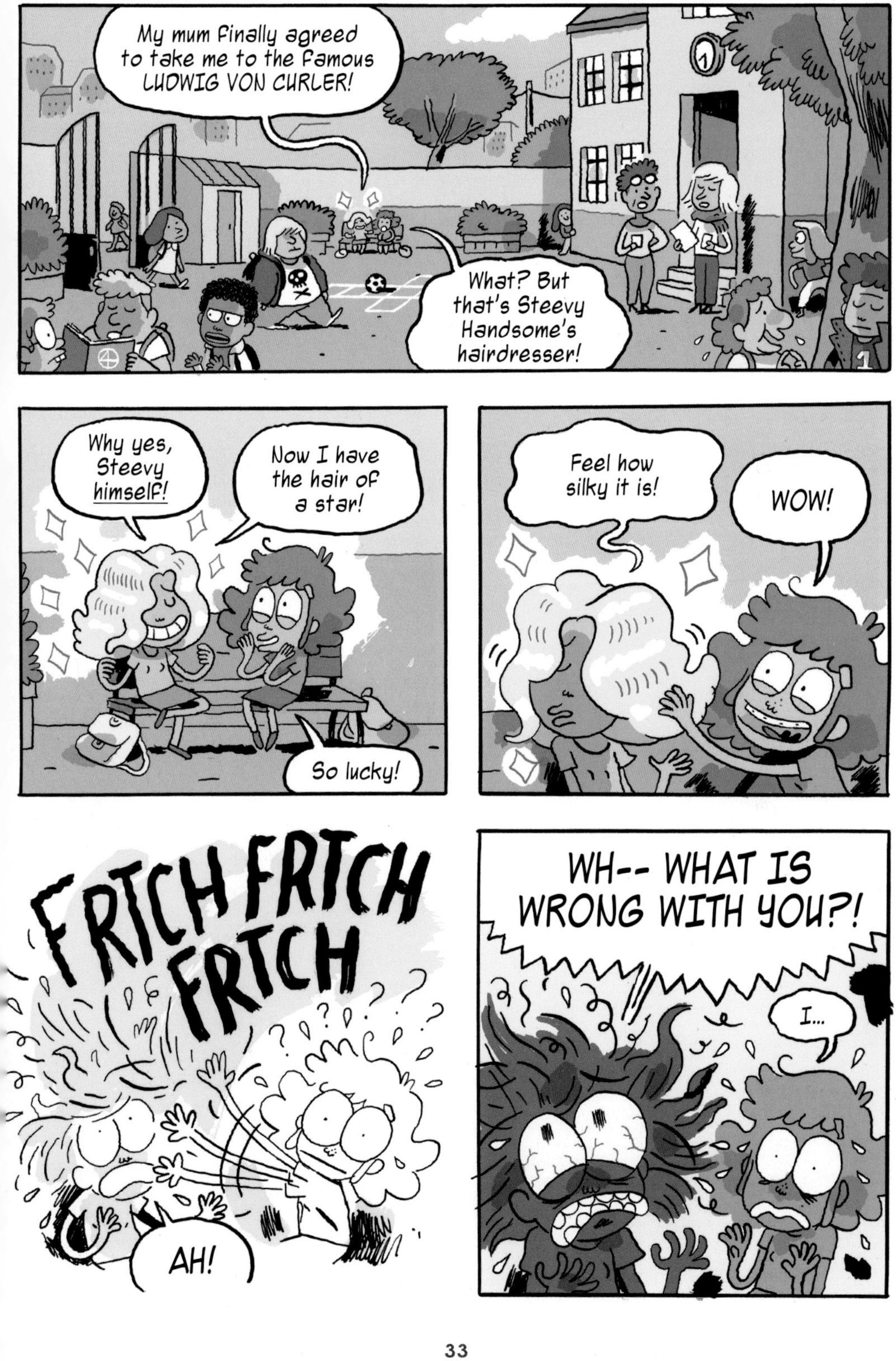

My mum finally agreed to take me to the famous LUDWIG VON CURLER!
What? But that's Steevy Handsome's hairdresser!
Why yes, Steevy himself!
Now I have the hair of a star!
So lucky!
Feel how silky it is!
WOW!
FRTCH FRTCH FRTCH FRTCH
AH!
WH-- WHAT IS WRONG WITH YOU?!
I...

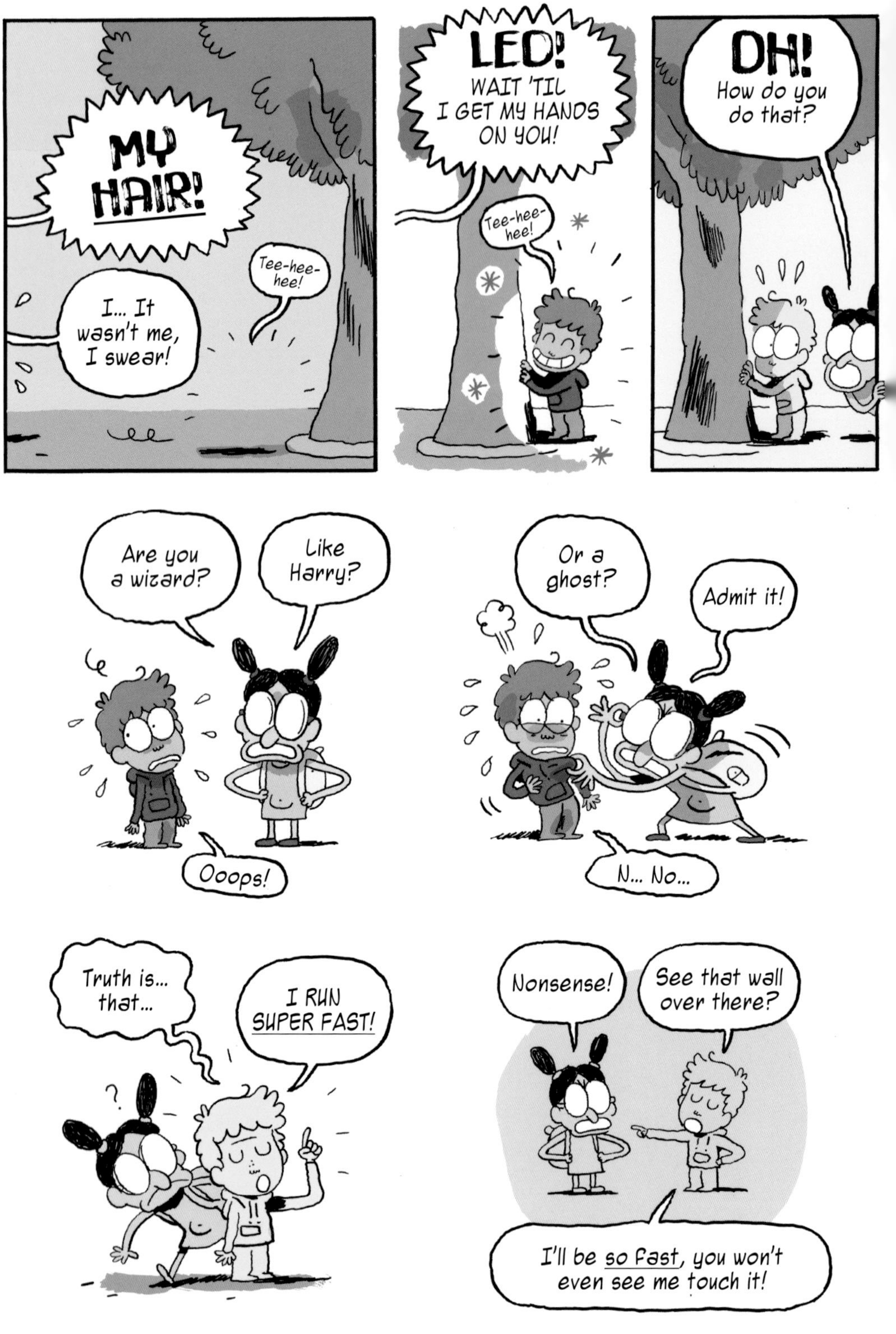
MY HAIR!
I... It wasn't me, I swear!
Tee-hee-hee!
LEO! WAIT 'TIL I GET MY HANDS ON YOU!
Tee-hee-hee!
OH! How do you do that?
Are you a wizard?
Like Harry?
Ooops!
Or a ghost?
Admit it!
N... No...
Truth is... that...
I RUN SUPER FAST!
Nonsense!
See that wall over there?
I'll be so fast, you won't even see me touch it!

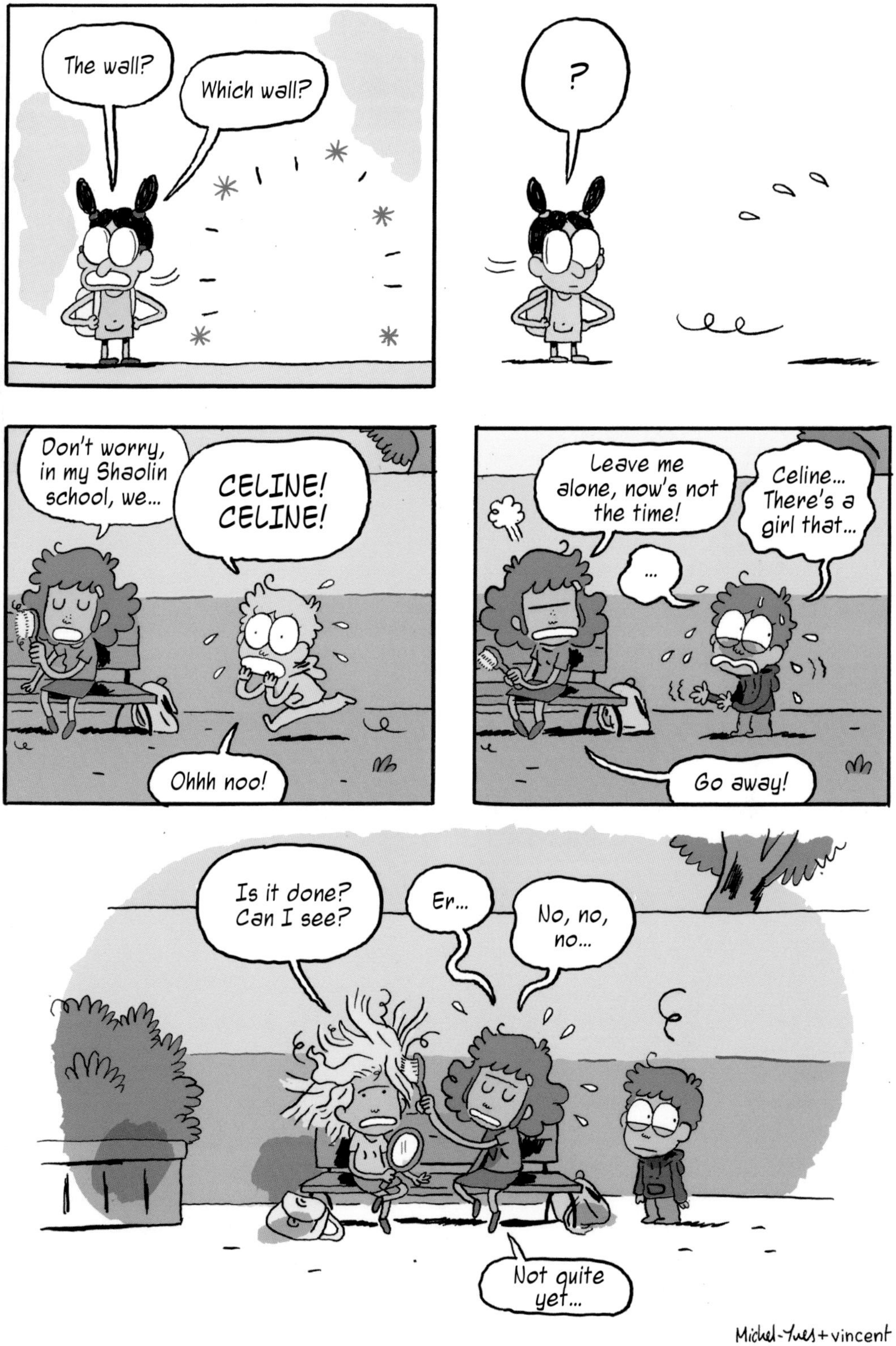
The wall?
Which wall?
?
Don't worry, in my Shaolin school, we...
CELINE! CELINE!
Ohhh noo!
Leave me alone, now's not the time!
Celine... There's a girl that...
...
Go away!
Is it done? Can I see?
Er...
No, no, no...
Not quite yet...
Michel-Yves + vincent

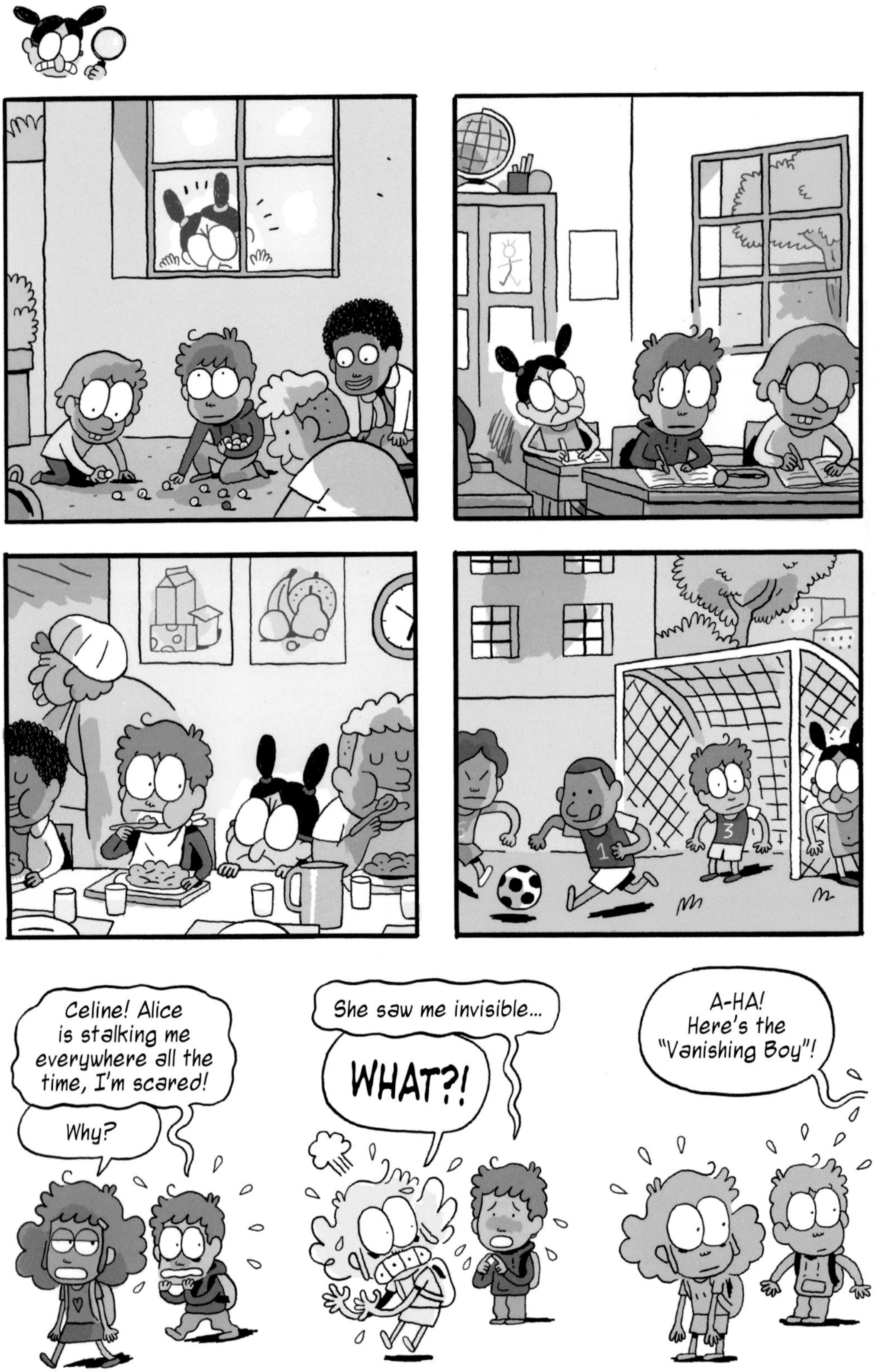
Celine! Alice is stalking me everywhere all the time, I'm scared!
Why?
She saw me invisible...
WHAT?!
A-HA! Here's the "Vanishing Boy"!

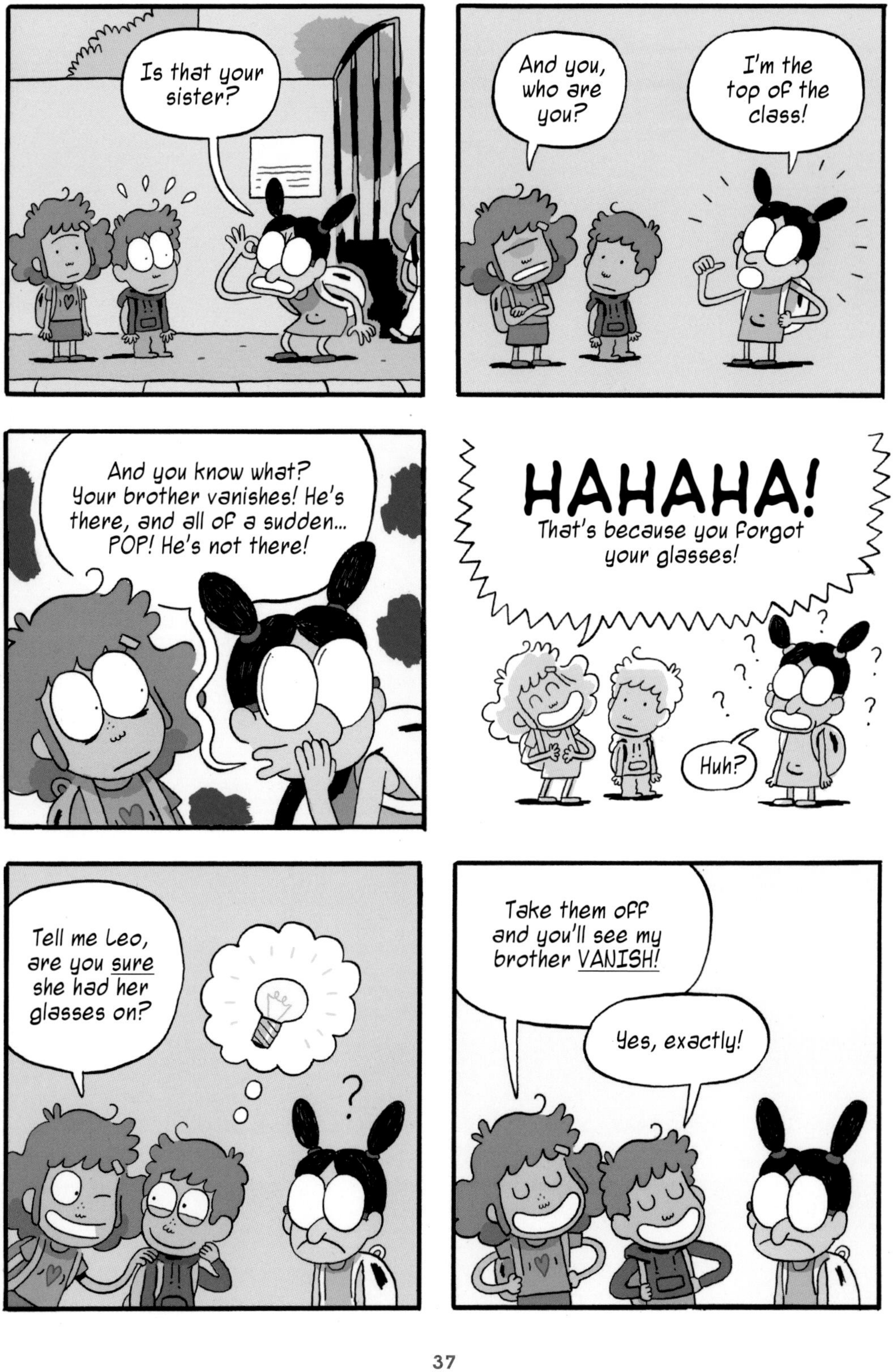
Is that your sister?
And you, who are you?
I'm the top of the class!
And you know what? Your brother vanishes! He's there, and all of a sudden... POP! He's not there!
HAHAHA!
That's because you forgot your glasses!
Huh?
Tell me Leo, are you sure she had her glasses on?
Take them off and you'll see my brother VANISH!
Yes, exactly!

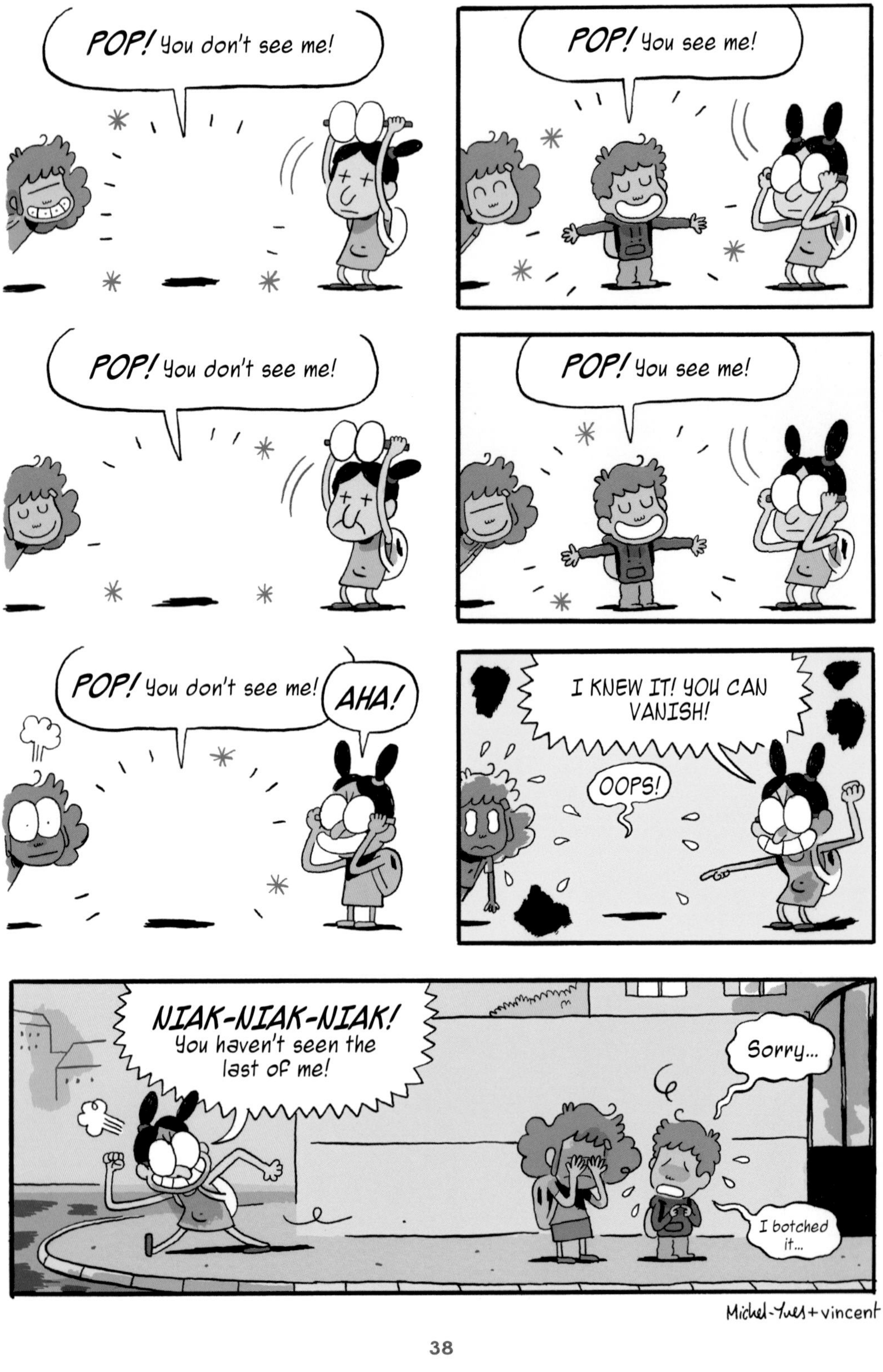
POP! You don't see me!
POP! You see me!
POP! You don't see me!
POP! You see me!
POP! You don't see me!
AHA!
I KNEW IT! YOU CAN VANISH!
OOPS!
NIAK-NIAK-NIAK! You haven't seen the last of me!
Sorry...
I botched it...
Michel-Yves + vincent

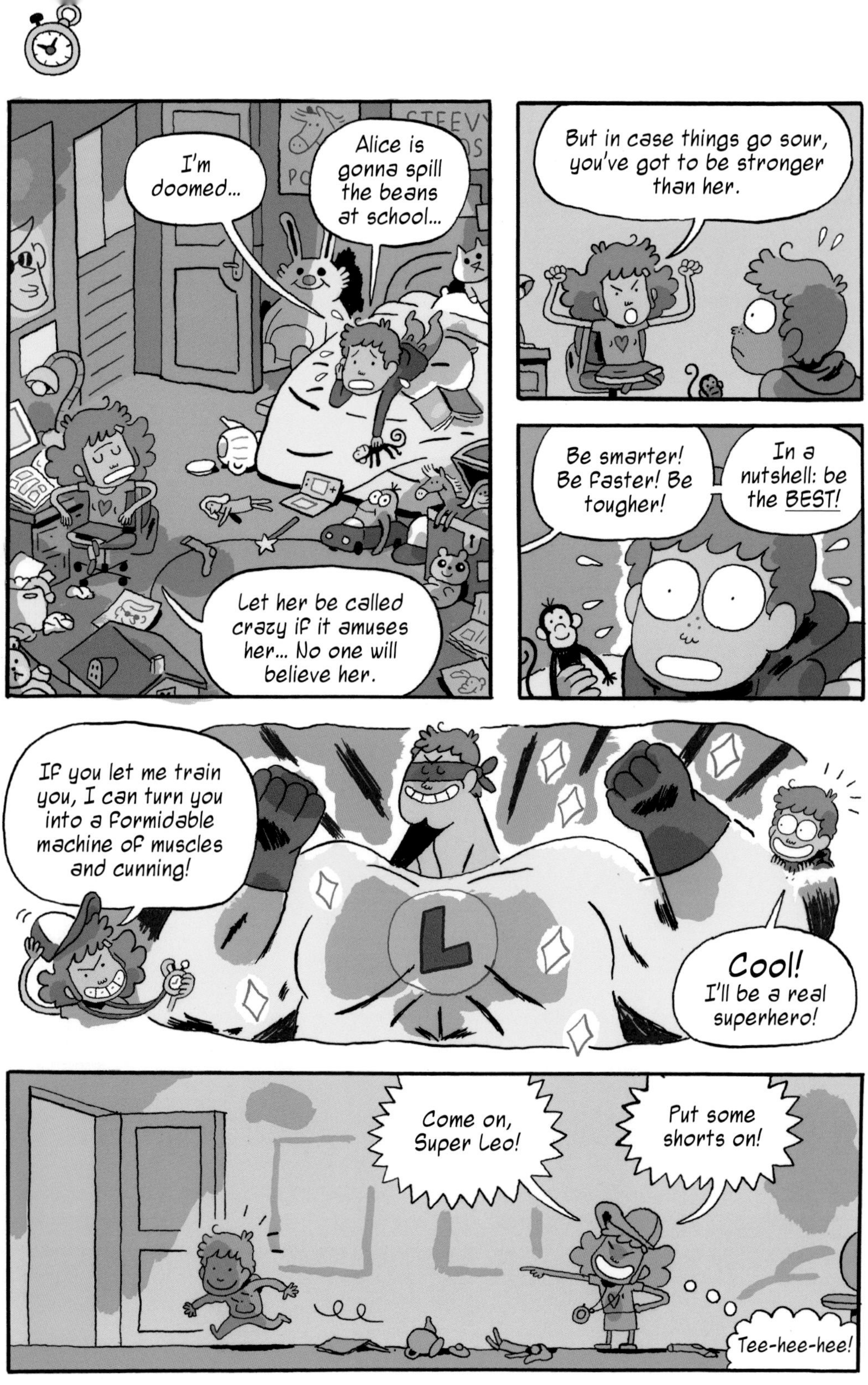
I'm doomed...
Alice is gonna spill the beans at school...
Let her be called crazy if it amuses her... No one will believe her.
But in case things go sour, you've got to be stronger than her.
Be smarter! Be faster! Be tougher!
In a nutshell: be the BEST!
If you let me train you, I can turn you into a formidable machine of muscles and cunning!
Cool! I'll be a real superhero!
Come on, Super Leo!
Put some shorts on!
Tee-hee-hee!

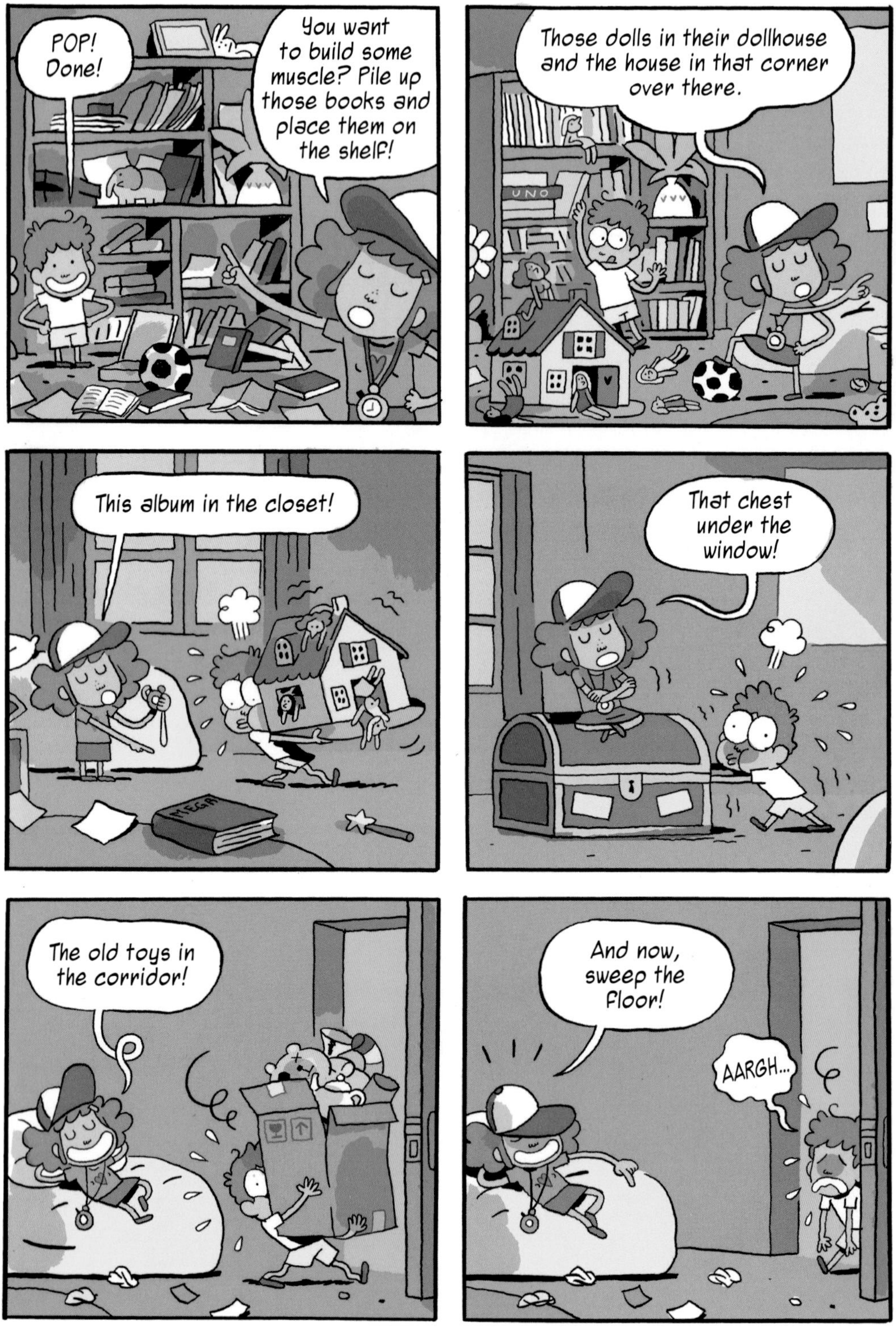
POP! Done!
You want to build some muscle? Pile up those books and place them on the shelf!
UNO
Those dolls in their dollhouse and the house in that corner over there.
This album in the closet!
MEGA
That chest under the window!
The old toys in the corridor!
And now, sweep the floor!
AARGH...

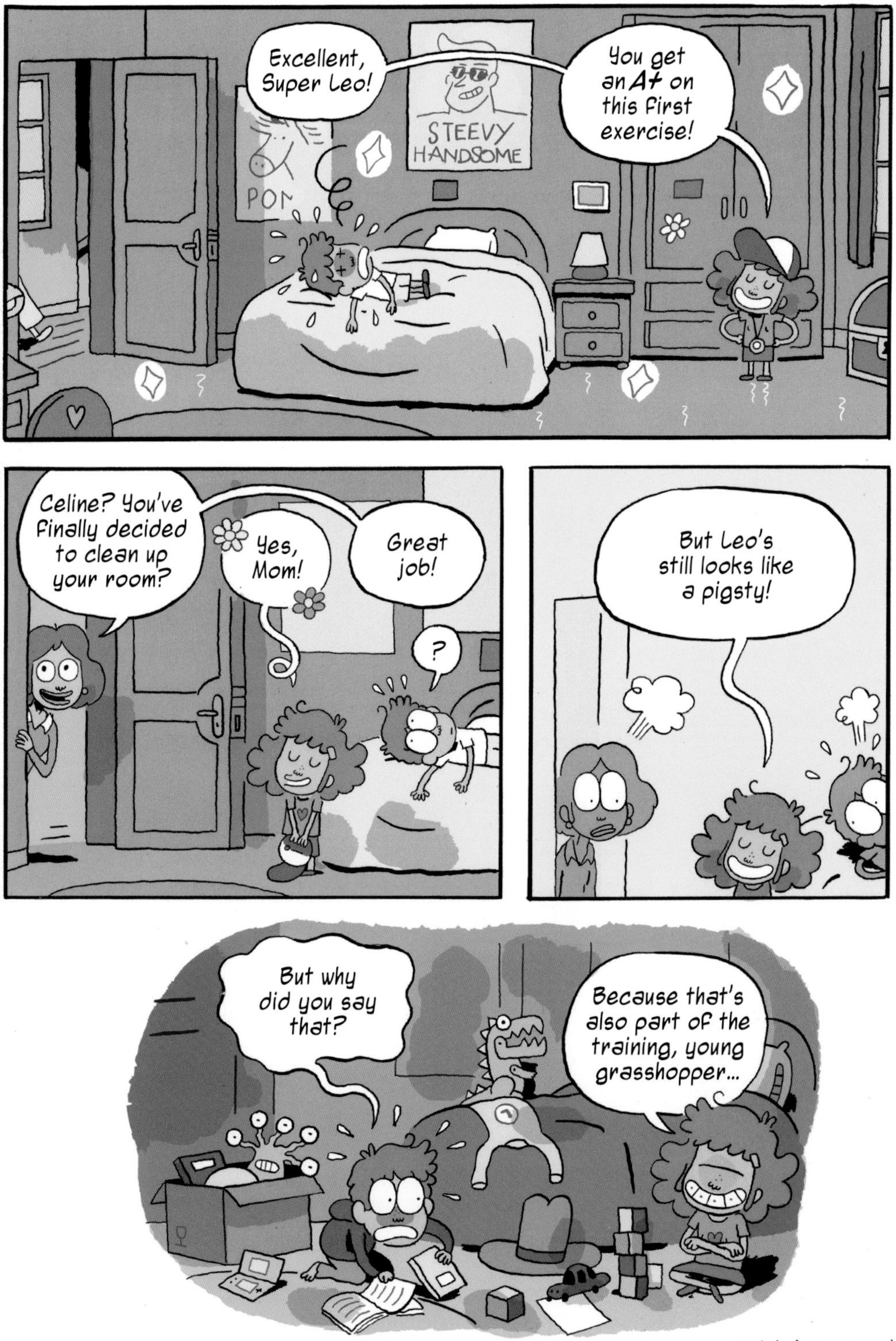
STEEVY HANDSOME
Excellent, Super Leo!
You get an A+ on this first exercise!
Celine? You've finally decided to clean up your room?
Yes, Mom!
Great job!
?
But Leo's still looks like a pigsty!
But why did you say that?
Because that's also part of the training, young grasshopper...

Michel-Yves + vincent

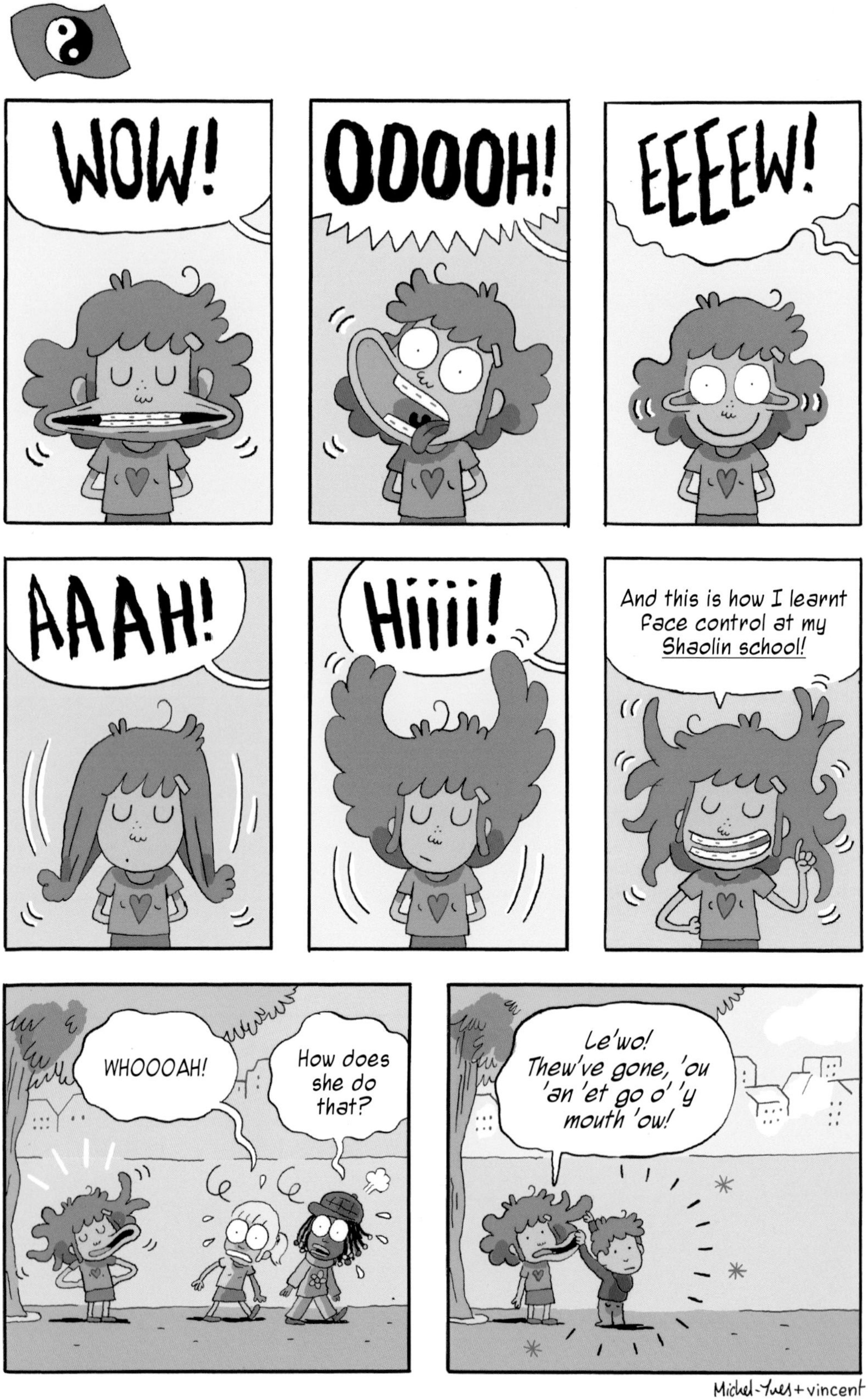
WOW!
OOOOH!
EEEEW!
AAAH!
Hiiii!
And this is how I learnt face control at my Shaolin school!
WHOOOAH!
How does she do that?
Le'wo! Thew've gone, 'ou 'an 'et go o' 'y mouth 'ow!
Michel-Yves + vincent

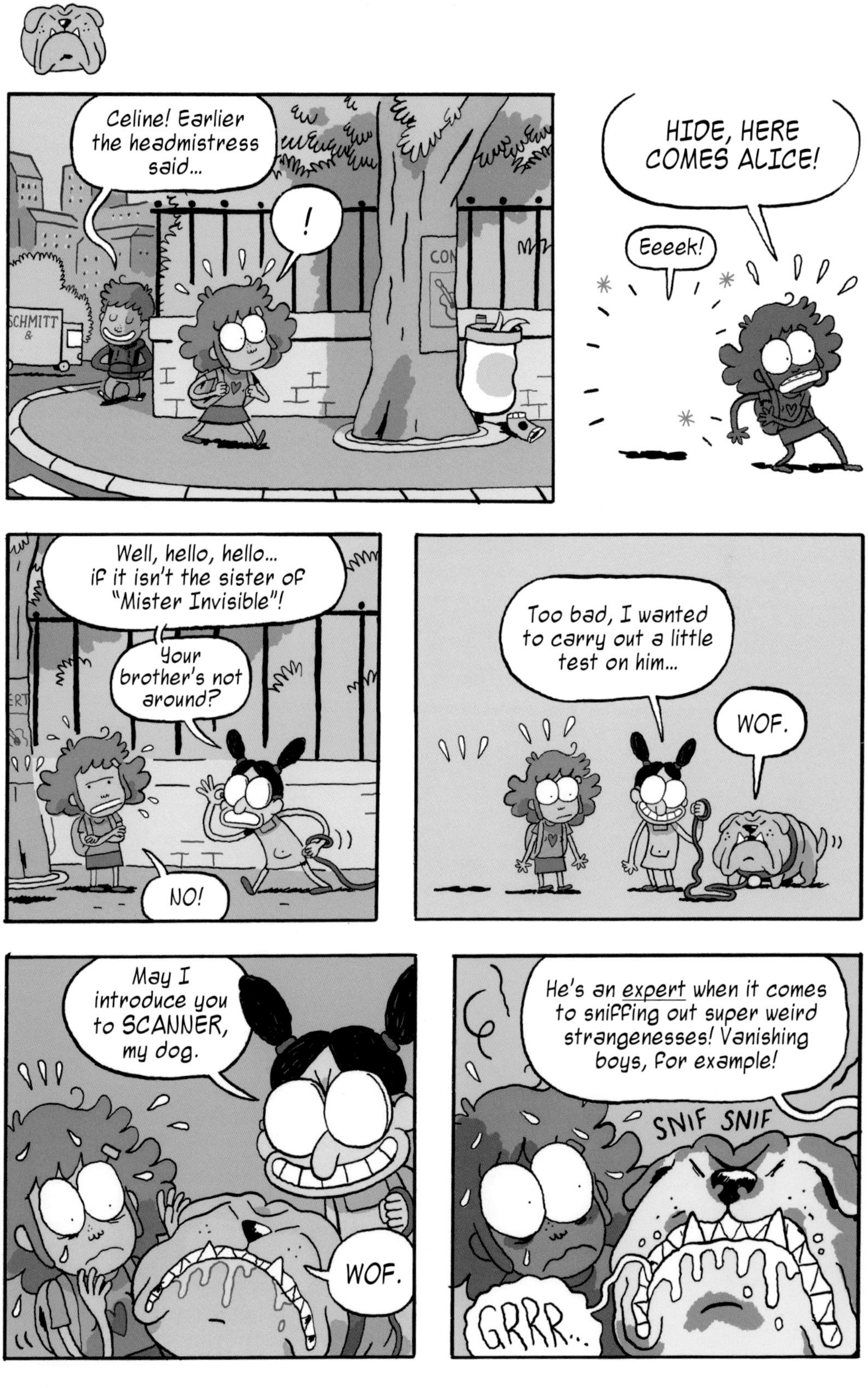
Celine! Earlier the headmistress said...
!
SCHMITT
HIDE, HERE COMES ALICE!
Eeeek!
Well, hello, hello... if it isn't the sister of "Mister Invisible"!
Your brother's not around?
NO!
Too bad, I wanted to carry out a little test on him...
WOF.
May I introduce you to SCANNER, my dog.
WOF.
He's an expert when it comes to sniffing out super weird strangenesses! Vanishing boys, for example!
SNIF SNIF
GRRR...

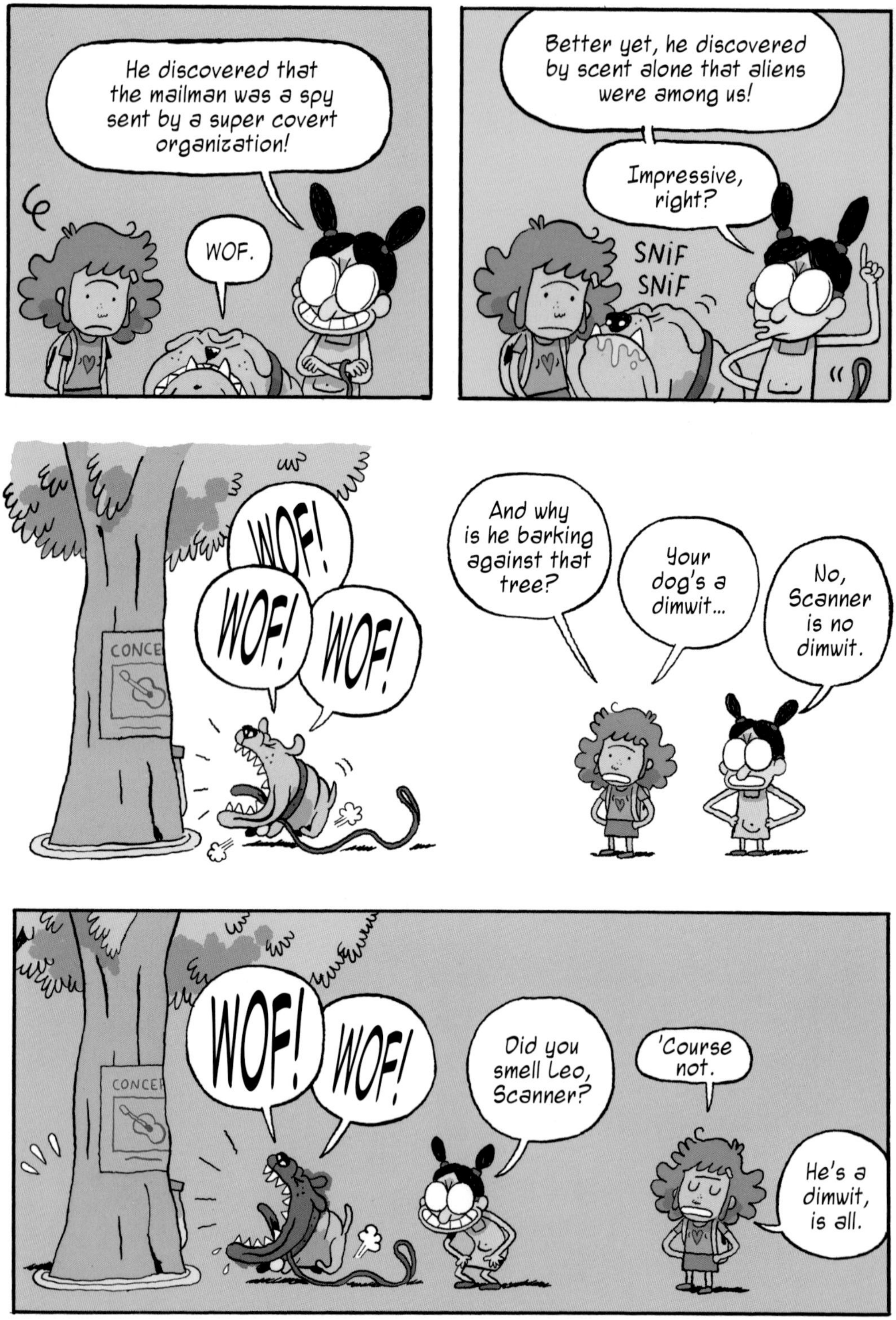
He discovered that the mailman was a spy sent by a super covert organization!
WOF.
Better yet, he discovered by scent alone that aliens were among us!
Impressive, right?
SNiF SNiF
WOF!
WOF!
WOF!
CONCE
And why is he barking against that tree?
Your dog's a dimwit...
No, Scanner is no dimwit.
WOF!
WOF!
CONCE
Did you smell Leo, Scanner?
'Course not.
He's a dimwit, is all.

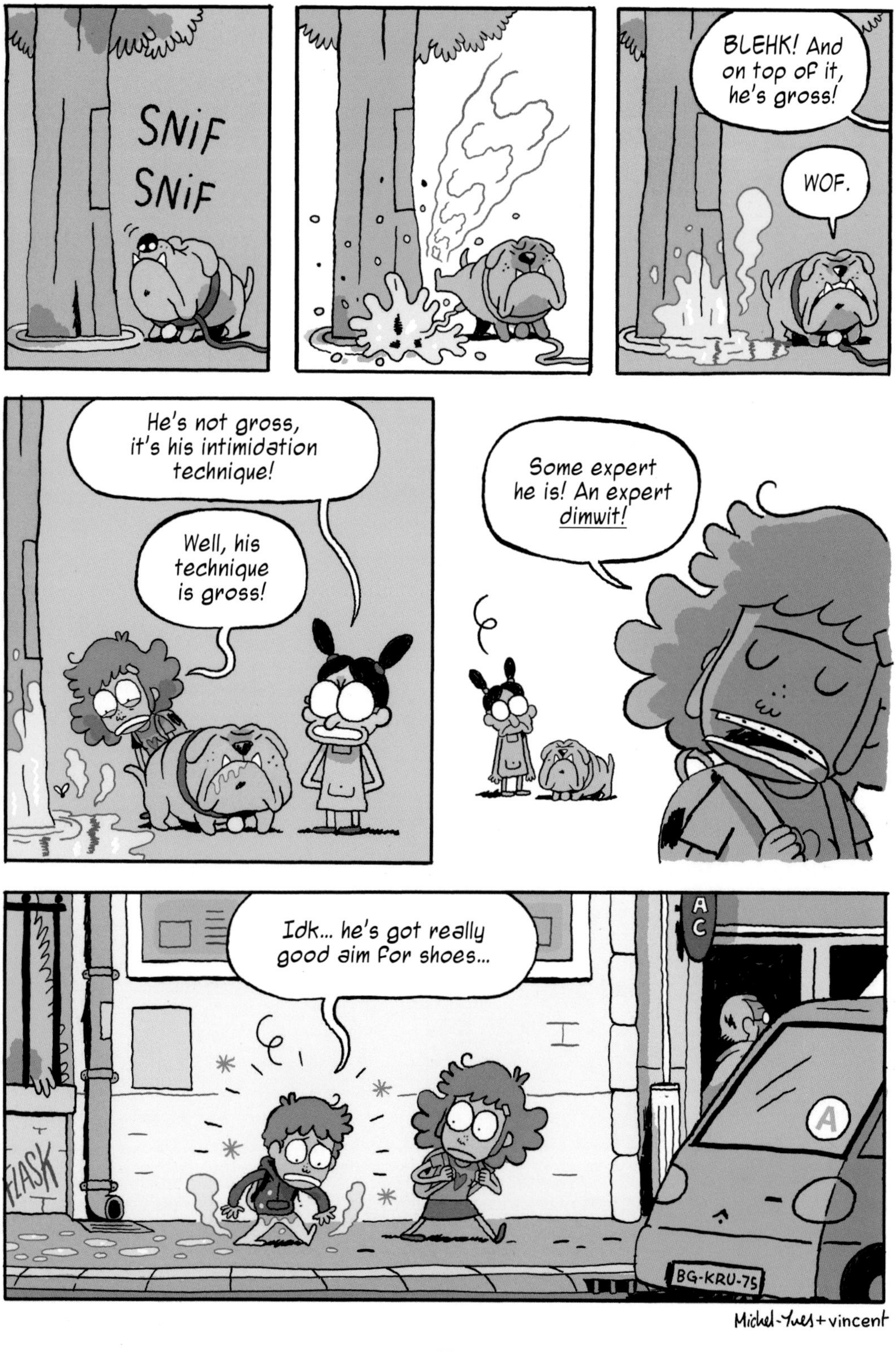
SNiF
SNiF
BLEHK! And on top of it, he's gross!
WOF.
He's not gross, it's his intimidation technique!
Well, his technique is gross!
Some expert he is! An expert dimwit!
Idk... he's got really good aim for shoes...
FLASK
AC
A
BG-KRU-75
Michel-Yves+vincent

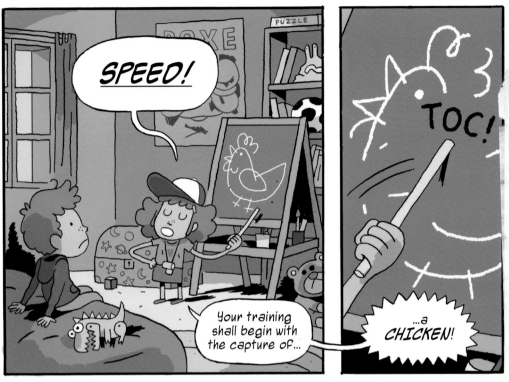

SPEED!

Your training shall begin with the capture of...

TOC!

...a CHICKEN!

A chicken?

Yeah, a chicken! They're super hard to catch! I saw that in a movie...

But there're no chickens in our place!

Er...

There's one in the fridge, but he doesn't run much anymore...

MILK

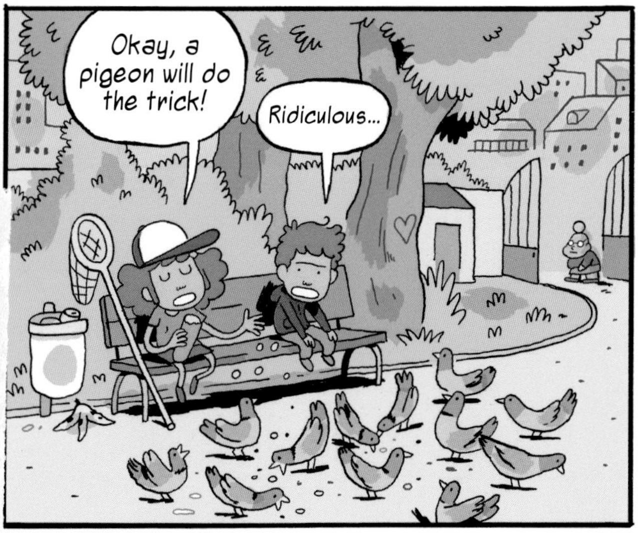
Okay, a pigeon will do the trick!
Ridiculous...

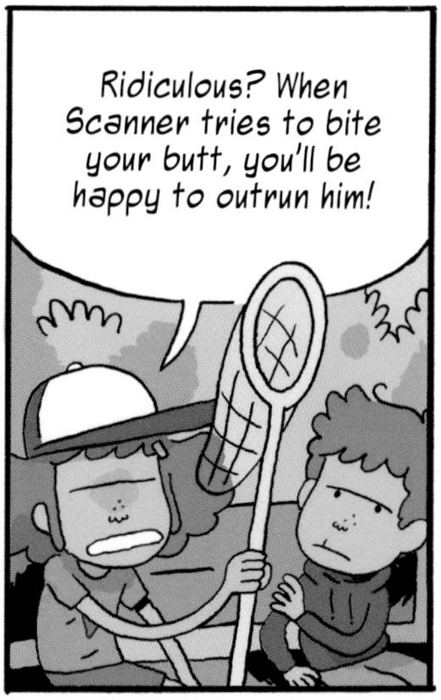
Ridiculous? When Scanner tries to bite your butt, you'll be happy to outrun him!

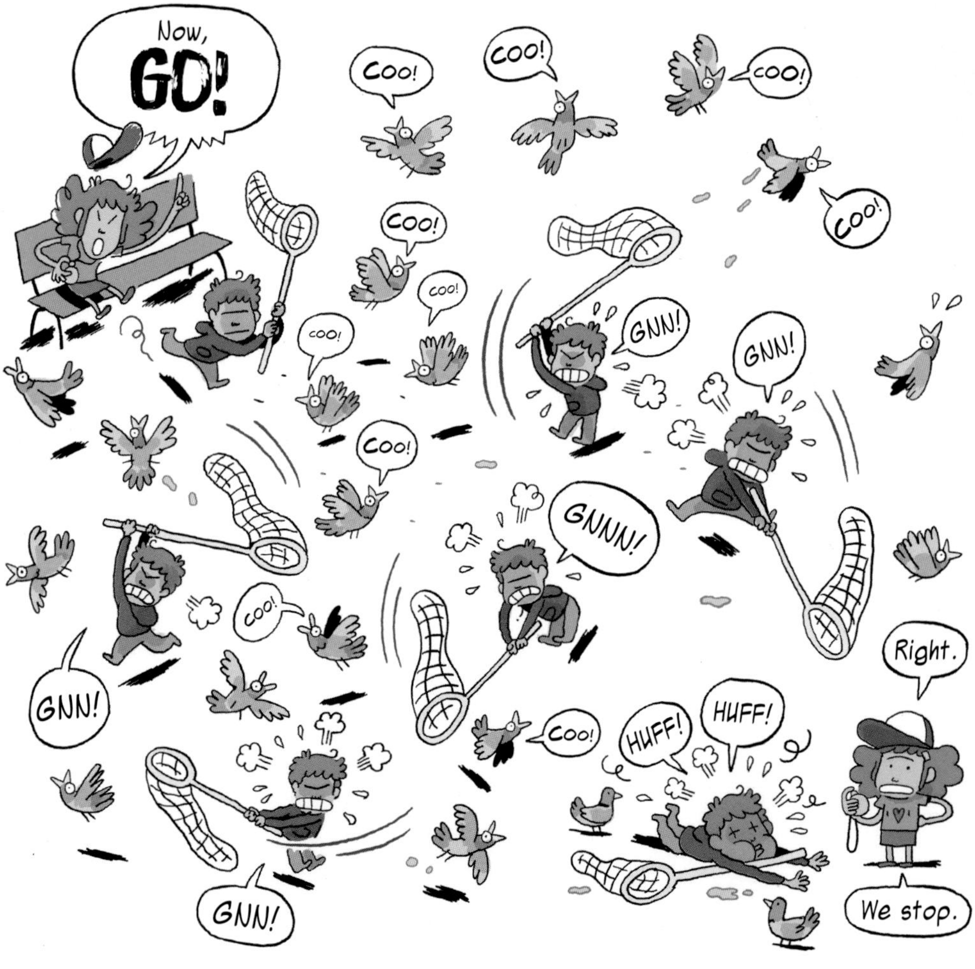
Now, GO!
COO!
COO!
COO!
COO!
COO!
COO!
COO!
GNN!
GNN!
COO!
GNNN!
COO!
GNN!
COO!
GNN!
HUFF!
HUFF!
Right.
We stop.

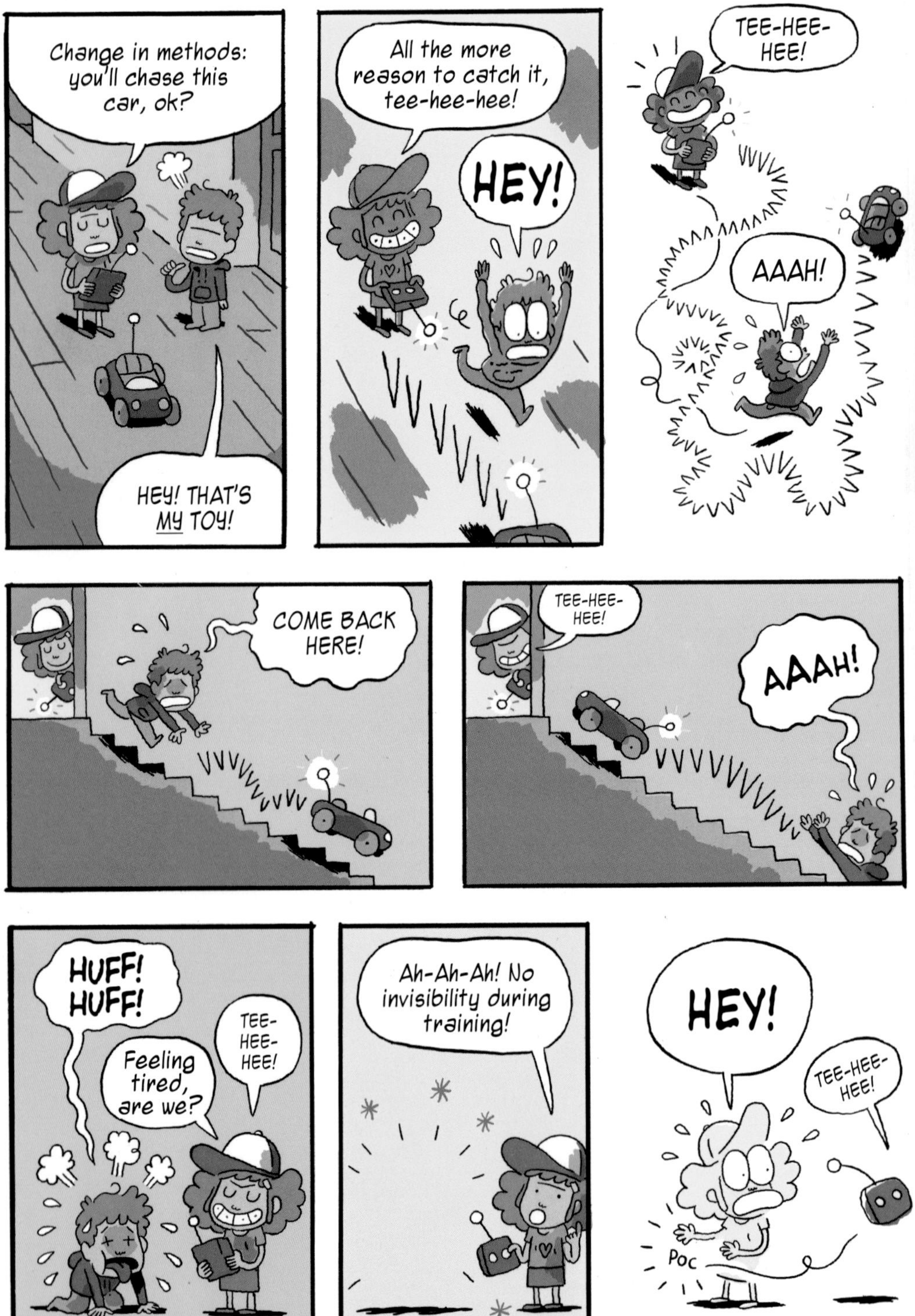
Change in methods: you'll chase this car, ok?
HEY! THAT'S MY TOY!
All the more reason to catch it, tee-hee-hee!
HEY!
TEE-HEE-HEE!
AAAH!
COME BACK HERE!
TEE-HEE-HEE!
AAAH!
HUFF! HUFF!
Feeling tired, are we?
TEE-HEE-HEE!
Ah-Ah-Ah! No invisibility during training!
HEY!
TEE-HEE-HEE!
Poc

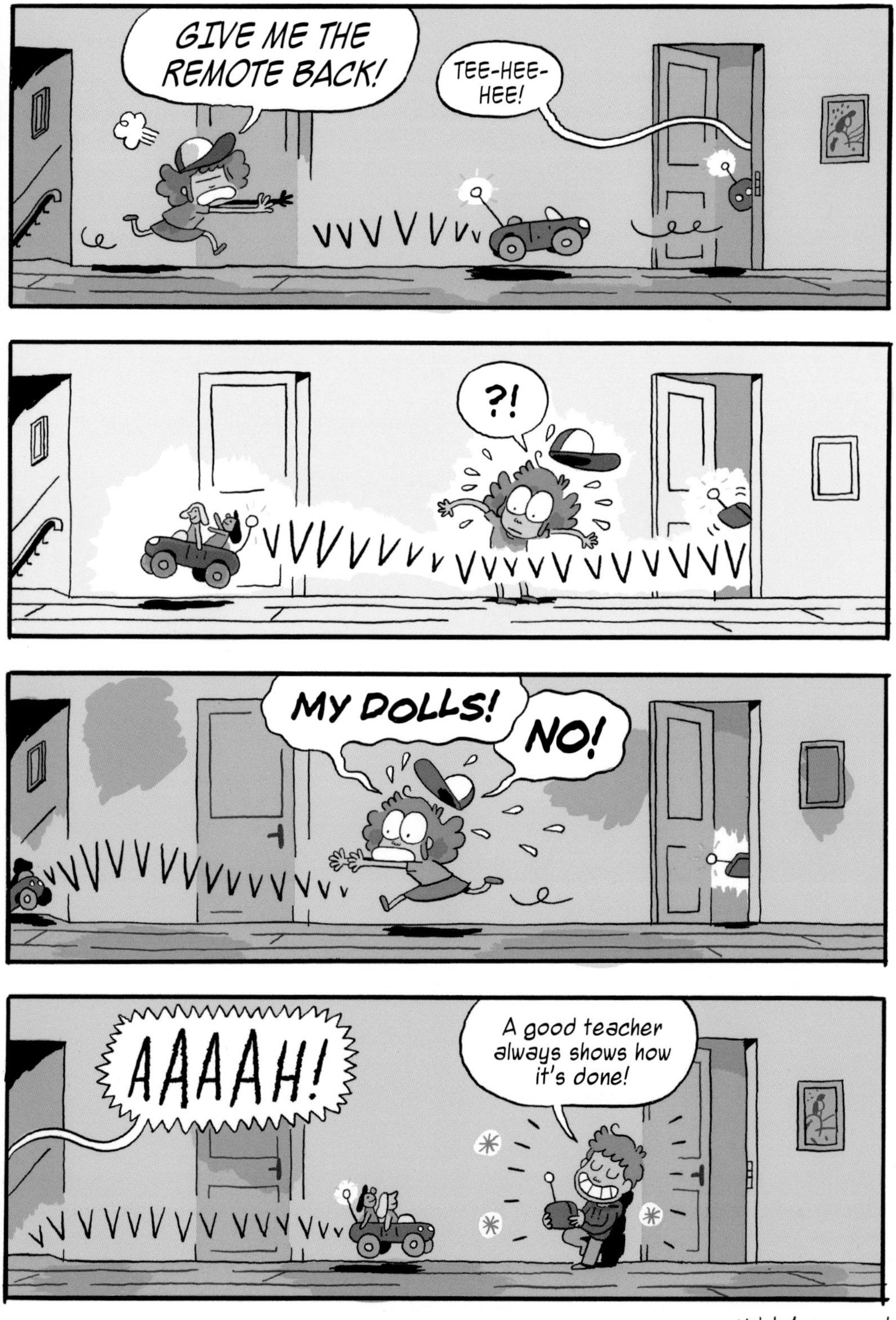
GIVE ME THE REMOTE BACK!
TEE-HEE-HEE!
?!
MY DOLLS!
NO!
AAAAH!
A good teacher always shows how it's done!
Michel-Yves + vincent

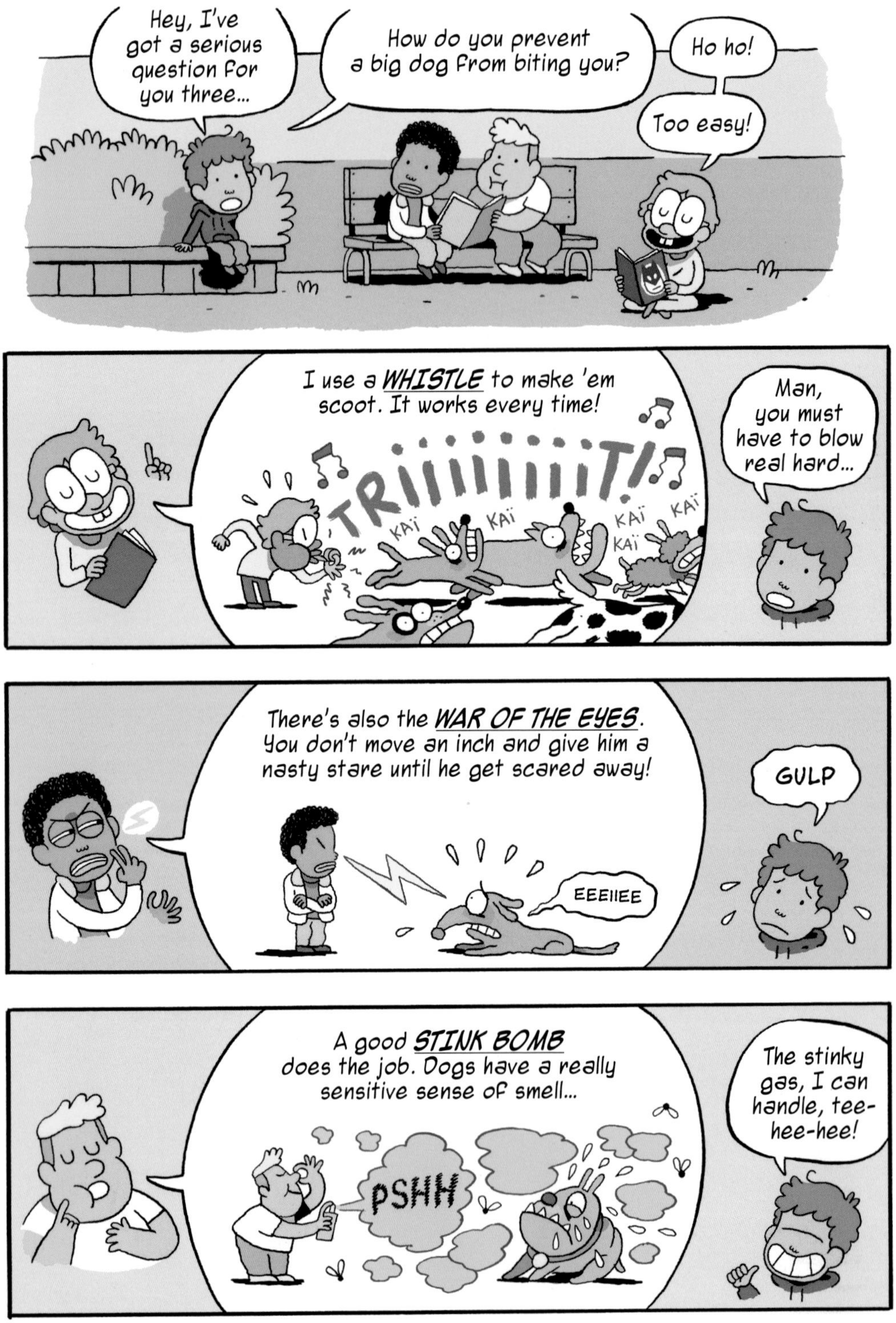
Hey, I've got a serious question for you three...
How do you prevent a big dog from biting you?
Ho ho!
Too easy!
I use a WHISTLE to make 'em scoot. It works every time!
TRIIIIIIIIT!
KAÏ
KAÏ
KAÏ
KAÏ
KAÏ
Man, you must have to blow real hard...
There's also the WAR OF THE EYES. You don't move an inch and give him a nasty stare until he get scared away!
EEEIIEE
GULP
A good STINK BOMB does the job. Dogs have a really sensitive sense of smell...
PSHH
The stinky gas, I can handle, tee-hee-hee!

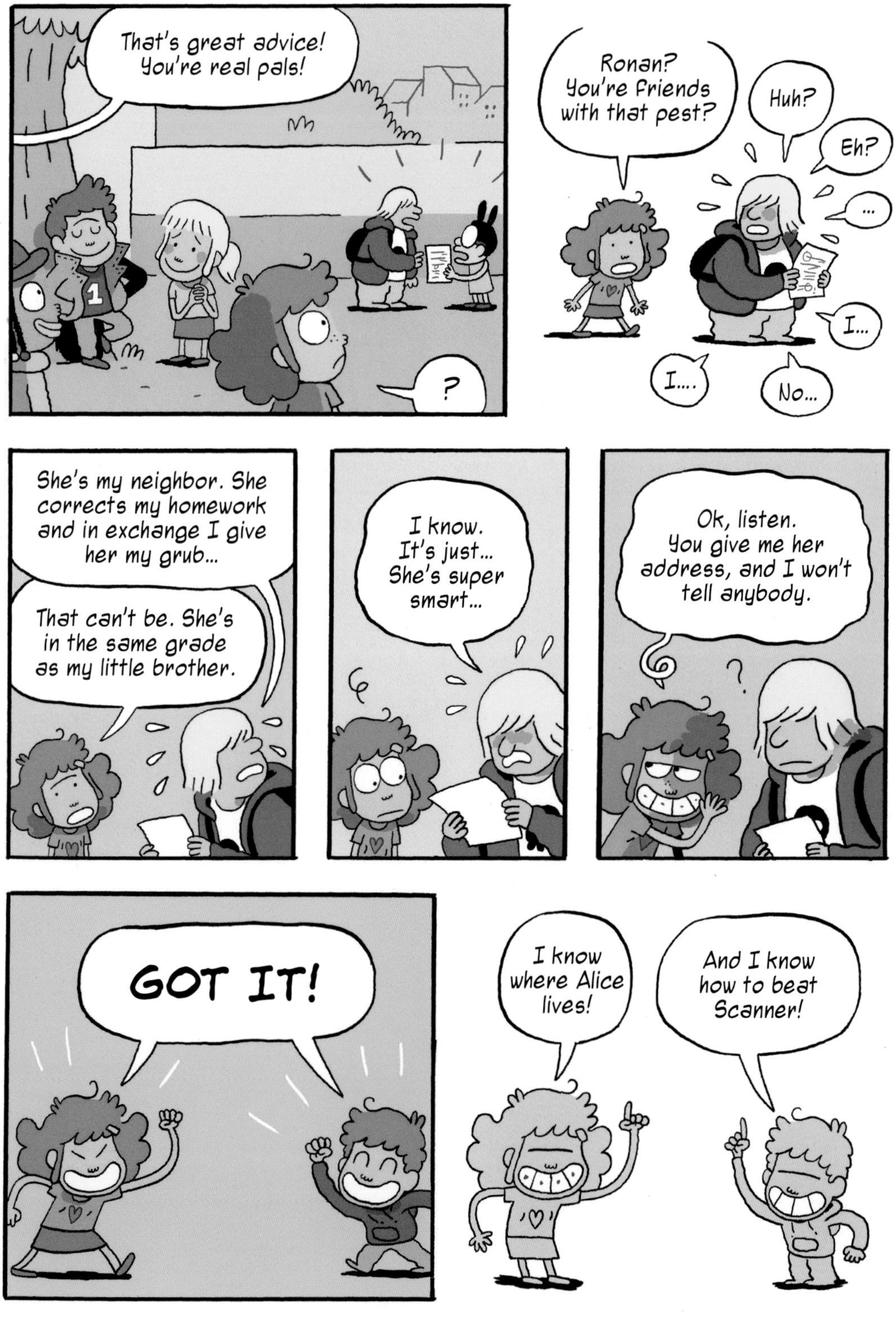
That's great advice! You're real pals!
?
Ronan? You're friends with that pest?
Huh?
Eh?
...
I...
No...
I....
She's my neighbor. She corrects my homework and in exchange I give her my grub...
That can't be. She's in the same grade as my little brother.
I know. It's just... She's super smart...
Ok, listen. You give me her address, and I won't tell anybody.
GOT IT!
I know where Alice lives!
And I know how to beat Scanner!

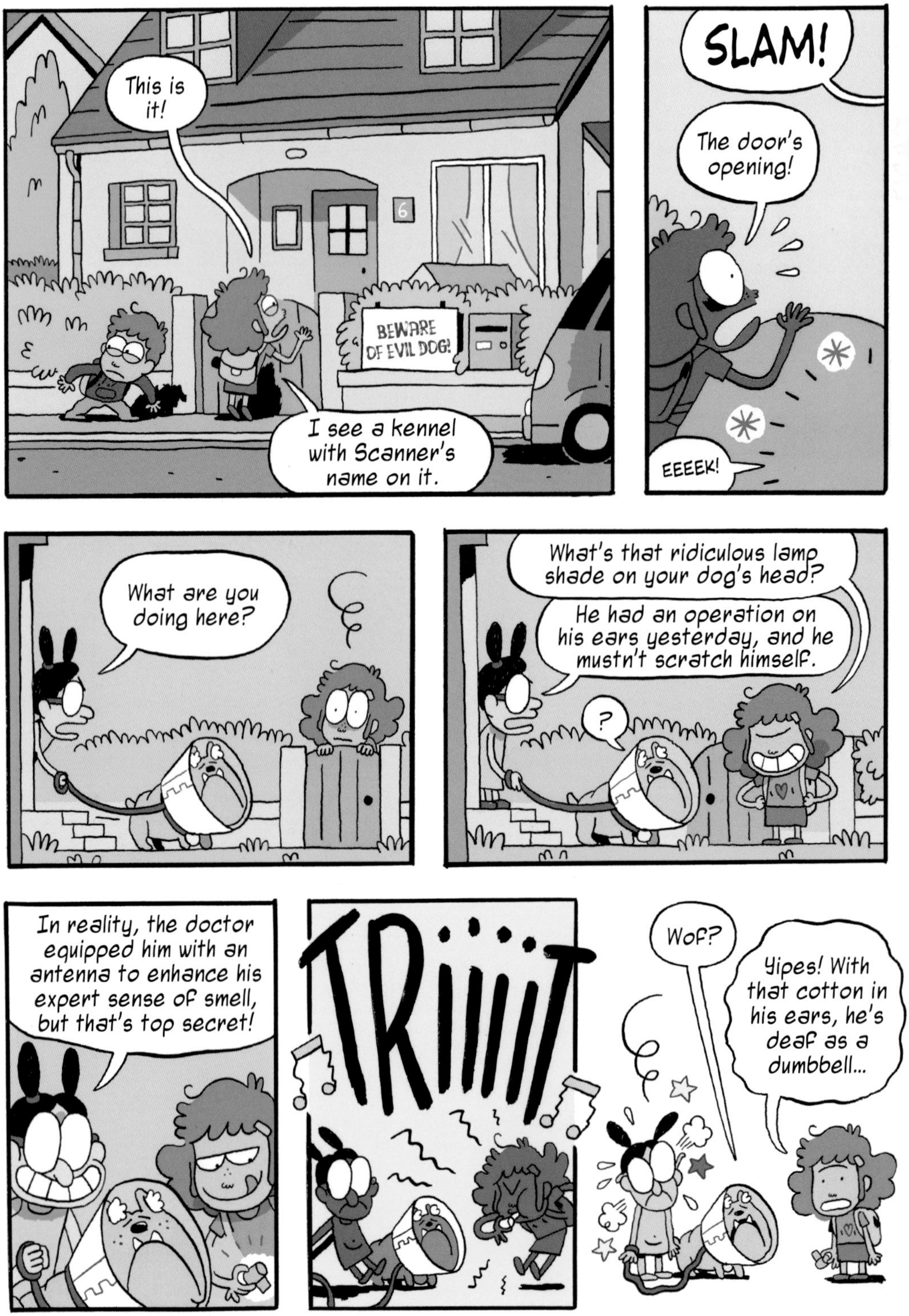
This is it!
BEWARE OF EVIL DOG!
6
I see a kennel with Scanner's name on it.
SLAM!
The door's opening!
EEEEK!
What are you doing here?
What's that ridiculous lamp shade on your dog's head?
He had an operation on his ears yesterday, and he mustn't scratch himself.
?
In reality, the doctor equipped him with an antenna to enhance his expert sense of smell, but that's top secret!
TRiiiiiT
Wof?
Yipes! With that cotton in his ears, he's deaf as a dumbbell...

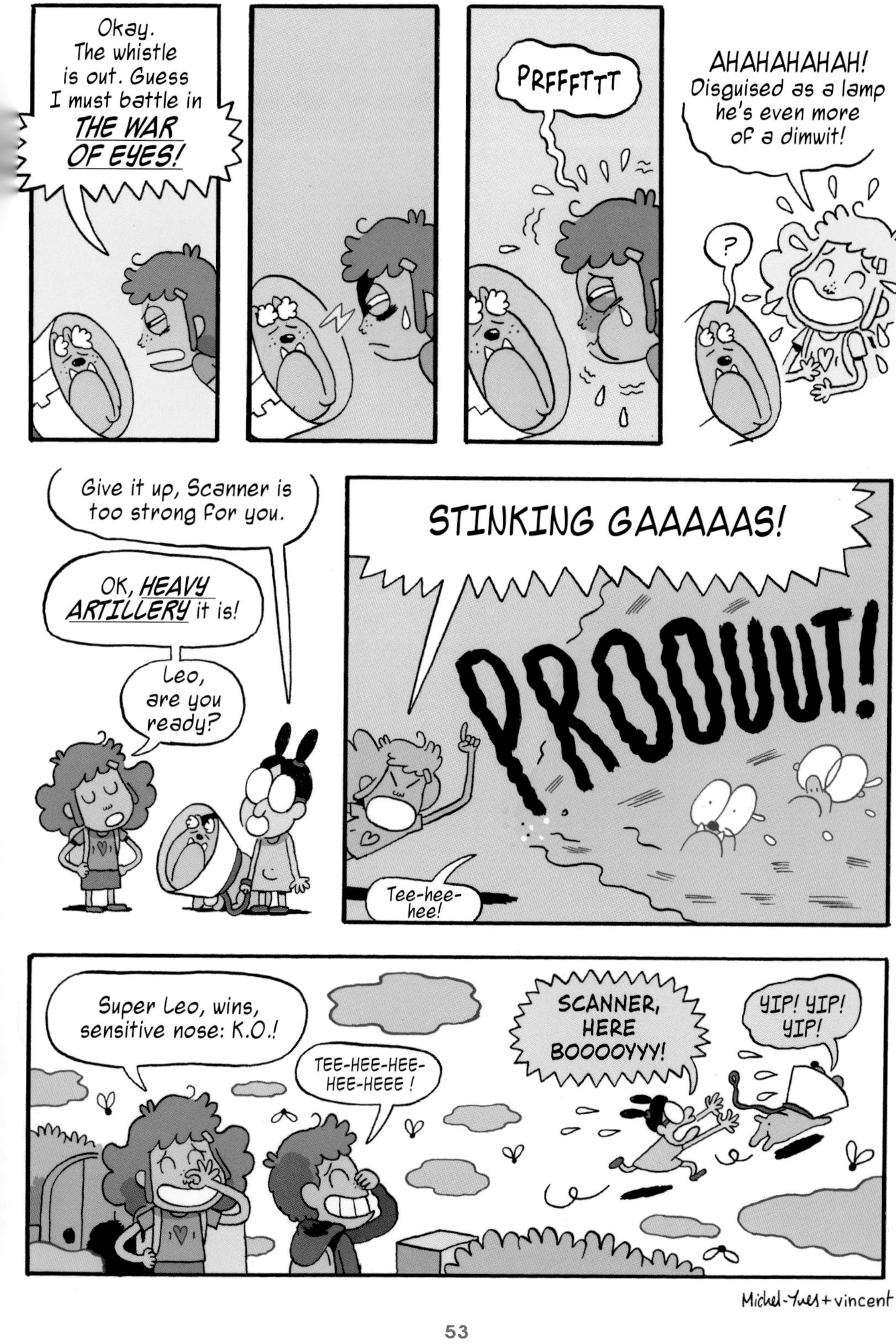

Okay. The whistle is out. Guess I must battle in THE WAR OF EYES!
PRFFFTTT
AHAHAHAHAH! Disguised as a lamp he's even more of a dimwit!
?
Give it up, Scanner is too strong for you.
OK, HEAVY ARTILLERY it is!
Leo, are you ready?
STINKING GAAAAAS!
PROOUUT!
Tee-hee-hee!
Super Leo, wins, sensitive nose: K.O.!
TEE-HEE-HEE-HEE-HEEE !
SCANNER, HERE BOOOOYYY!
YIP! YIP! YIP!

Michel-Yves + vincent

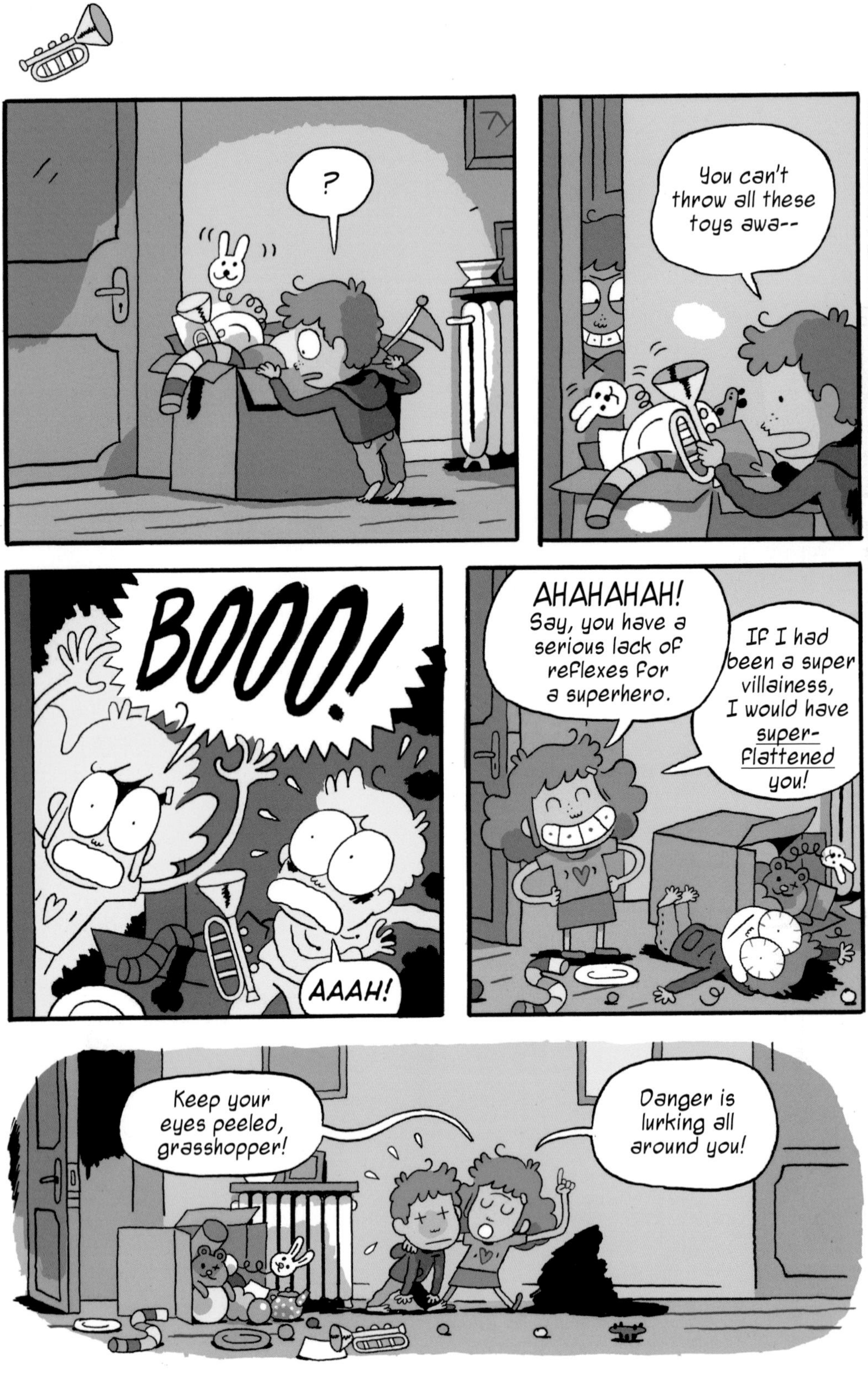
?
You can't throw all these toys awa--
BOOO!
AAAH!
AHAHAHAH! Say, you have a serious lack of reflexes for a superhero.
If I had been a super villainess, I would have super-flattened you!
Keep your eyes peeled, grasshopper!
Danger is lurking all around you!

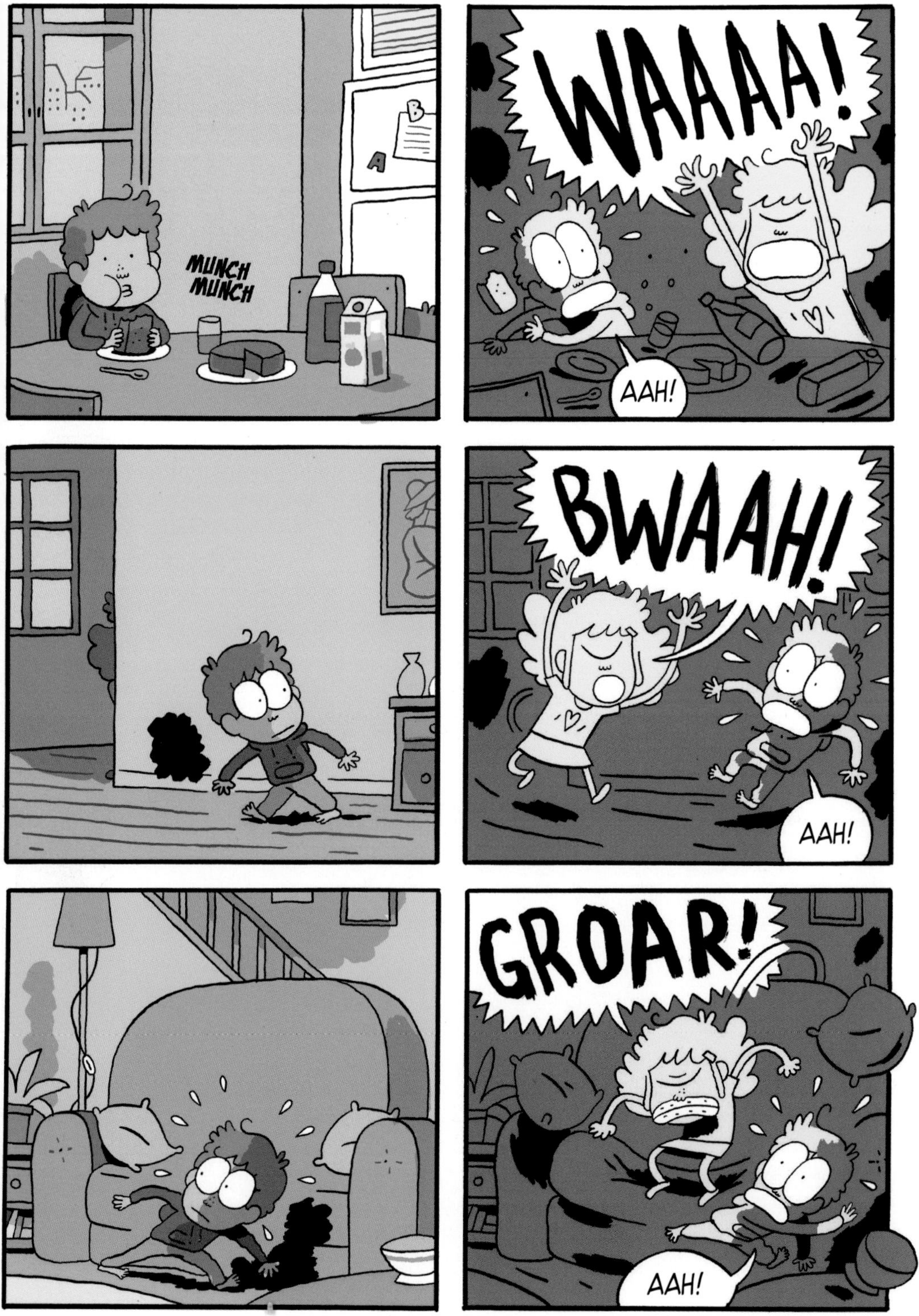
MUNCH
MUNCH
B
A
WAAAAA!
AAH!
BWAAAH!
AAH!
GROAR!
AAH!

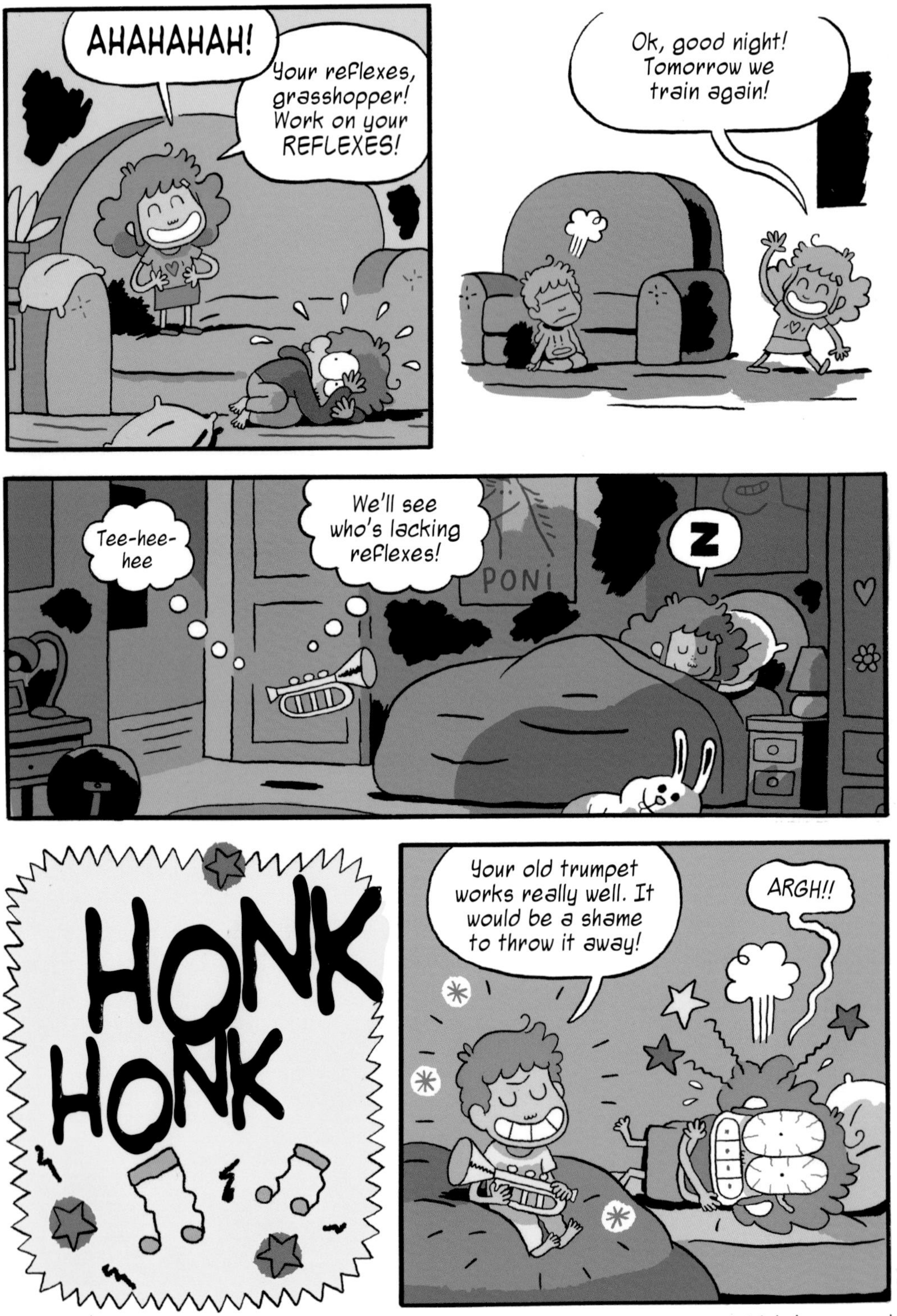
AHAHAHAH!
Your reflexes, grasshopper! Work on your REFLEXES!
Ok, good night! Tomorrow we train again!
Tee-hee-hee
We'll see who's lacking reflexes!
PONI
Z
HONK HONK
Your old trumpet works really well. It would be a shame to throw it away!
ARGH!!
Michel-Yves + vincent

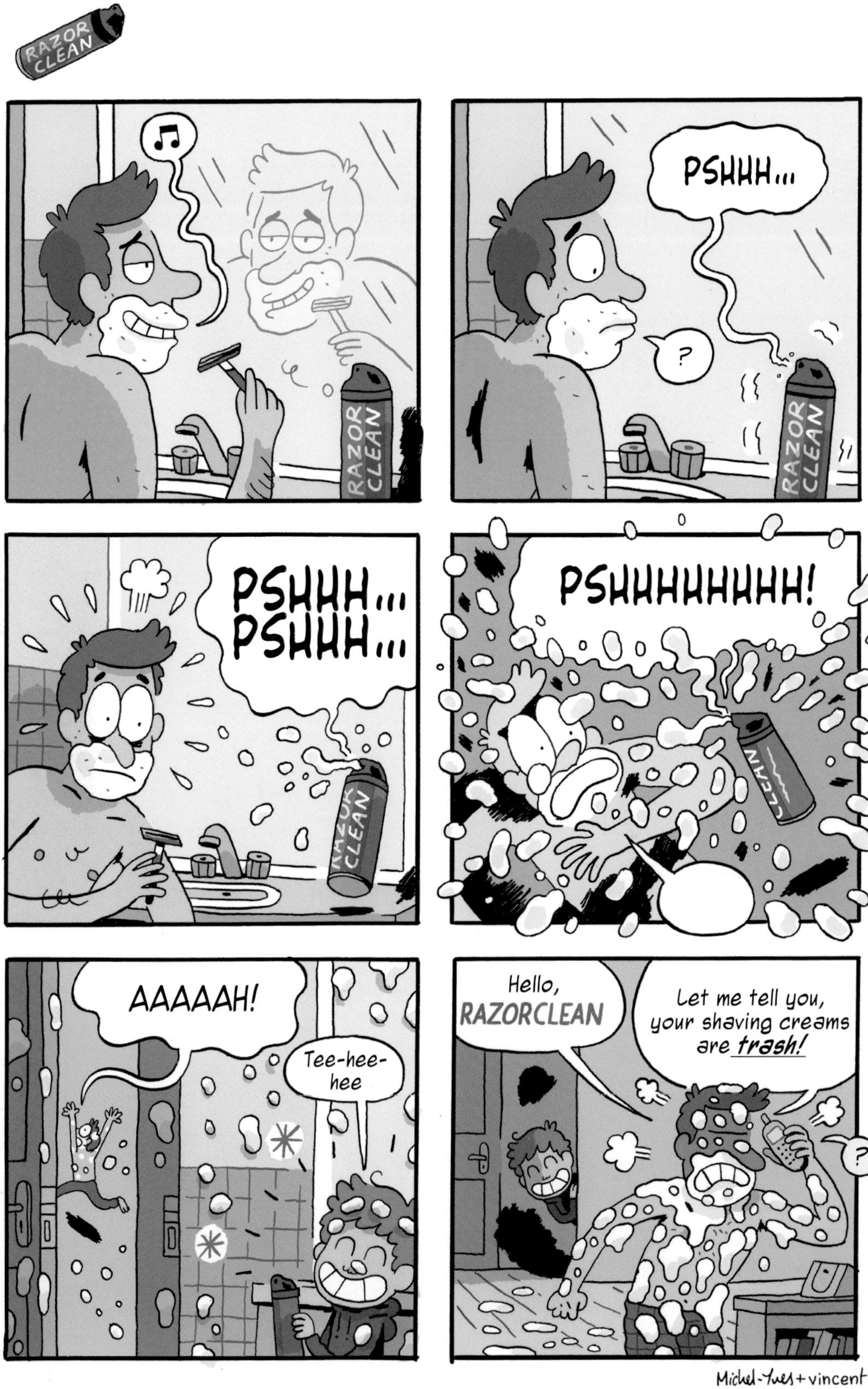
RAZOR CLEAN
RAZOR CLEAN
PSHHH...
?
RAZOR CLEAN
PSHHH... PSHHH...
RAZOR CLEAN
PSHHHHHHHH!
CLEAN
AAAAAH!
Tee-hee-hee
Hello, RAZORCLEAN
Let me tell you, your shaving creams are *trash!*
?

Michel-Yves + vincent

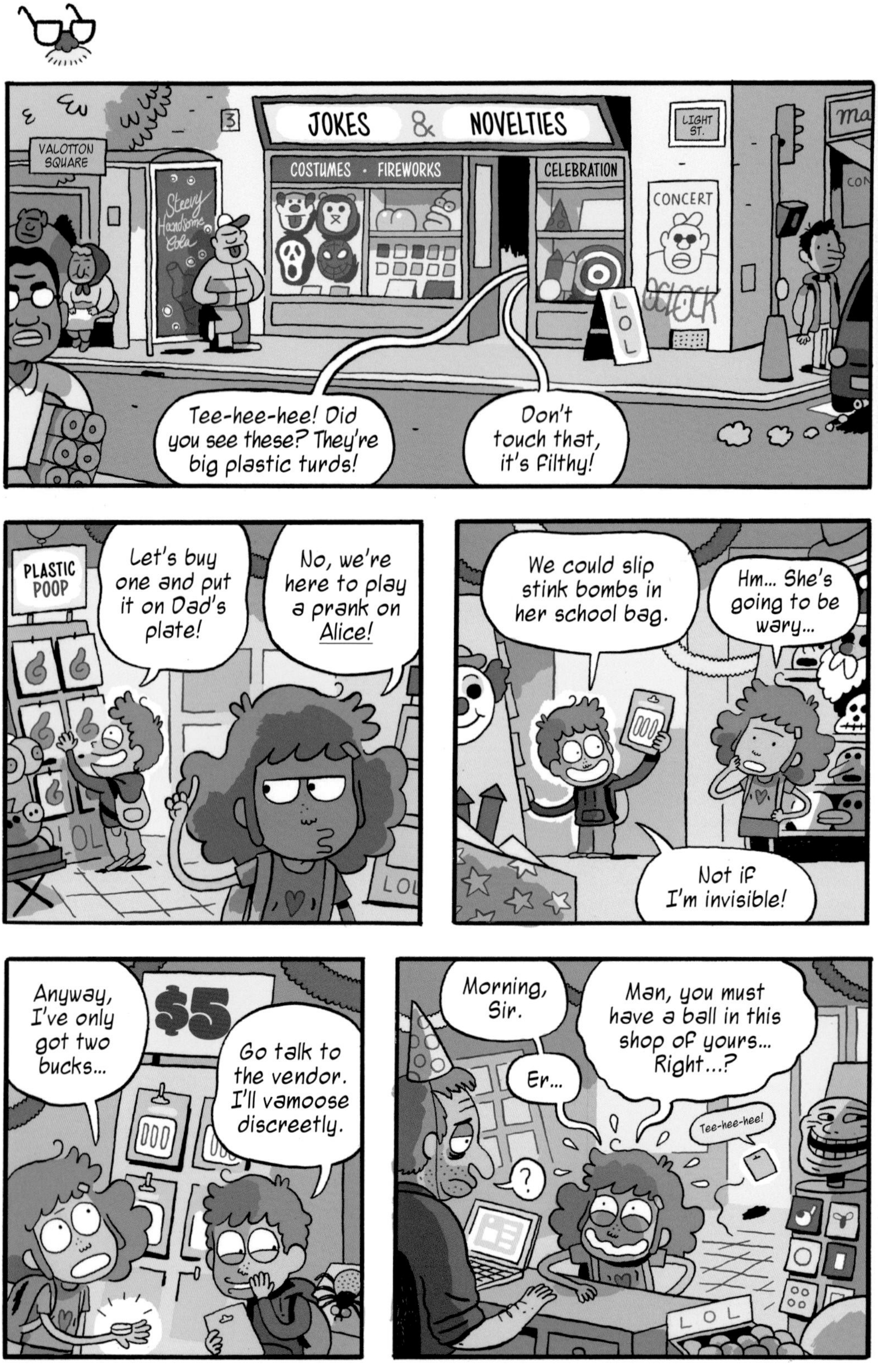
VALOTTON SQUARE
JOKES & NOVELTIES
COSTUMES · FIREWORKS
CELEBRATION
LIGHT ST.
CONCERT
LOL
Tee-hee-hee! Did you see these? They're big plastic turds!
Don't touch that, it's filthy!
PLASTIC POOP
Let's buy one and put it on Dad's plate!
No, we're here to play a prank on Alice!
We could slip stink bombs in her school bag.
Hm... She's going to be wary...
Not if I'm invisible!
Anyway, I've only got two bucks...
$5
Go talk to the vendor. I'll vamoose discreetly.
Morning, Sir.
Er...
Man, you must have a ball in this shop of yours... Right...?
Tee-hee-hee!
?
LOL

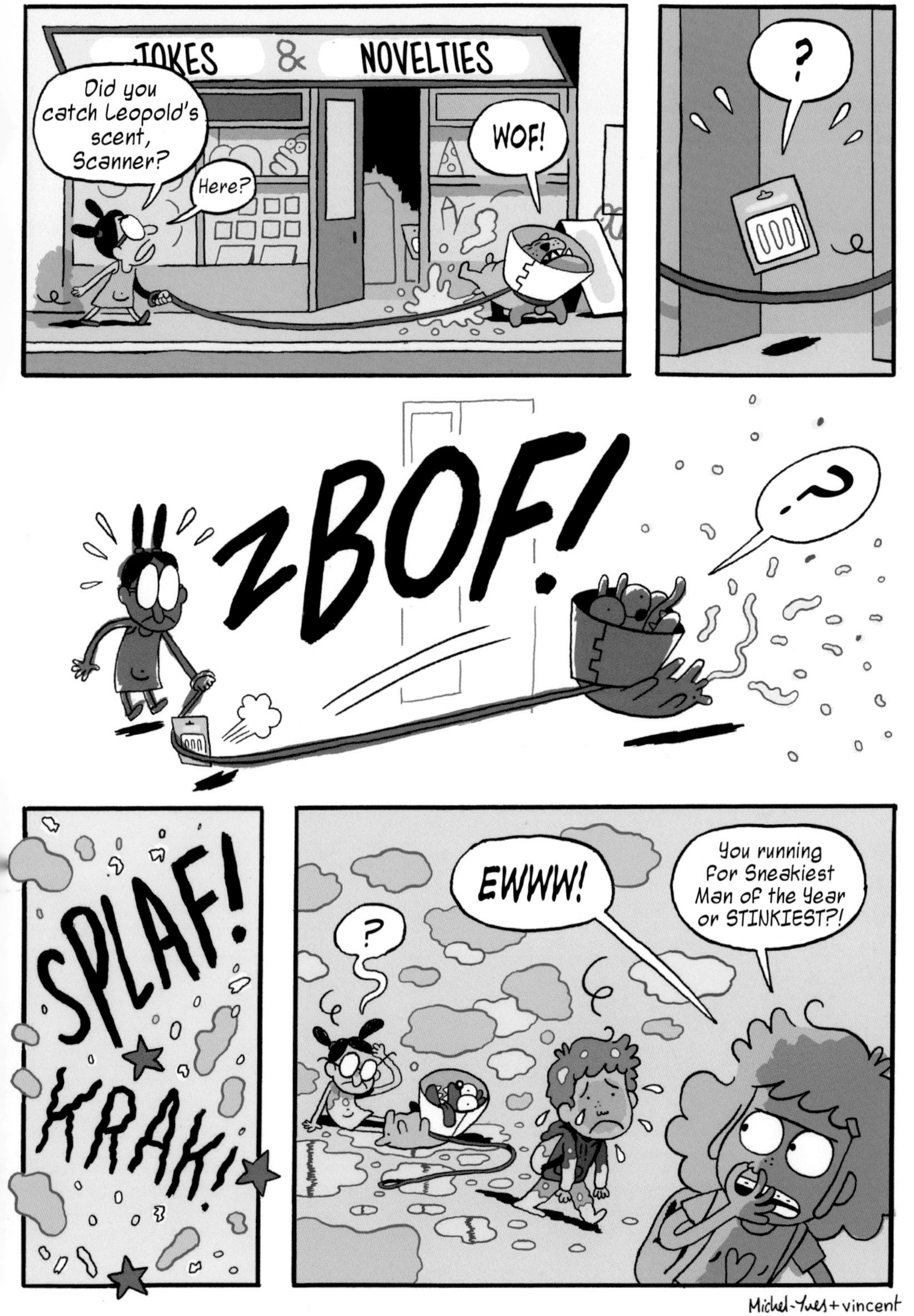
JOKES & NOVELTIES
Did you catch Leopold's scent, Scanner?
Here?
WOF!
?
ZBOF!
?
SPLAF!
KRAK!
?
EWWW!
You running for Sneakiest Man of the Year or STINKIEST?!
Michel-Yves + vincent

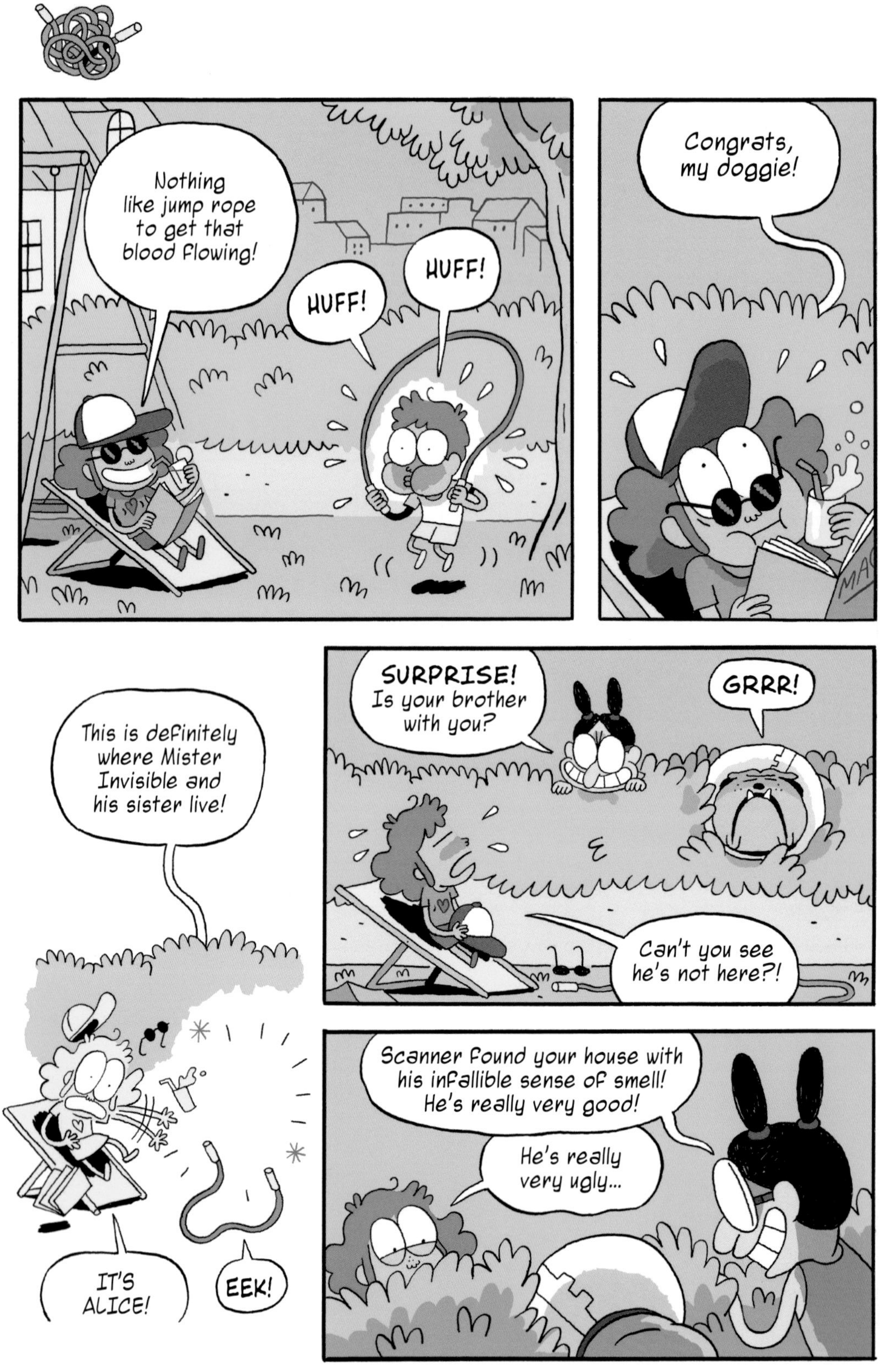

Nothing like jump rope to get that blood flowing!
HUFF!
HUFF!
Congrats, my doggie!
This is definitely where Mister Invisible and his sister live!
IT'S ALICE!
EEK!
SURPRISE! Is your brother with you?
GRRR!
Can't you see he's not here?!
Scanner found your house with his infallible sense of smell! He's really very good!
He's really very ugly...

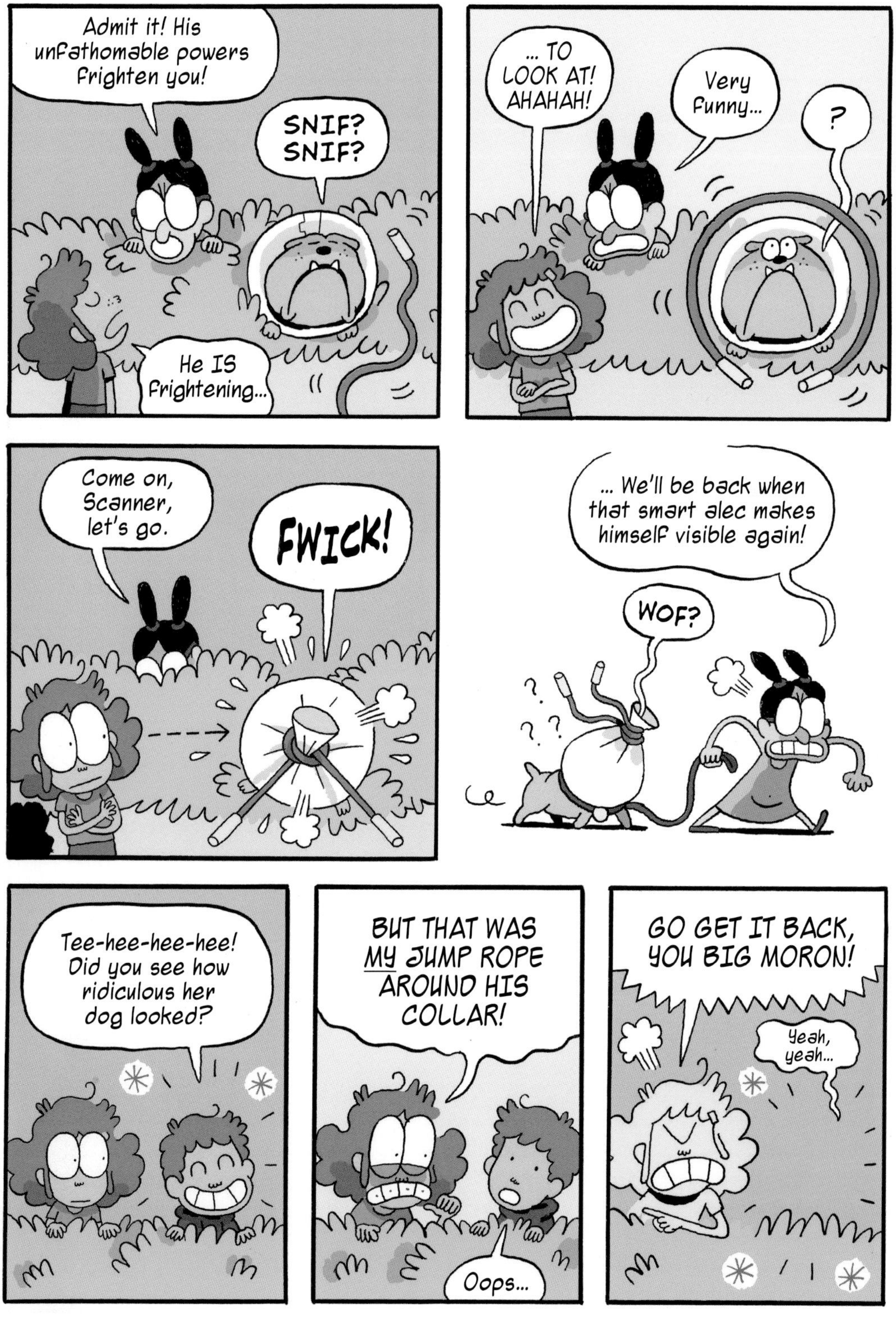

Admit it! His unfathomable powers frighten you!
SNIF? SNIF?
He IS frightening...
... TO LOOK AT! AHAHAH!
Very funny...
?
Come on, Scanner, let's go.
FWICK!
... We'll be back when that smart alec makes himself visible again!
WOF?
Tee-hee-hee-hee! Did you see how ridiculous her dog looked?
BUT THAT WAS MY JUMP ROPE AROUND HIS COLLAR!
Oops...
GO GET IT BACK, YOU BIG MORON!
Yeah, yeah...

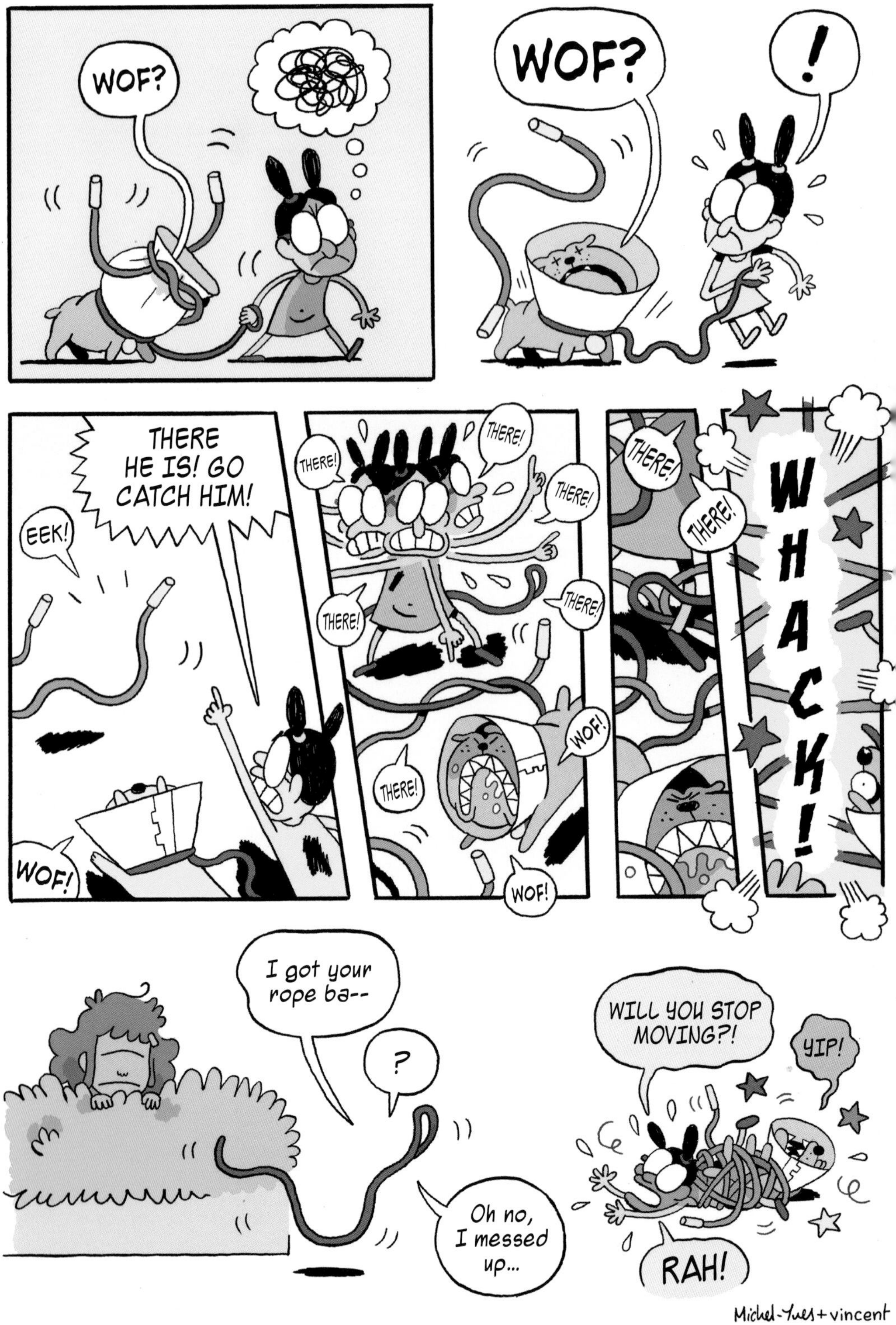

WOF?
WOF?
!
THERE HE IS! GO CATCH HIM!
EEK!
WOF!
THERE!
THERE!
THERE!
THERE!
THERE!
THERE!
WOF!
WOF!
THERE!
THERE!
WHACK!
I got your rope ba--
?
Oh no, I messed up...
WILL YOU STOP MOVING?!
YIP!
RAH!
Michel-Yves + vincent

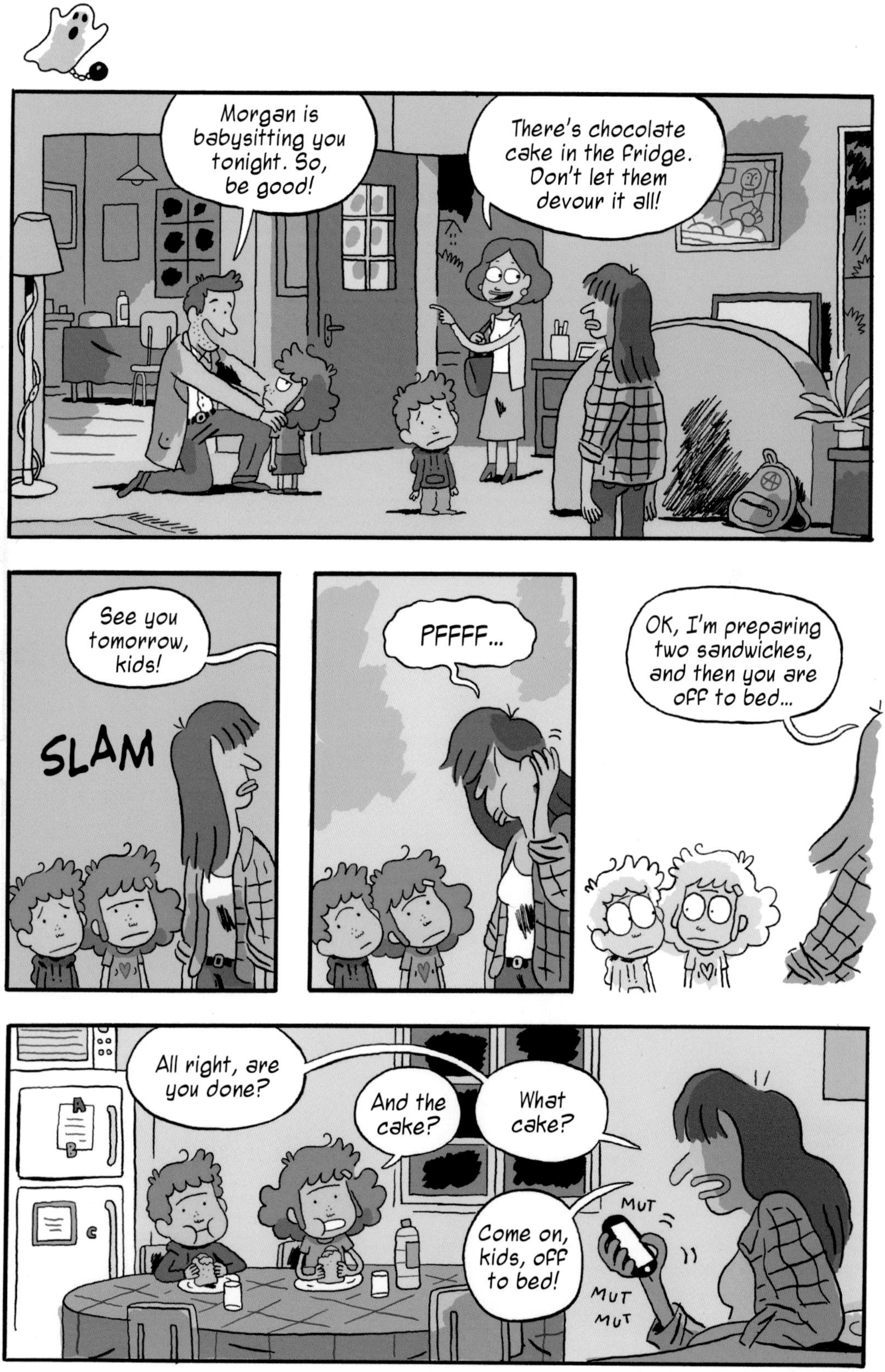
Morgan is babysitting you tonight. So, be good!
There's chocolate cake in the fridge. Don't let them devour it all!
See you tomorrow, kids!
SLAM
PFFFF...
OK, I'm preparing two sandwiches, and then you are off to bed...
All right, are you done?
And the cake?
What cake?
Come on, kids, off to bed!
MUT
MUT
MUT

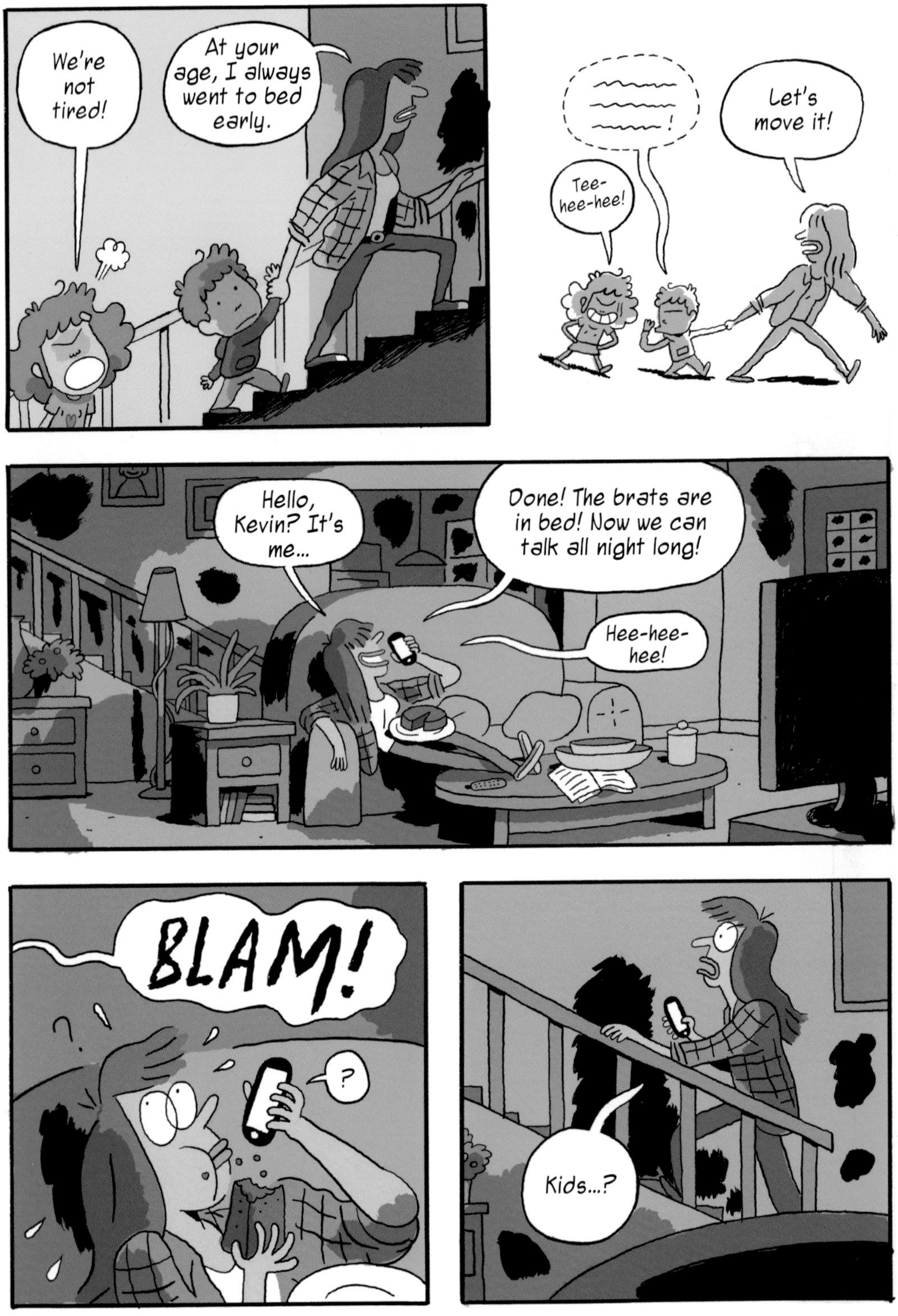
We're not tired!
At your age, I always went to bed early.
~~~~ ~~~~ ~~~~!
Let's move it!
Tee-hee-hee!
Hello, Kevin? It's me...
Done! The brats are in bed! Now we can talk all night long!
Hee-hee-hee!
BLAM!
?
?
Kids...?
~~~~

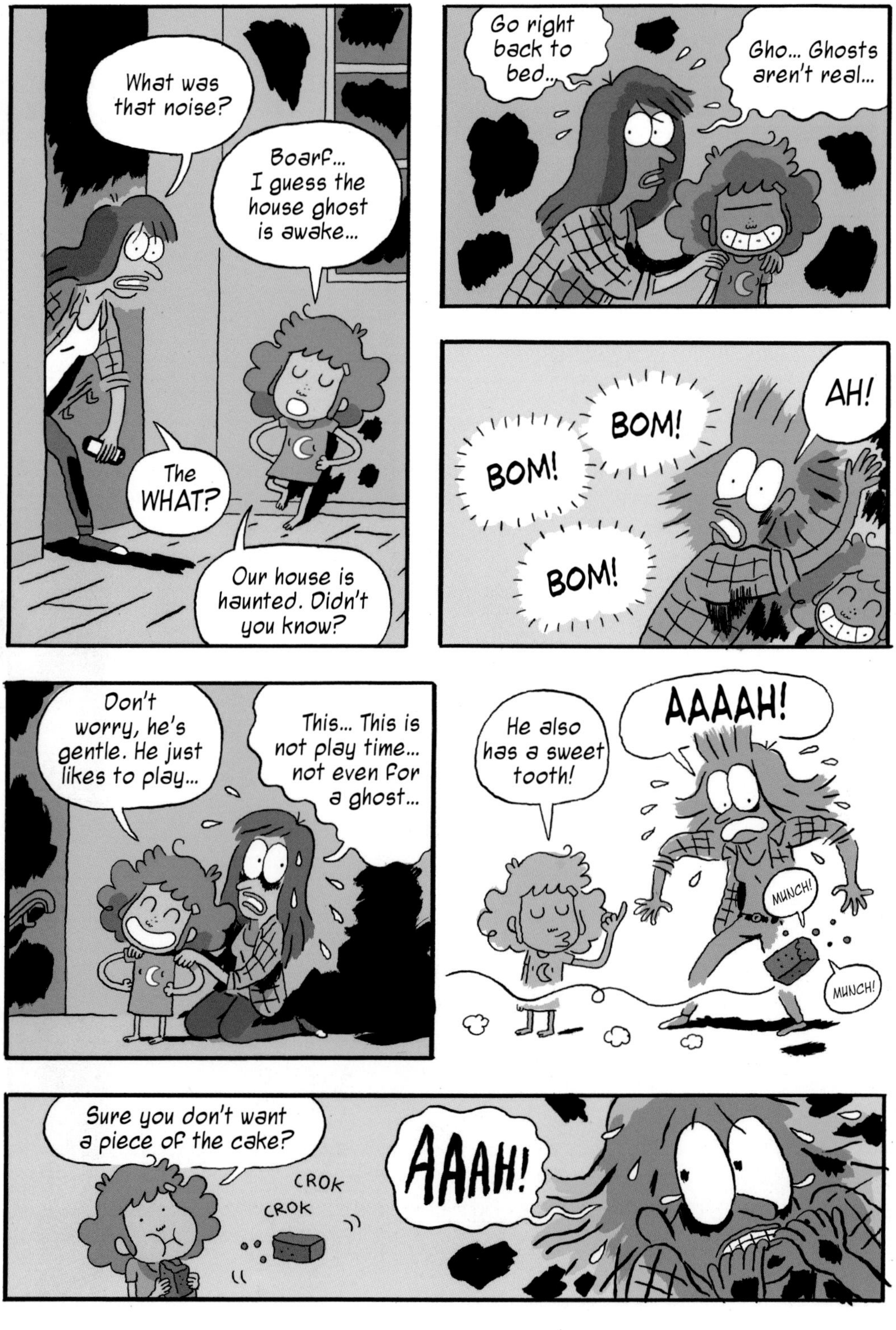
What was that noise?
Boarf... I guess the house ghost is awake...
The WHAT?
Our house is haunted. Didn't you know?
Go right back to bed...
Gho... Ghosts aren't real...
AH!
BOM!
BOM!
BOM!
Don't worry, he's gentle. He just likes to play...
This... This is not play time... not even for a ghost...
He also has a sweet tooth!
AAAAH!
MUNCH!
MUNCH!
Sure you don't want a piece of the cake?
CROK
CROK
AAAH!

Go on, play with him!
No... No... Wa... way!
POC
BOOHOOHOOH!
AH!
CLICK!
NOOOO! The lights!
AAAAH! He touched my arm!
He likes you.
He's going to play with you ALL NIGHT, tee-hee-hee!
KLAK KLAK KLAK! Come and get me, Kevin!
KLAK KLAK KLAK!

Michel-Yves+vincent

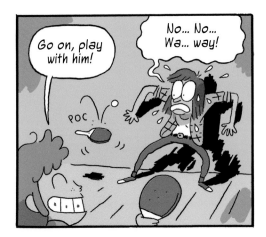

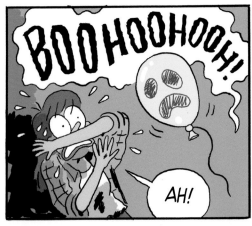

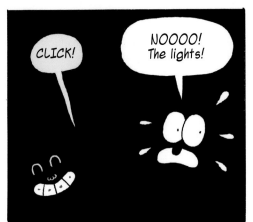

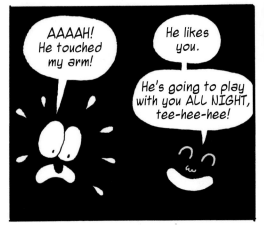

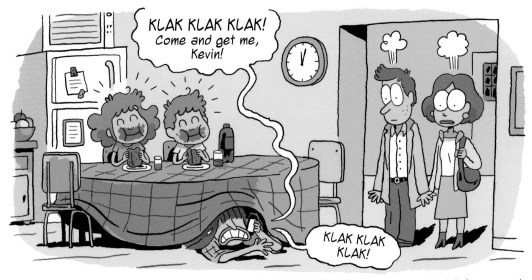

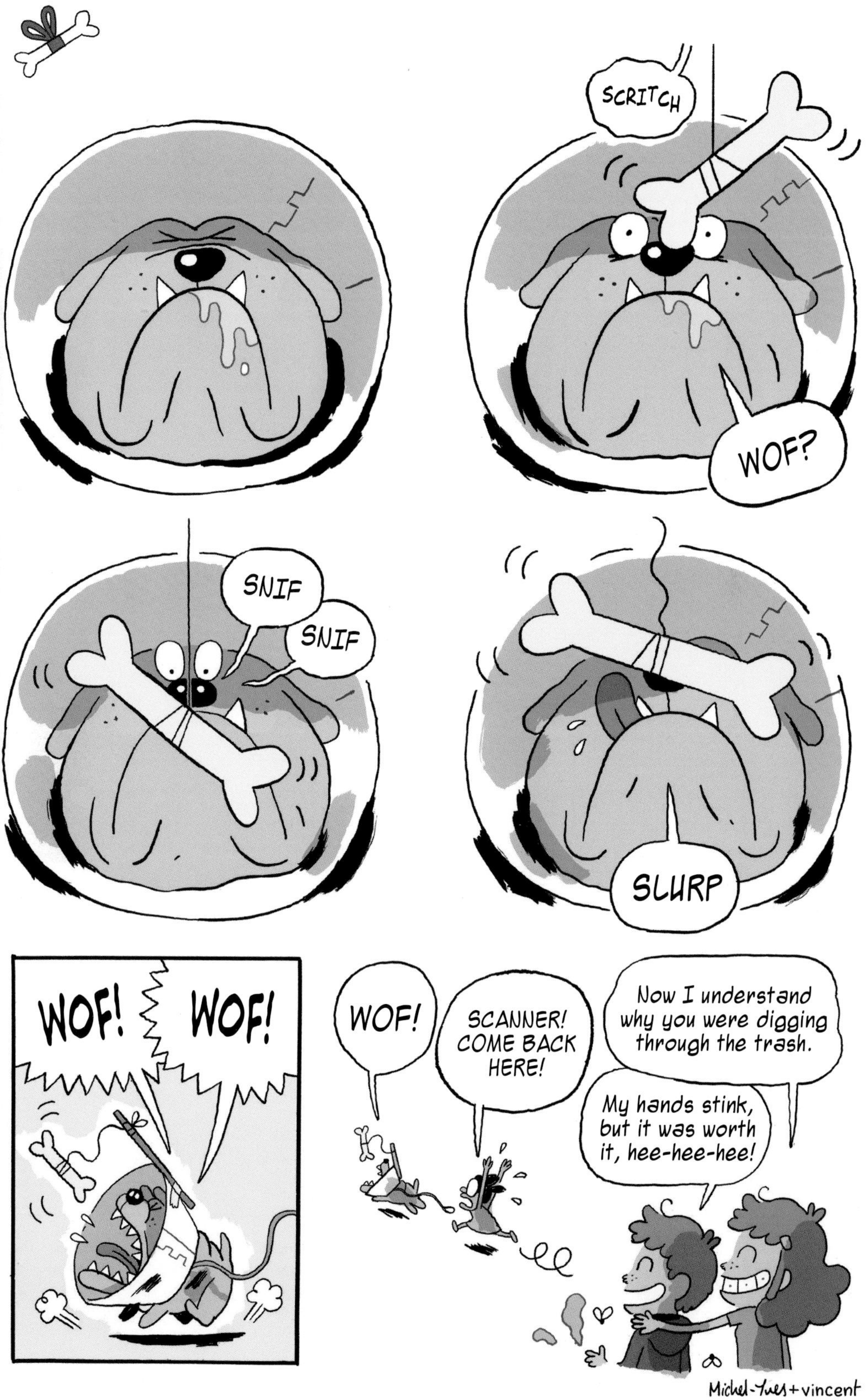
SCRITCH
WOF?
SNIF
SNIF
SLURP
WOF! WOF!
WOF!
SCANNER! COME BACK HERE!
Now I understand why you were digging through the trash.
My hands stink, but it was worth it, hee-hee-hee!
Michel-Yves + vincent

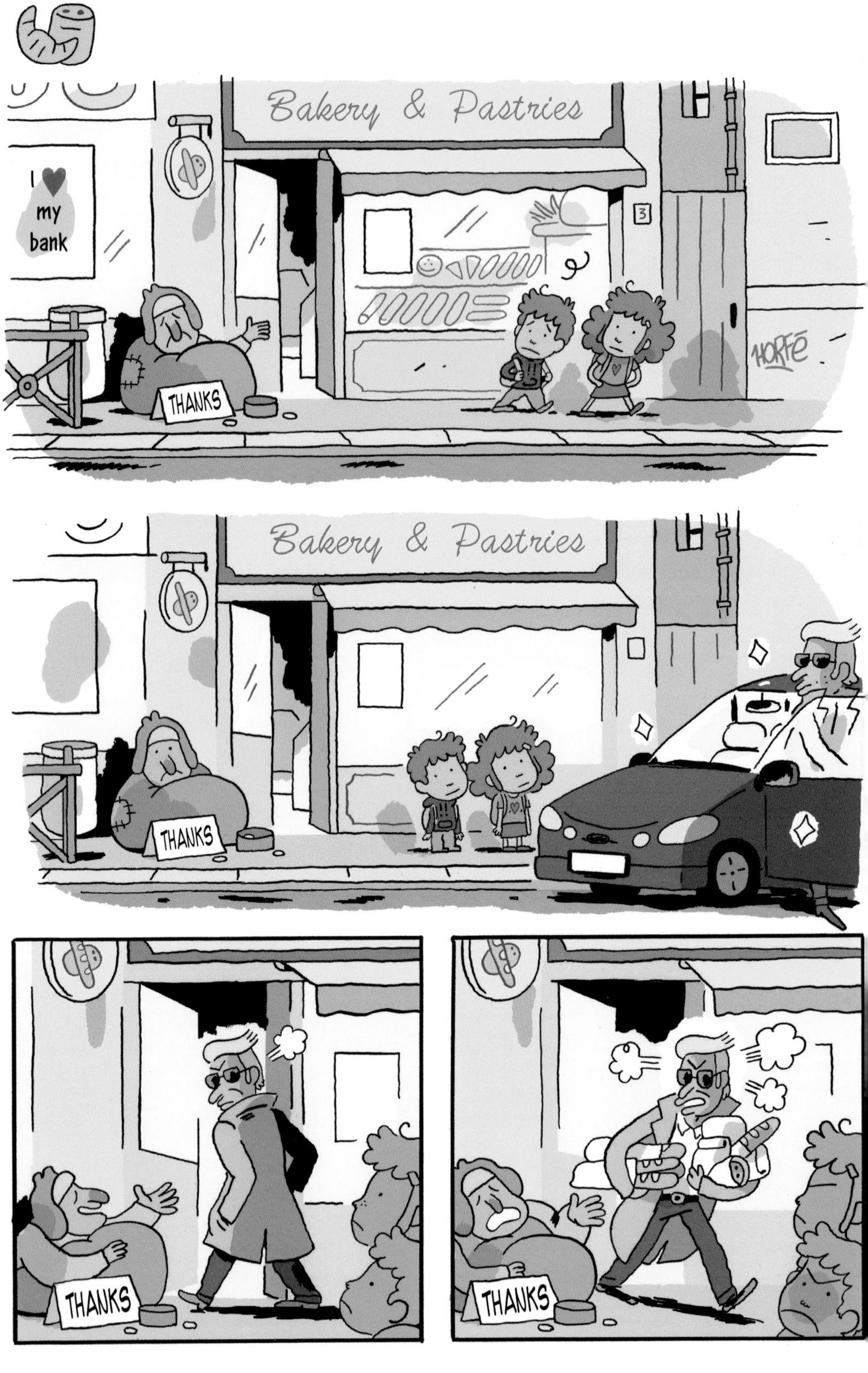
Bakery & Pastries
I ♥ my bank
THANKS
3
HORFÉ
Bakery & Pastries
THANKS
THANKS
THANKS

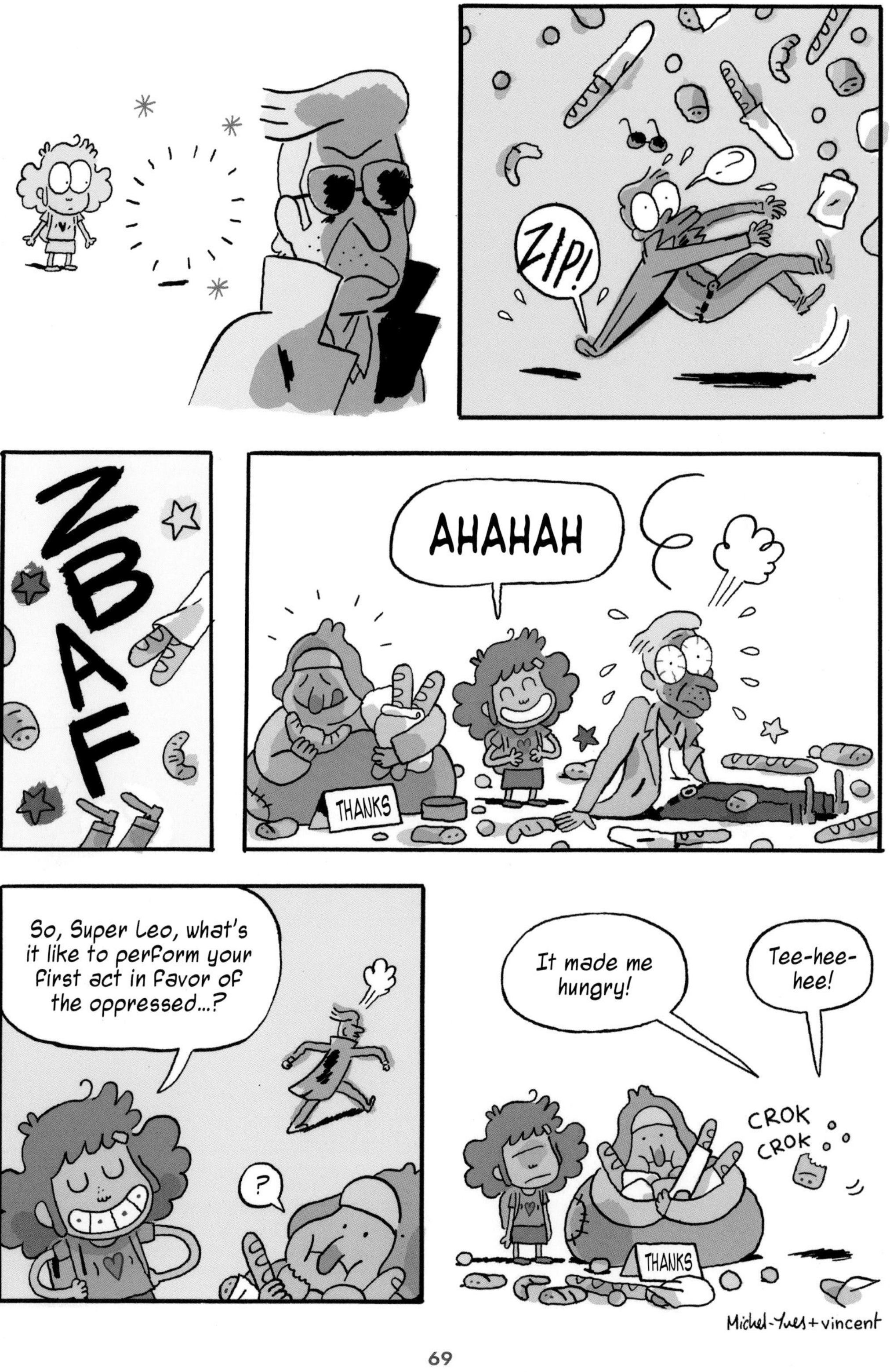
ZIP!
ZBAF
AHAHAH
THANKS
So, Super Leo, what's it like to perform your first act in favor of the oppressed...?
?
It made me hungry!
Tee-hee-hee!
CROK CROK
THANKS

Michel-Yves+vincent

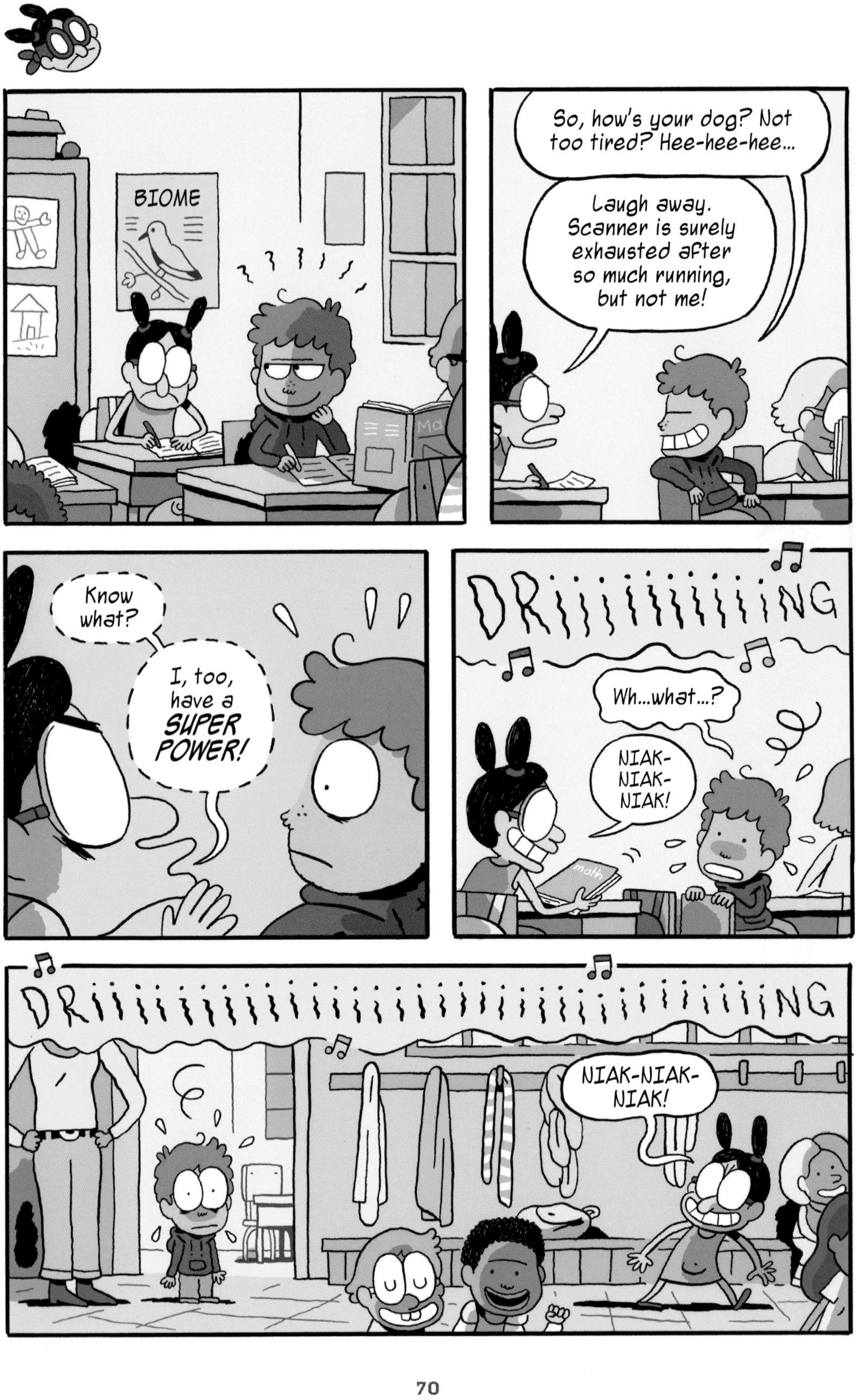

BIOME
So, how's your dog? Not too tired? Hee-hee-hee...
Laugh away. Scanner is surely exhausted after so much running, but not me!
Know what?
I, too, have a SUPER POWER!
DRiiiiiiiiiiiNG
Wh...what...?
NIAK-NIAK-NIAK!
math
DRiiiiiiiiiiiiiiiiiiiiiiiiiiiiiiiiNG
NIAK-NIAK-NIAK!

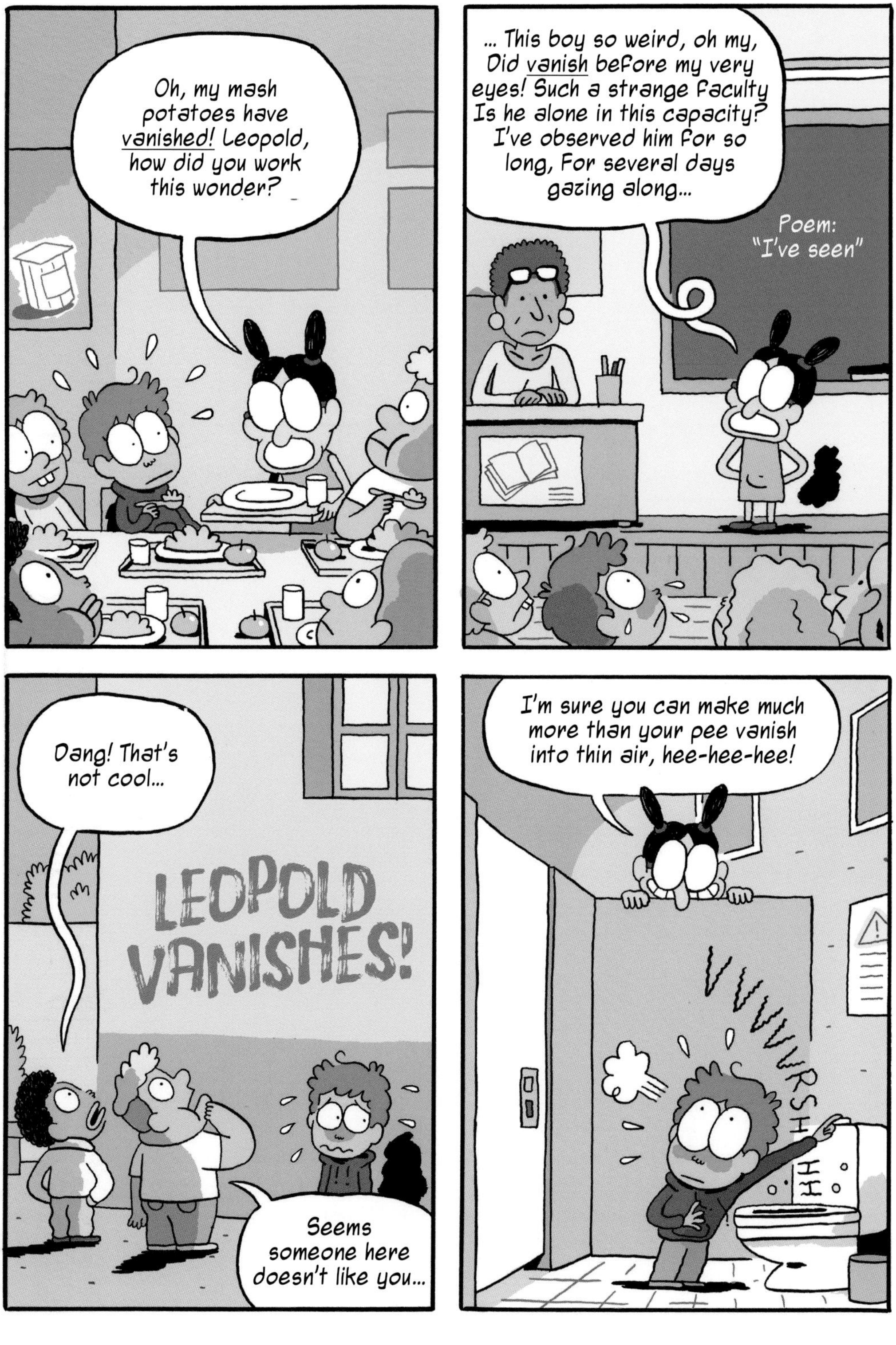
Oh, my mash potatoes have vanished! Leopold, how did you work this wonder?
... This boy so weird, oh my, Did vanish before my very eyes! Such a strange faculty Is he alone in this capacity? I've observed him for so long, For several days gazing along...
Poem: "I've seen"
Dang! That's not cool...
LEOPOLD VANISHES!
Seems someone here doesn't like you...
I'm sure you can make much more than your pee vanish into thin air, hee-hee-hee!
VVVVVRSHHH

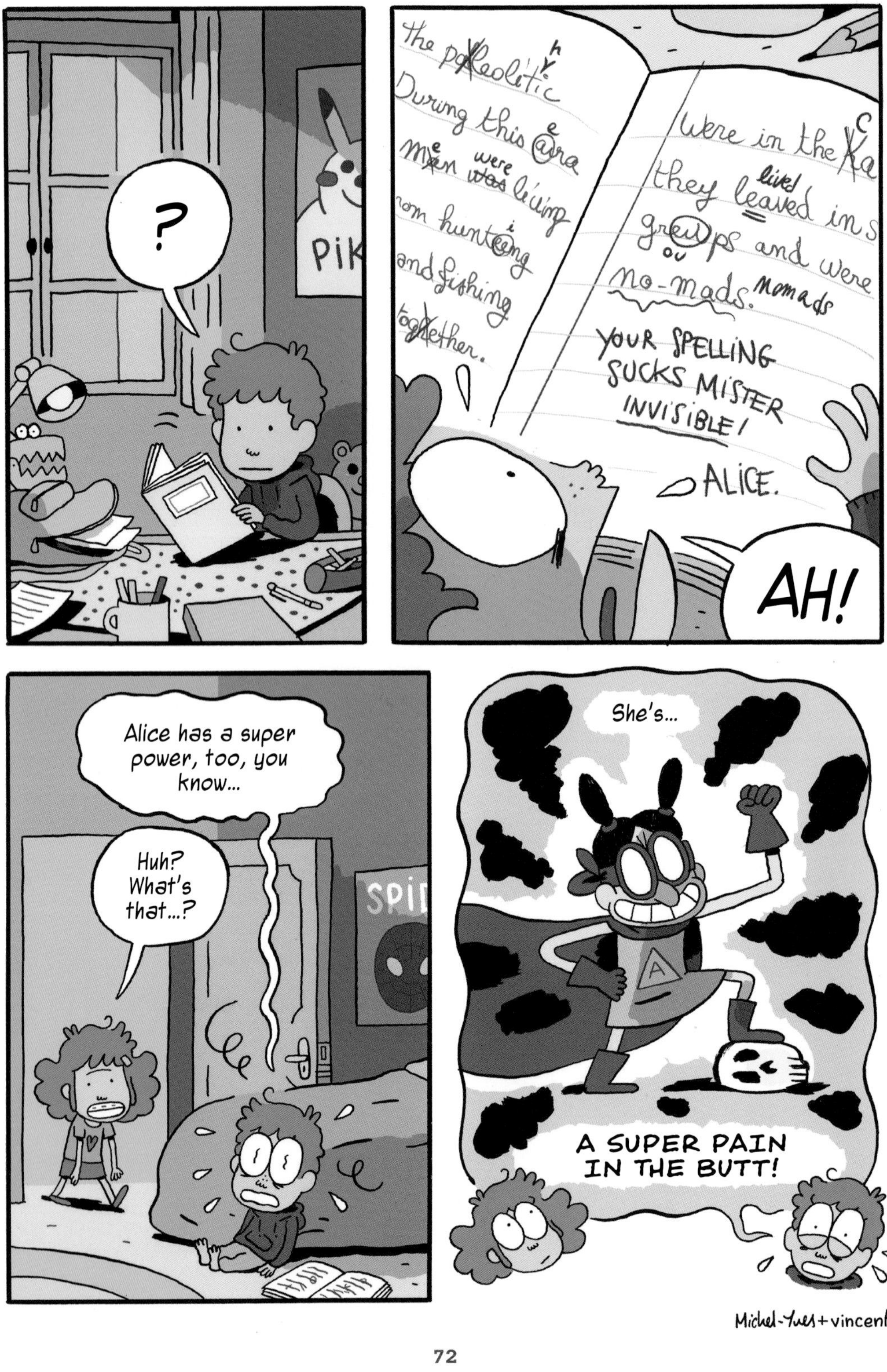
?
During this @ra
they leaved in s
greups and were
no-mads.
YOUR SPELLING SUCKS MISTER INVISIBLE!
ALICE.
AH!
Alice has a super power, too, you know...
Huh? What's that...?
She's...
A SUPER PAIN IN THE BUTT!

Michel-Yves+vincent

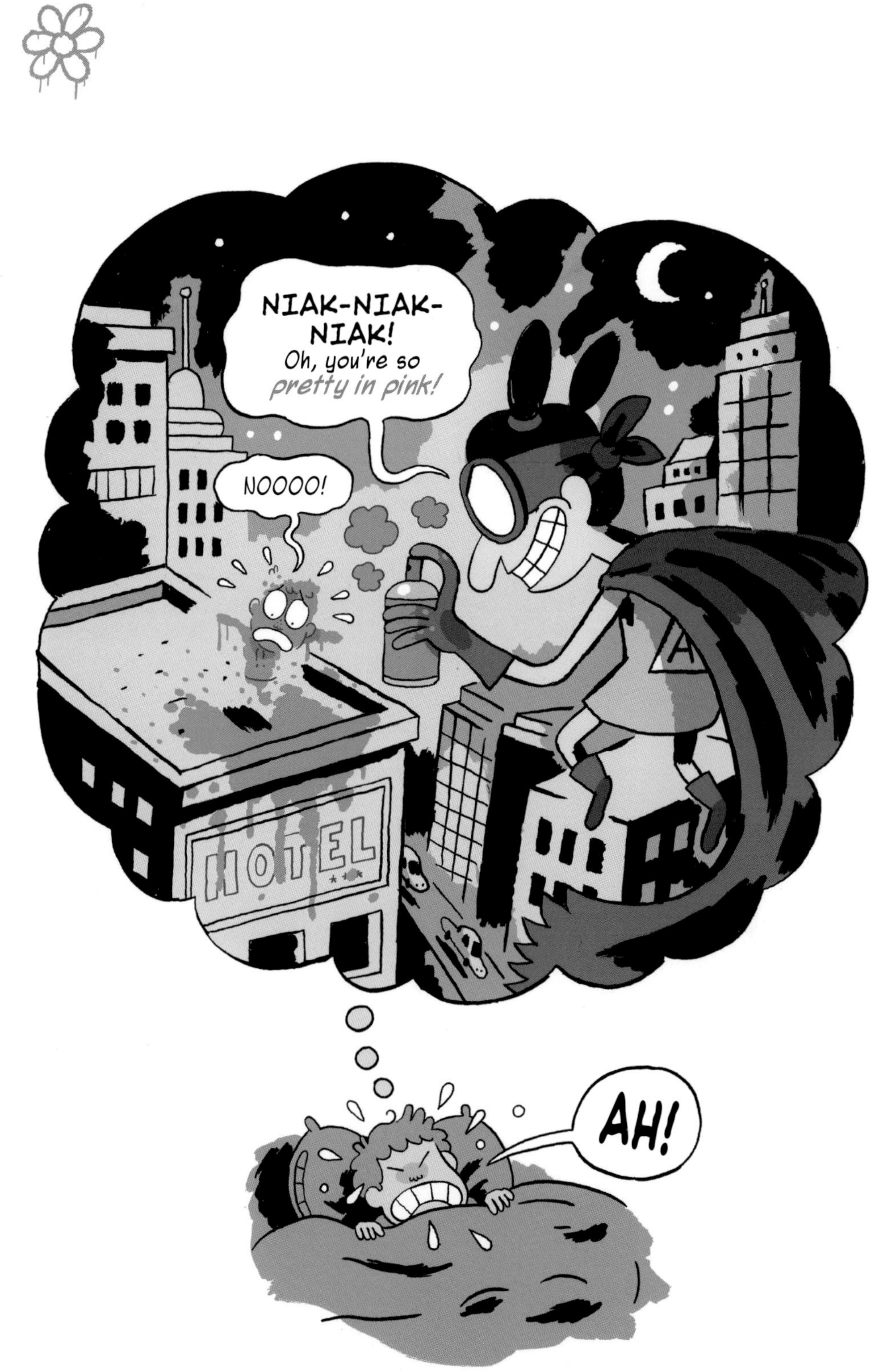
NIAK-NIAK-NIAK!
Oh, you're so pretty in pink!
NOOOO!
HOTEL
AH!

Michel-Yves + vincent

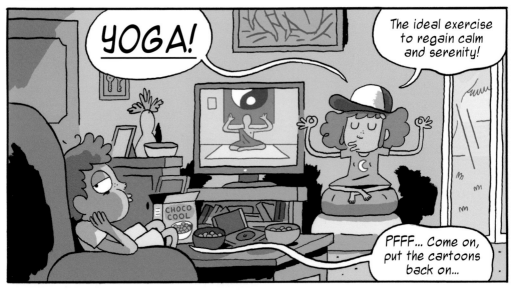

YOGA!

The ideal exercise to regain calm and serenity!

CHOCO COOL

PFFF... Come on, put the cartoons back on...

Mom does yoga. We'll ask her to take us to her class.

I don't want to! Being calm sucks...

A superhero is always serene, even in the face of danger.

I learned that at my Shaolin school when I...

Hey! Ho!

Your imaginary school! It's just make believe for Valentine and Julie.

Yeah... well. Yoga is cool.

And anyway, I already told mom. She's excited for us to do a family activity!

WHAT?

Ah, there you are, my sweethearts! Get ready, we're off to take pretty photos for your yoga passes.

74

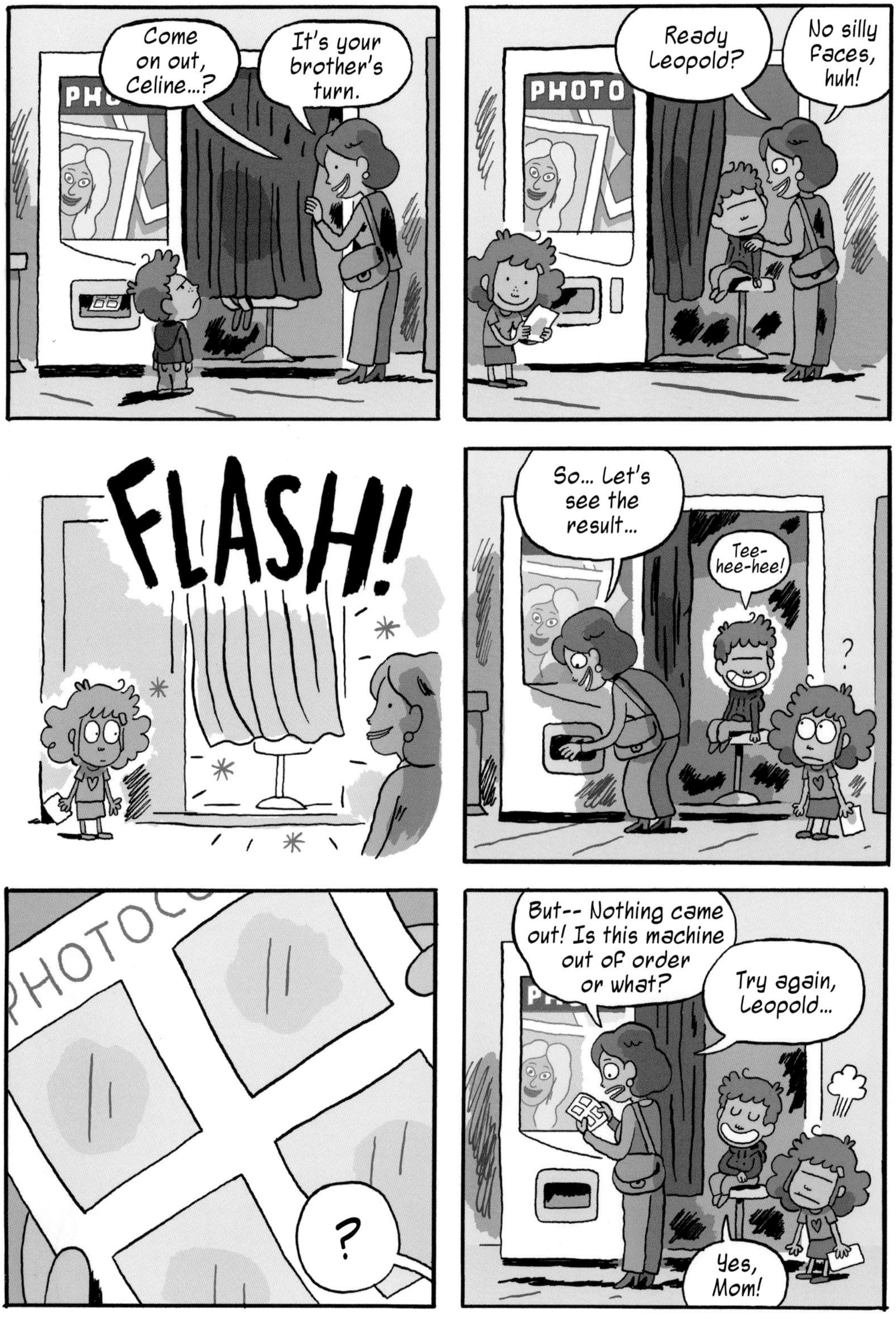
Come on out, Celine...?
It's your brother's turn.
Ready Leopold?
No silly faces, huh!
PHOTO
FLASH!
So... Let's see the result...
Tee-hee-hee!
?
PHOTOCO
?
But-- Nothing came out! Is this machine out of order or what?
Try again, Leopold...
Yes, Mom!

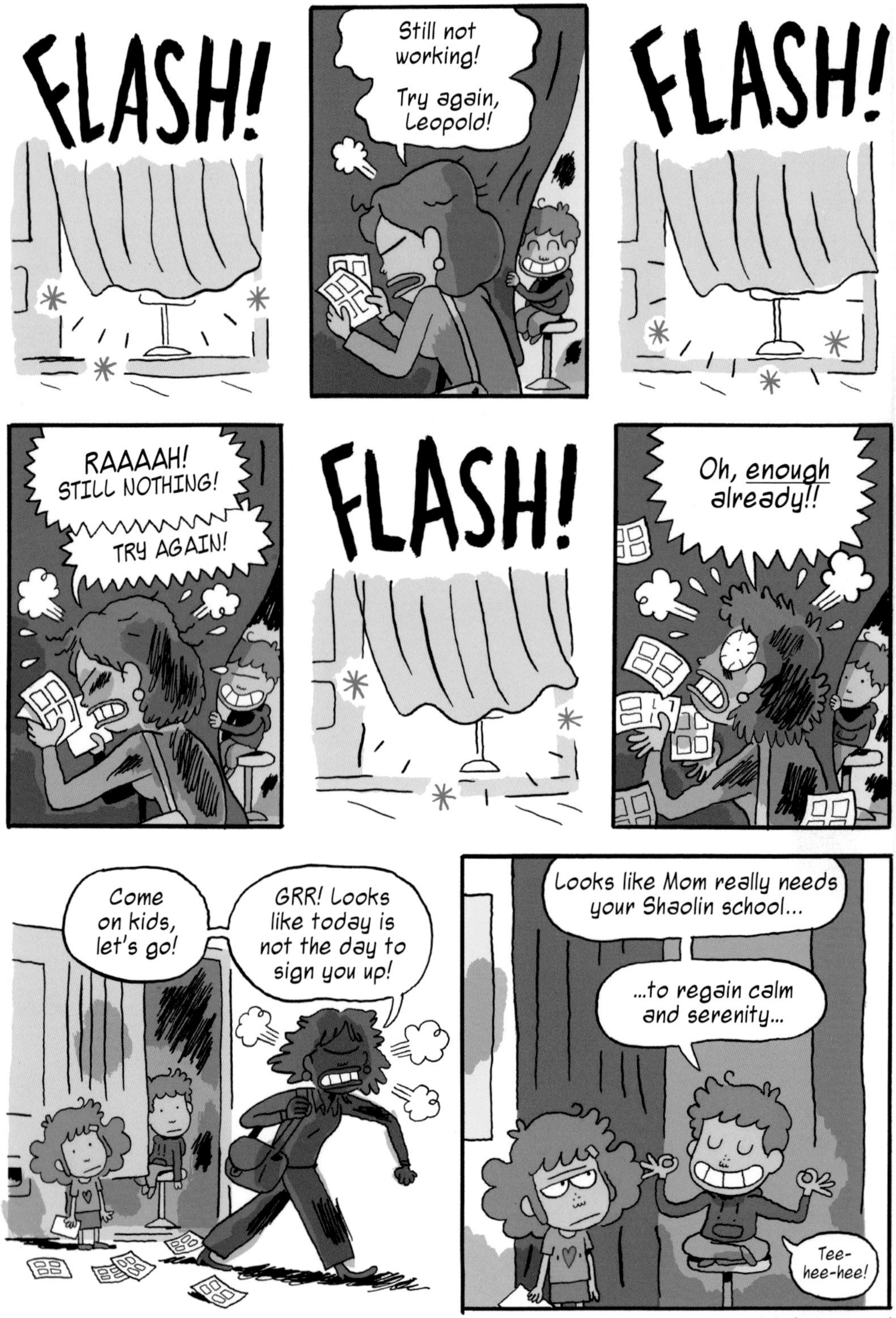
FLASH!
Still not working!
Try again, Leopold!
FLASH!
RAAAAH! STILL NOTHING!
TRY AGAIN!
FLASH!
Oh, enough already!!
Come on kids, let's go!
GRR! Looks like today is not the day to sign you up!
Looks like Mom really needs your Shaolin school...
...to regain calm and serenity...
Tee-hee-hee!
Michel-Yves+vincent

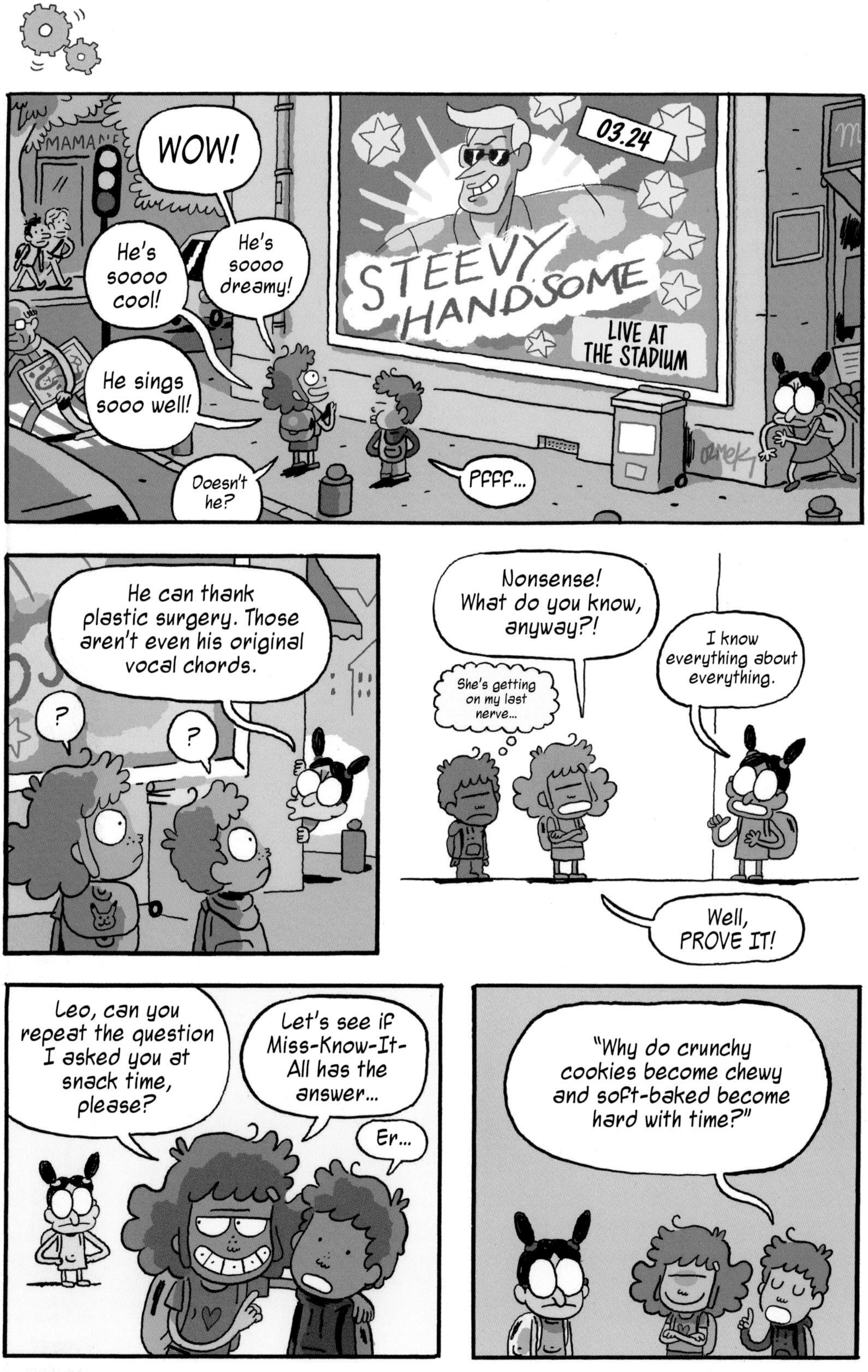
MAMANE
03.24
STEEVY HANDSOME
LIVE AT THE STADIUM
WOW!
He's soooo cool!
He's soooo dreamy!
He sings sooo well!
Doesn't he?
PFFF...
He can thank plastic surgery. Those aren't even his original vocal chords.
?
?
Nonsense! What do you know, anyway?!
She's getting on my last nerve...
I know everything about everything.
Well, PROVE IT!
Leo, can you repeat the question I asked you at snack time, please?
Let's see if Miss-Know-It-All has the answer...
Er...
"Why do crunchy cookies become chewy and soft-baked become hard with time?"

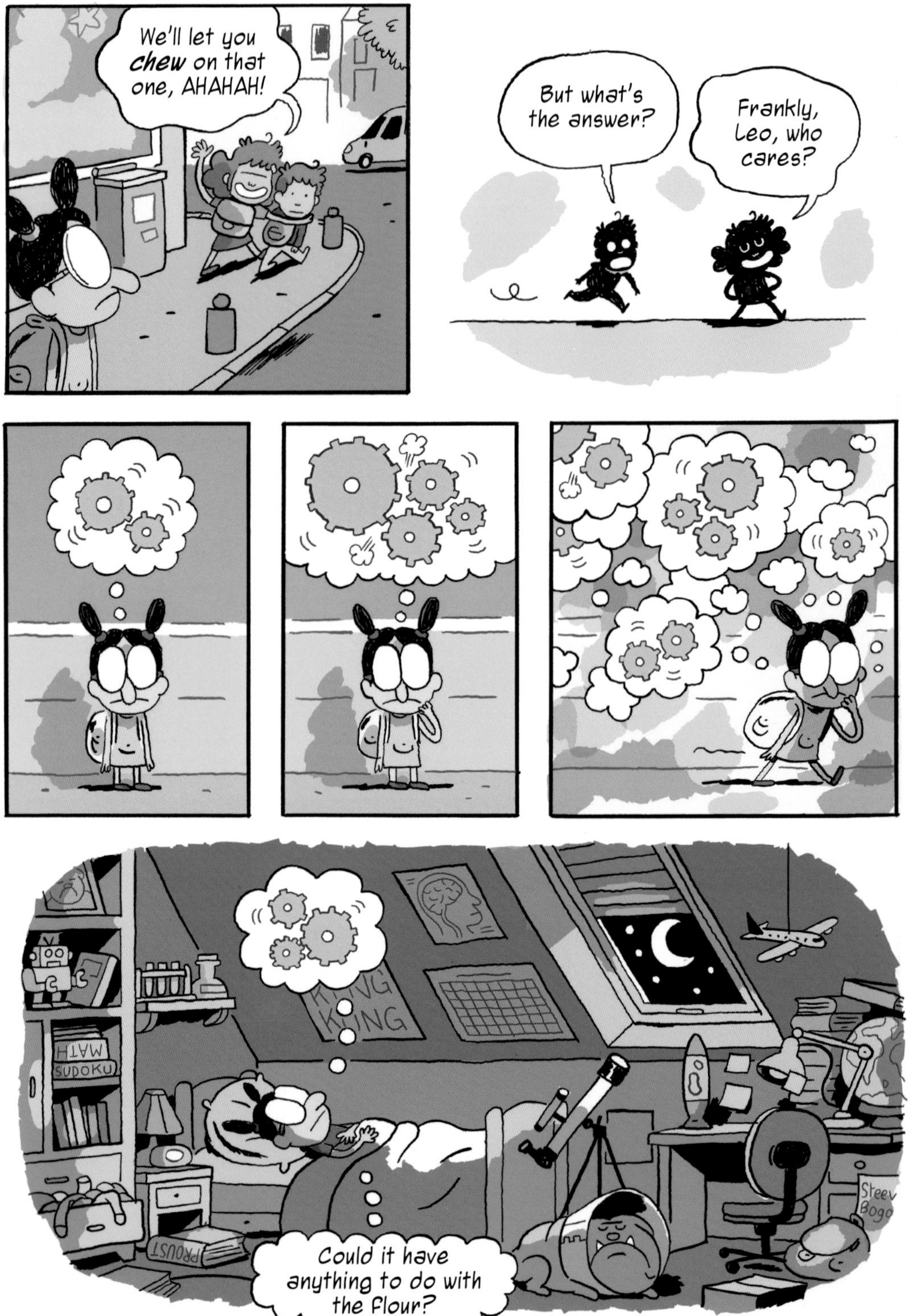
We'll let you **chew** on that one, AHAHAH!
But what's the answer?
Frankly, Leo, who cares?
SUDOKU
PROUST
Could it have anything to do with the flour?
Michel-Yves + vincent

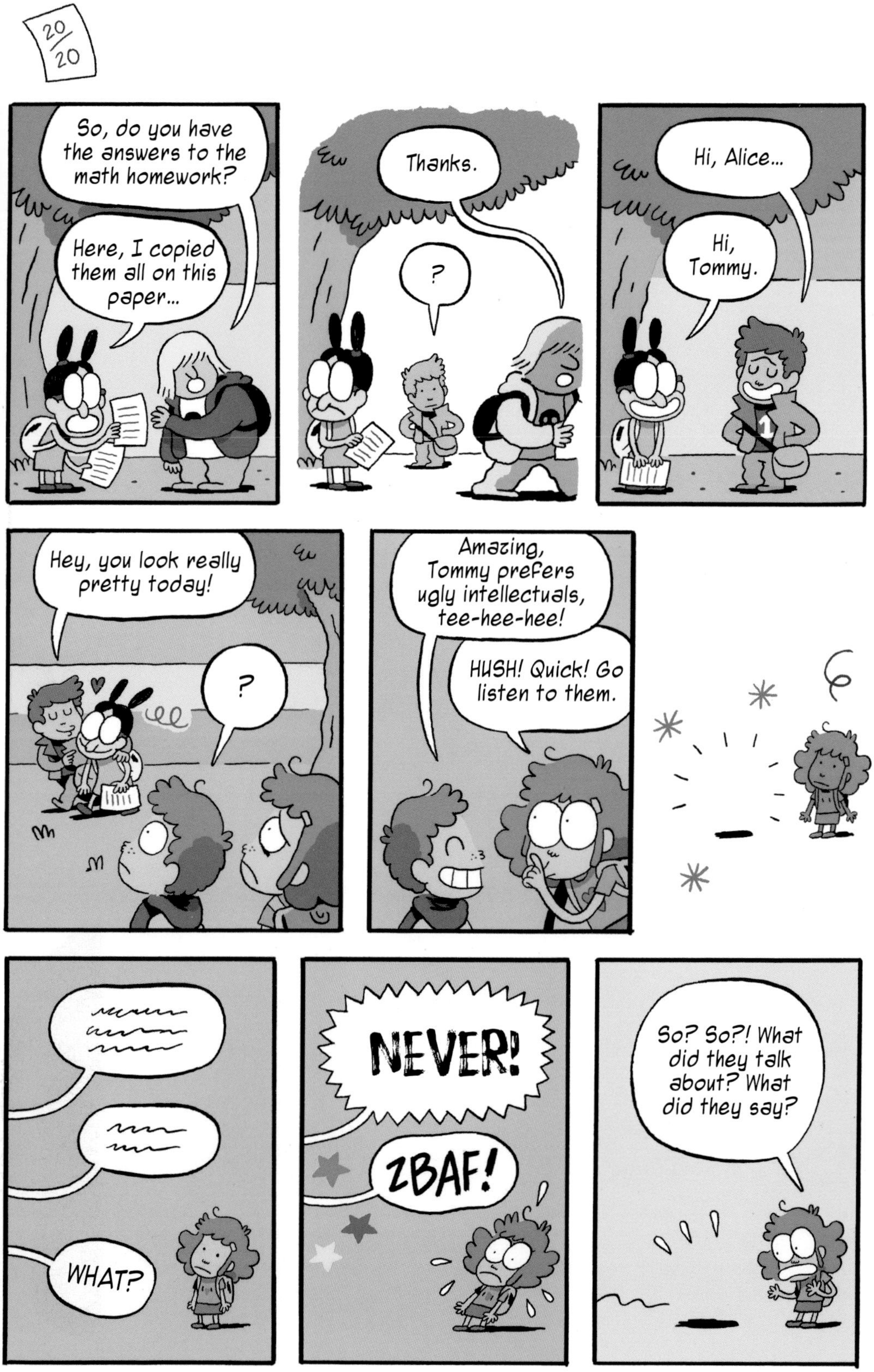
20/20
So, do you have the answers to the math homework?
Here, I copied them all on this paper...
Thanks.
?
Hi, Alice...
Hi, Tommy.
Hey, you look really pretty today!
?
Amazing, Tommy prefers ugly intellectuals, tee-hee-hee!
HUSH! Quick! Go listen to them.
WHAT?
NEVER!
ZBAF!
So? So?! What did they talk about? What did they say?

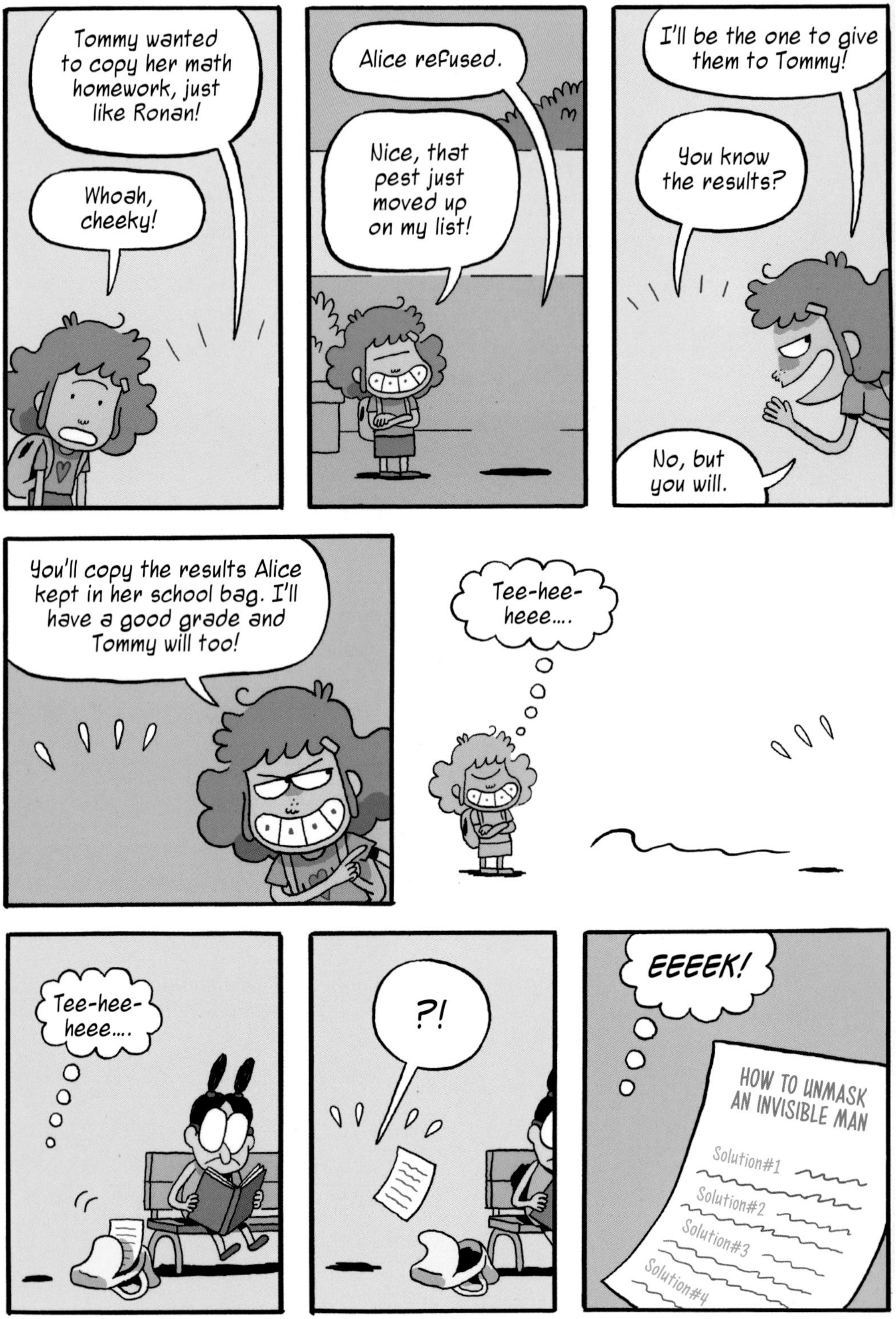
Tommy wanted to copy her math homework, just like Ronan!
Whoah, cheeky!
Alice refused.
Nice, that pest just moved up on my list!
I'll be the one to give them to Tommy!
You know the results?
No, but you will.
You'll copy the results Alice kept in her school bag. I'll have a good grade and Tommy will too!
Tee-hee-heee....
Tee-hee-heee....
?!
EEEEK!
HOW TO UNMASK AN INVISIBLE MAN
Solution#1
Solution#2
Solution#3
Solution#4

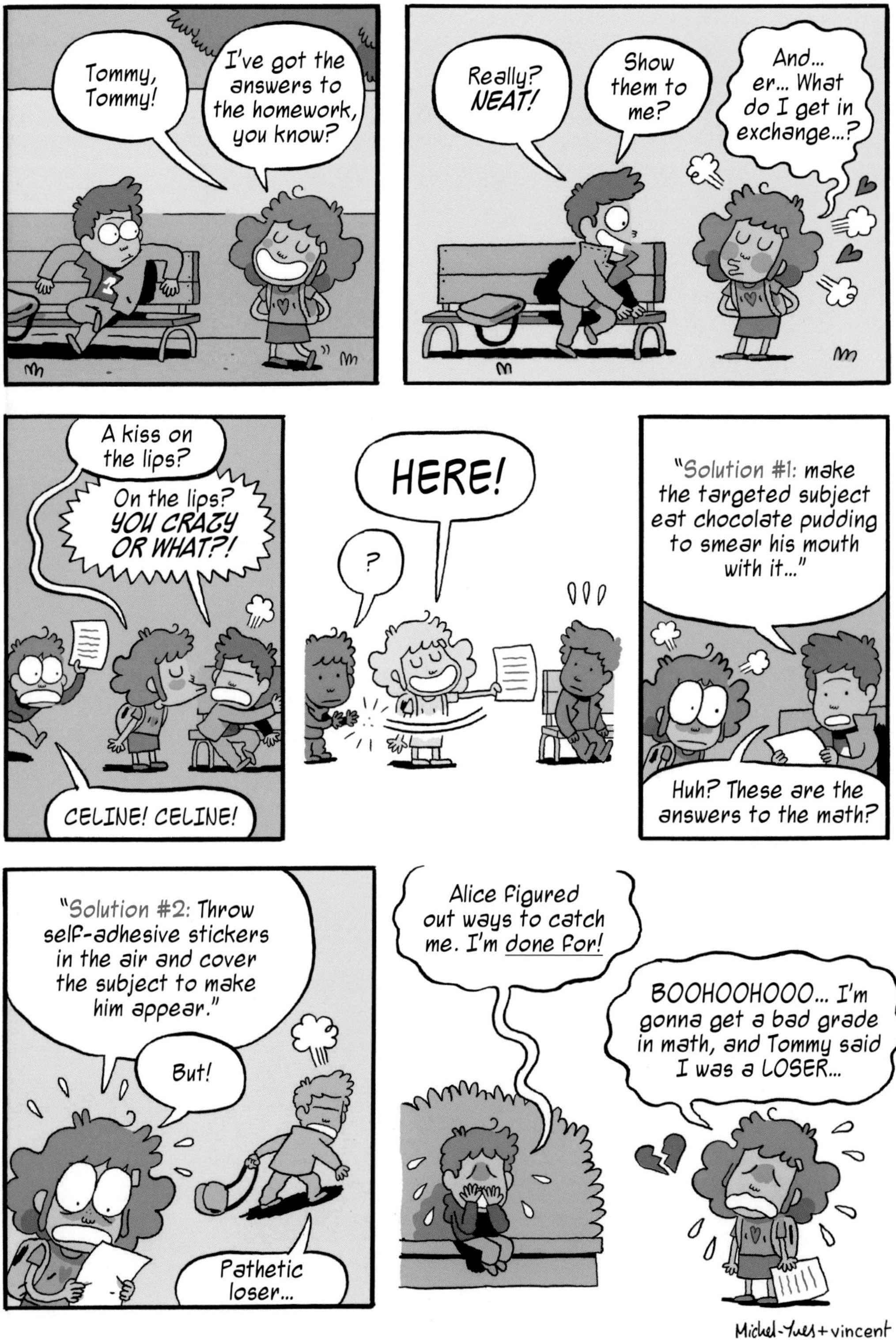
Tommy, Tommy!
I've got the answers to the homework, you know?
Really? NEAT!
Show them to me?
And... er... What do I get in exchange...?
A kiss on the lips?
On the lips? YOU CRAZY OR WHAT?!
CELINE! CELINE!
HERE!
?
"Solution #1: make the targeted subject eat chocolate pudding to smear his mouth with it..."
Huh? These are the answers to the math?
"Solution #2: Throw self-adhesive stickers in the air and cover the subject to make him appear."
But!
Pathetic loser...
Alice figured out ways to catch me. I'm done for!
BOOHOOHOOO... I'm gonna get a bad grade in math, and Tommy said I was a LOSER...
Michel-Yves+vincent

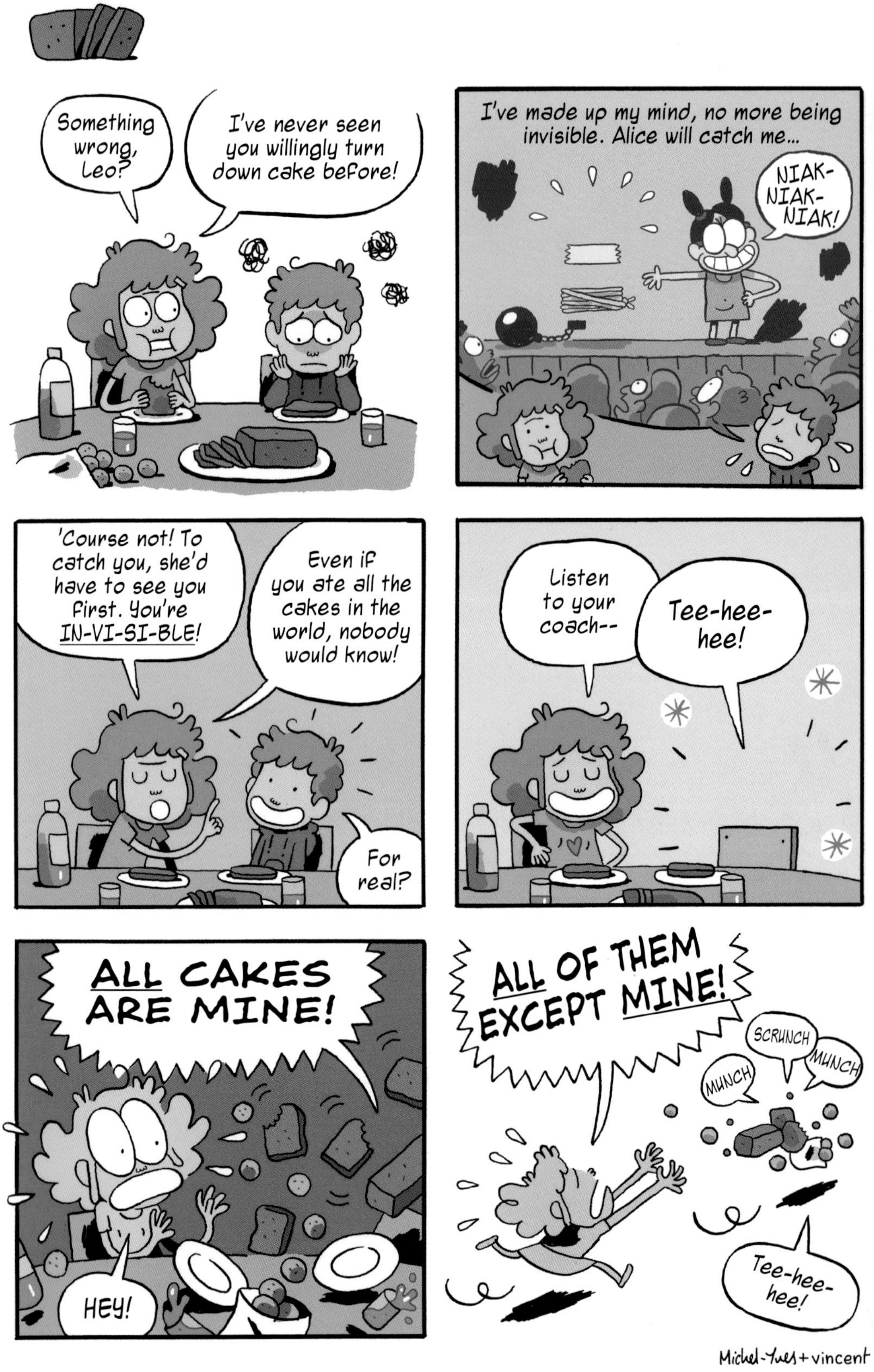

Something wrong, Leo?
I've never seen you willingly turn down cake before!
I've made up my mind, no more being invisible. Alice will catch me...
NIAK-NIAK-NIAK!
'Course not! To catch you, she'd have to see you first. You're IN-VI-SI-BLE!
Even if you ate all the cakes in the world, nobody would know!
For real?
Listen to your coach--
Tee-hee-hee!
ALL CAKES ARE MINE!
HEY!
ALL OF THEM EXCEPT MINE!
SCRUNCH
MUNCH
MUNCH
Tee-hee-hee!
Michel-Yves + vincent

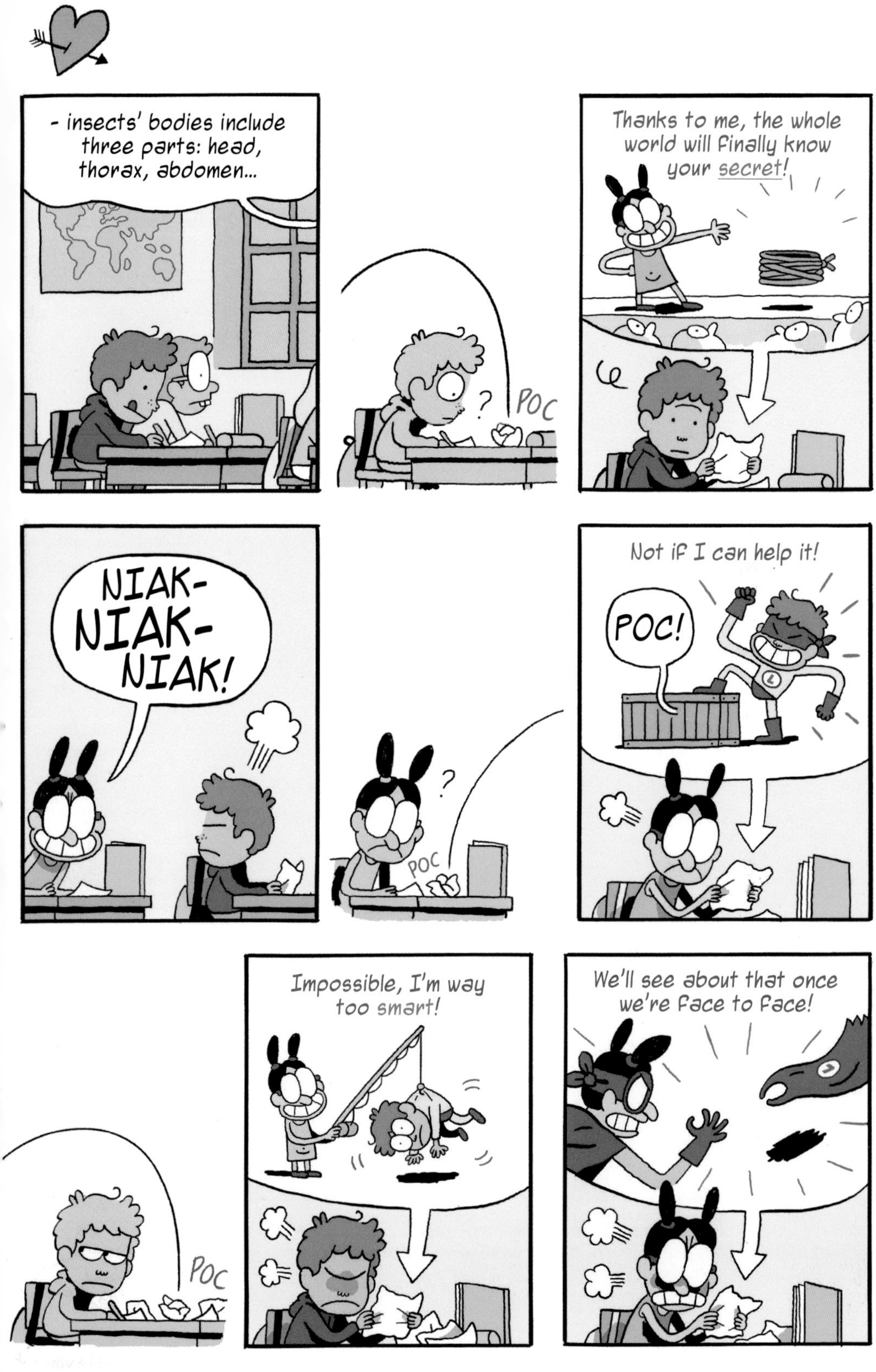
- insects' bodies include three parts: head, thorax, abdomen...
POC
Thanks to me, the whole world will finally know your secret!
NIAK-NIAK-NIAK!
POC
Not if I can help it!
POC!
Impossible, I'm way too smart!
POC
We'll see about that once we're face to face!

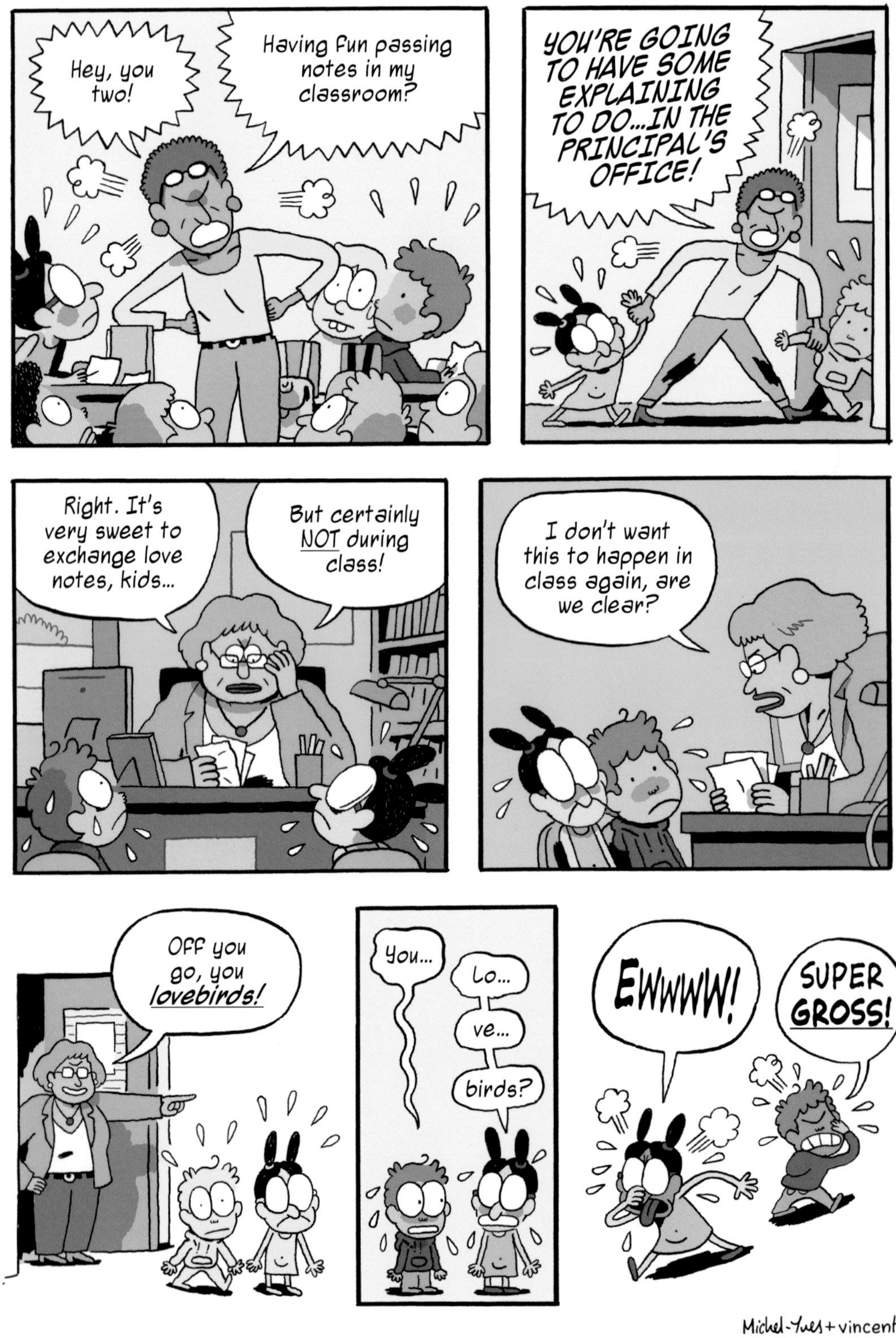
Hey, you two!
Having fun passing notes in my classroom?
YOU'RE GOING TO HAVE SOME EXPLAINING TO DO...IN THE PRINCIPAL'S OFFICE!
Right. It's very sweet to exchange love notes, kids...
But certainly NOT during class!
I don't want this to happen in class again, are we clear?
Off you go, you lovebirds!
You...
Lo...
ve...
birds?
EWWWW!
SUPER GROSS!

Michel-Yves + vincent

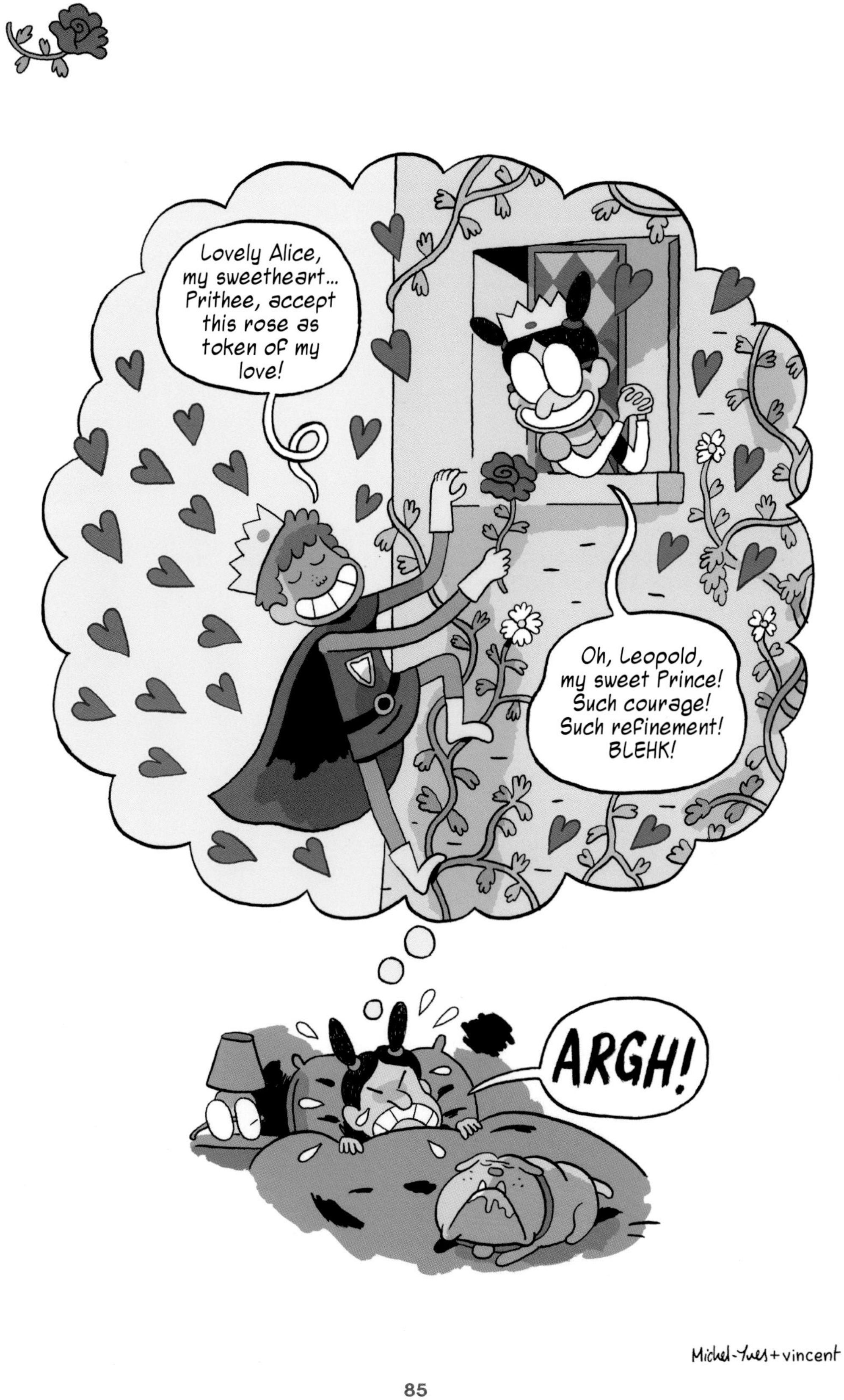
Lovely Alice, my sweetheart... Prithee, accept this rose as token of my love!
Oh, Leopold, my sweet Prince! Such courage! Such refinement! BLEHK!
ARGH!
Michel-Yves + vincent

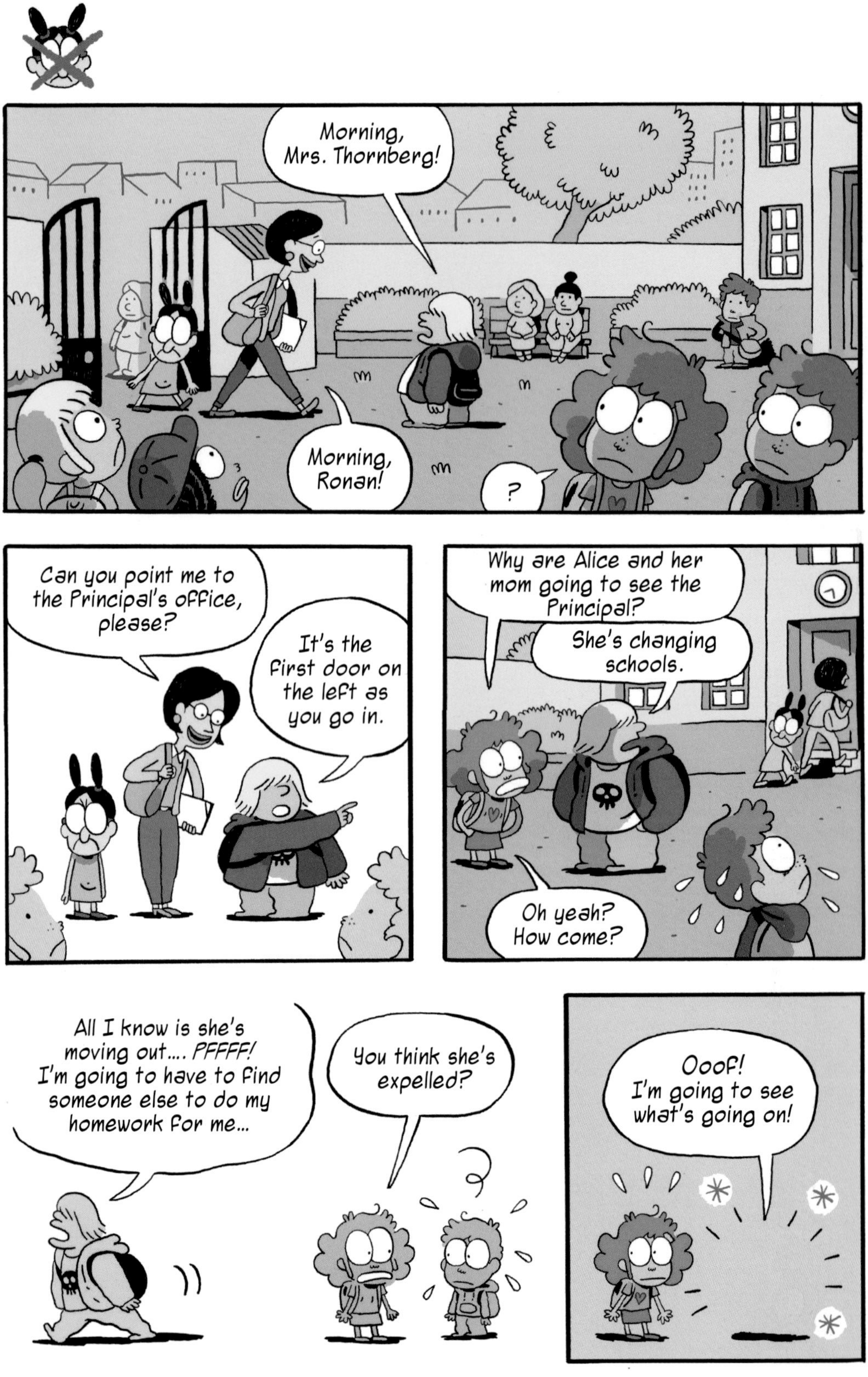
Morning,
Mrs. Thornberg!
Morning,
Ronan!
?
Can you point me to the Principal's office, please?
It's the first door on the left as you go in.
Why are Alice and her mom going to see the Principal?
She's changing schools.
Oh yeah? How come?
All I know is she's moving out.... PFFFF! I'm going to have to find someone else to do my homework for me...
You think she's expelled?
Ooof! I'm going to see what's going on!

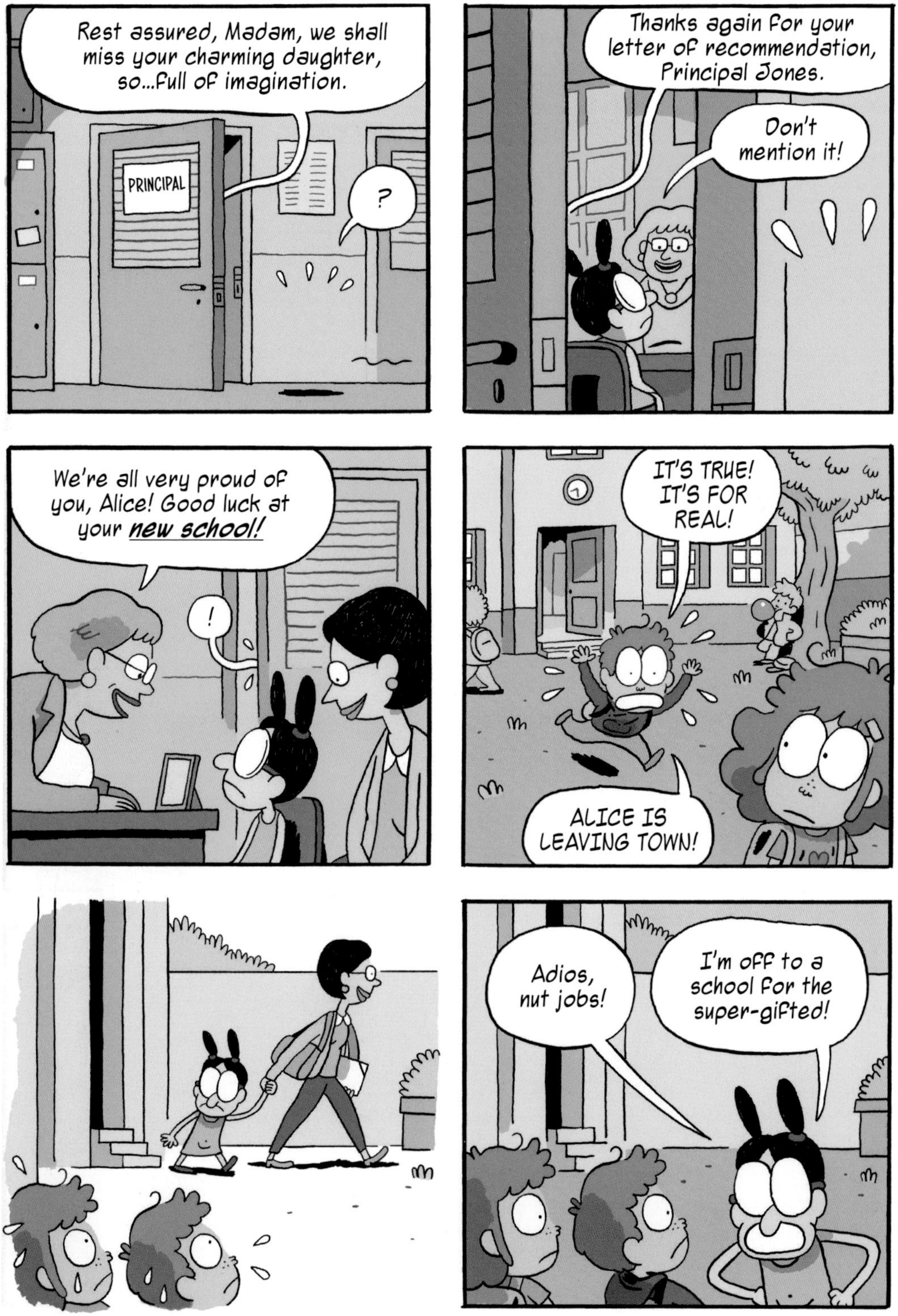
Rest assured, Madam, we shall miss your charming daughter, so...full of imagination.
PRINCIPAL
?
Thanks again for your letter of recommendation, Principal Jones.
Don't mention it!
We're all very proud of you, Alice! Good luck at your new school!
!
IT'S TRUE! IT'S FOR REAL!
ALICE IS LEAVING TOWN!
Adios, nut jobs!
I'm off to a school for the super-gifted!

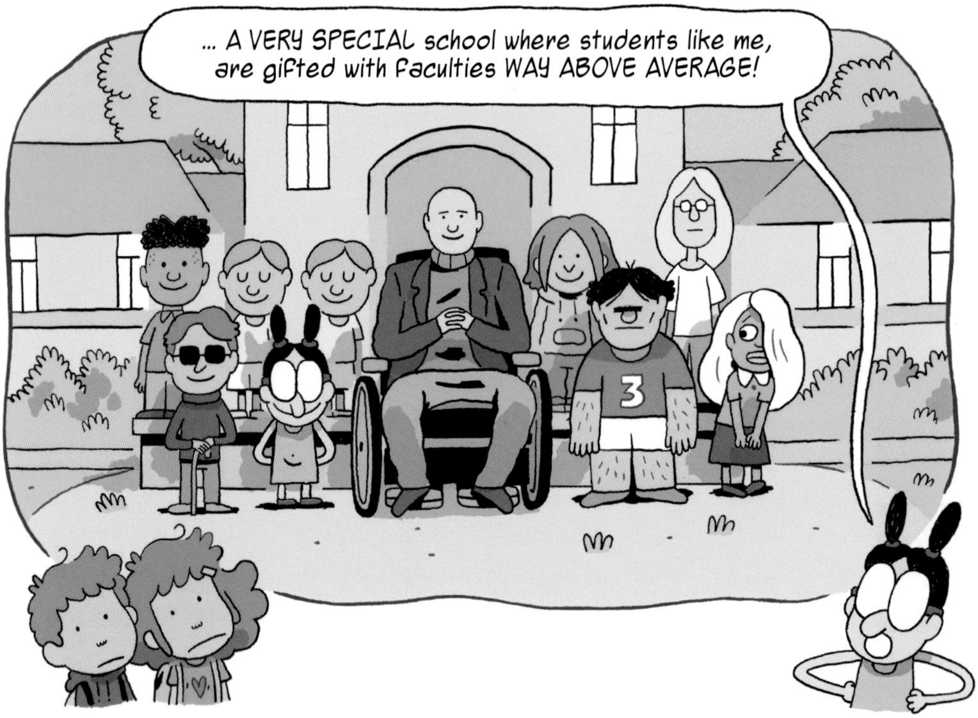
... A VERY SPECIAL school where students like me, are gifted with faculties WAY ABOVE AVERAGE!

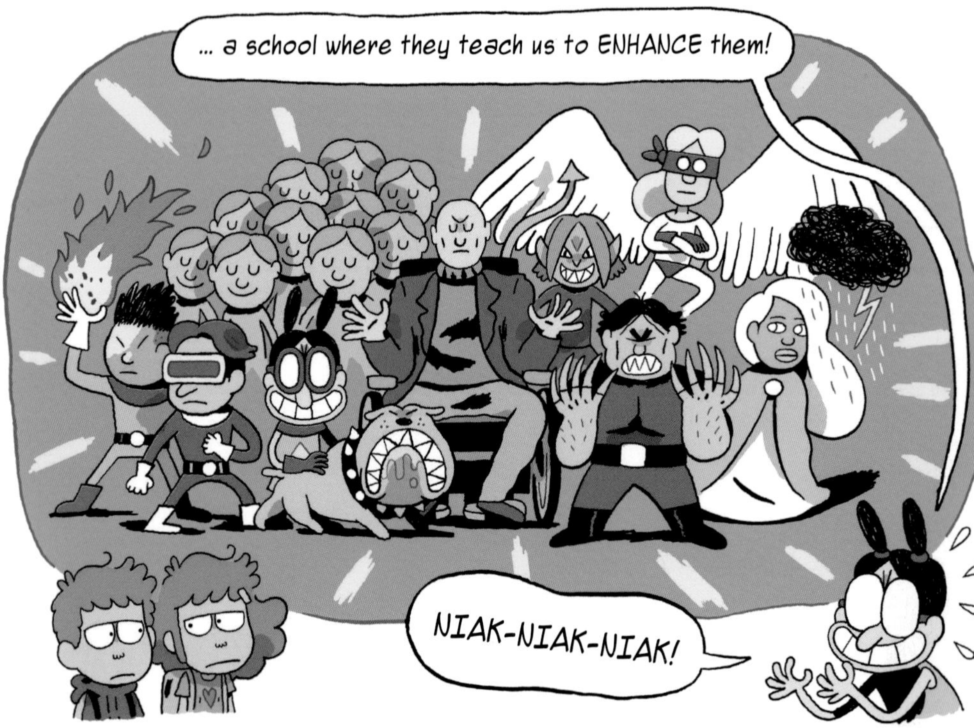
... a school where they teach us to ENHANCE them!
NIAK-NIAK-NIAK!

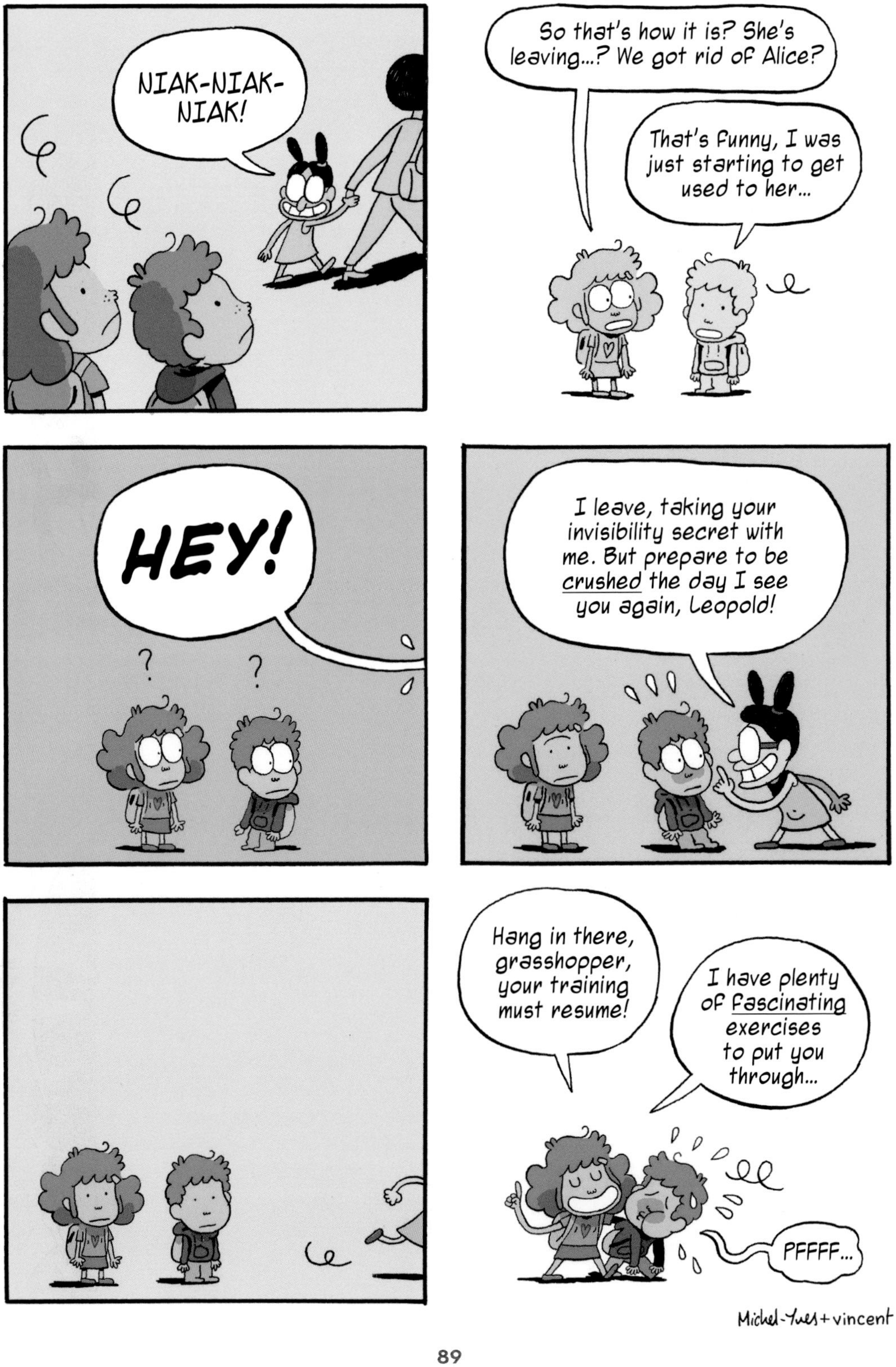
NIAK-NIAK-NIAK!
So that's how it is? She's leaving...? We got rid of Alice?
That's funny, I was just starting to get used to her...
HEY!
?
?
I leave, taking your invisibility secret with me. But prepare to be crushed the day I see you again, Leopold!
Hang in there, grasshopper, your training must resume!
I have plenty of fascinating exercises to put you through...
PFFFF...
Michel-Yves + vincent

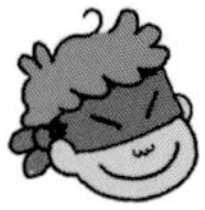

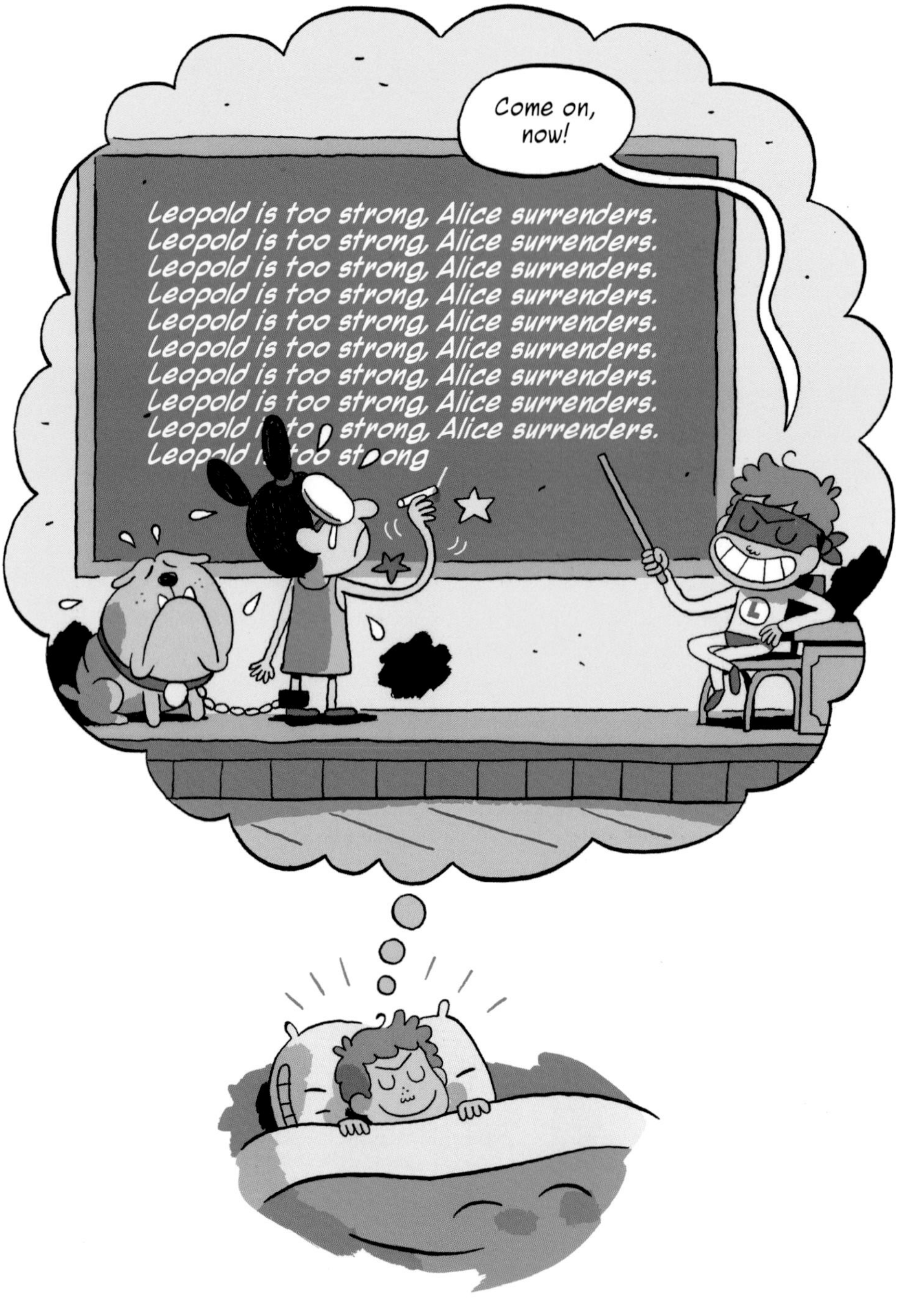

Come on, now!
Leopold is too strong, Alice surrenders.
Leopold is too strong, Alice surrenders.
Leopold is too strong, Alice surrenders.
Leopold is too strong, Alice surrenders.
Leopold is too strong, Alice surrenders.
Leopold is too strong, Alice surrenders.
Leopold is too strong, Alice surrenders.
Leopold is too strong, Alice surrenders.
Leopold strong, Alice surrenders.
Leop too st ong

Michel-Yves + vincent

SPOT THE DIFFERENCES

Play WITH Leopold

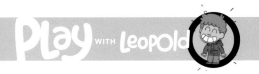

Leo messed around in Celine's room! It's up to you, dear reader, to spot the 12 differences!

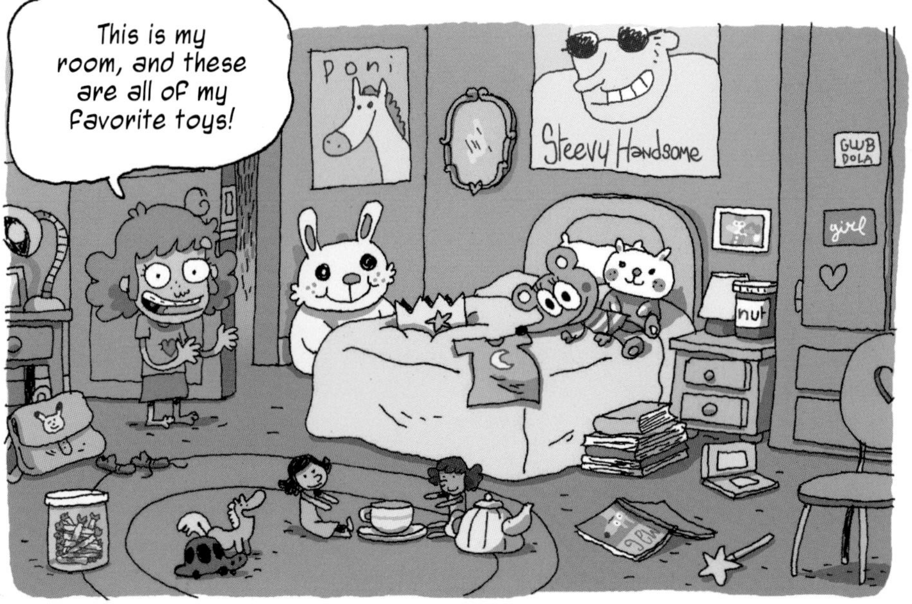
This is my room, and these are all of my favorite toys!
poni
Steevy Handsome
GWB DOLA
girl
nut

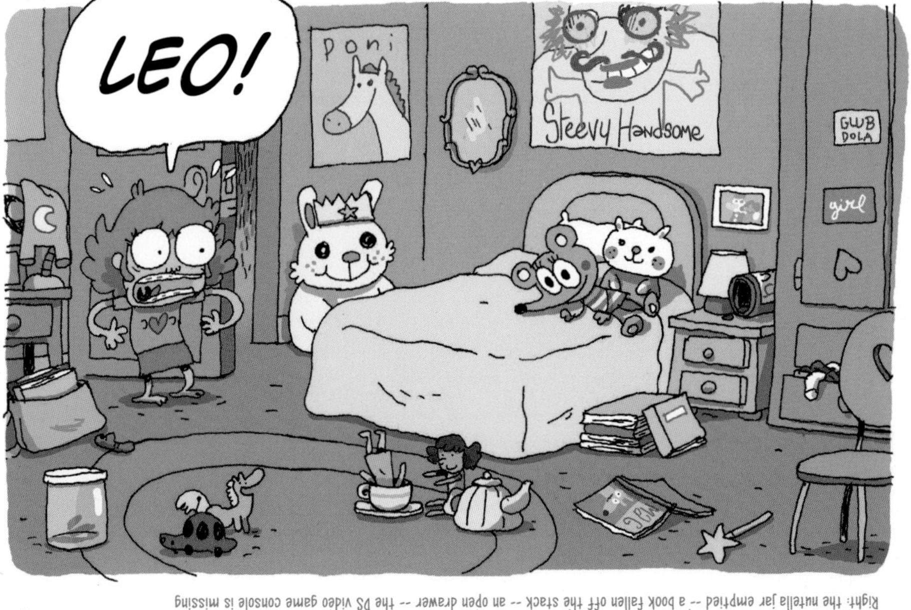
LEO!
poni
Steevy Handsome
GWB DOLA
girl

Answers:
Left: the blue t-shirt from the bed on the lamp -- the open school bag -- a pink slipper is missing -- the empty curly wurly jar -- the backwards red car
Center: the bed's crown on the yellow rabbit -- the poster of Steevy Handsome with make up -- a doll on the floor sunk head first into a tea cup
Right: the nutella jar emptied -- a book fallen off the stack -- an open drawer -- the PS video game console is missing

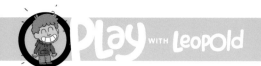

ON THE RUN!

Leopold has managed to escape once again, but he won't get away so easily. Help Alice to trace his steps by using the same path he did.

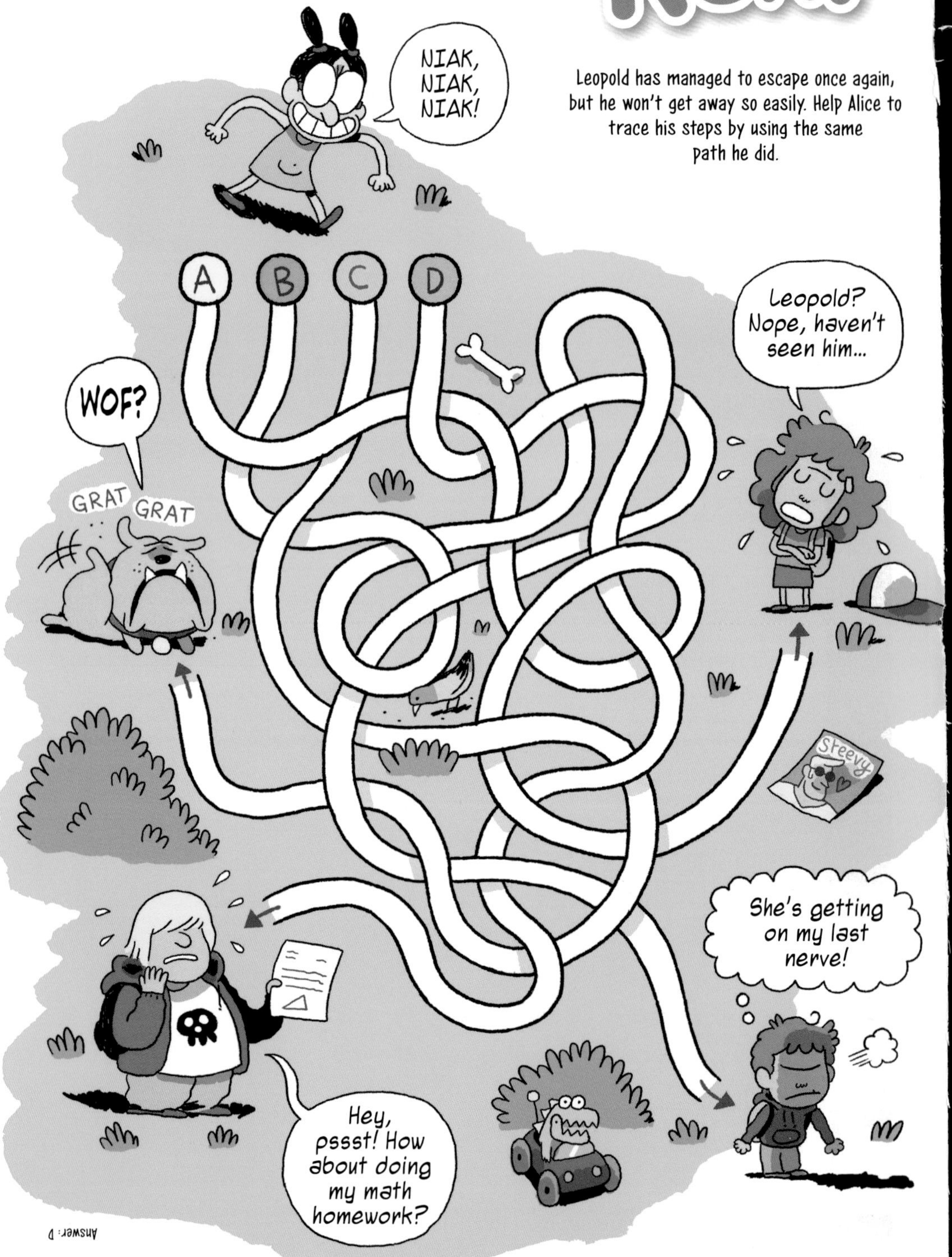
NIAK, NIAK, NIAK!
A
B
C
D
Leopold? Nope, haven't seen him...
WOF?
GRAT GRAT
Steevy
She's getting on my last nerve!
Hey, pssst! How about doing my math homework?

Answer: D

WHO'S AFRAID?

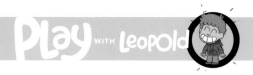

At night, danger is lurking around every corner! And Celine and Leopold might be caught in its grasp! Can you help them identify this threat? Answer the questions and follow the instructions...

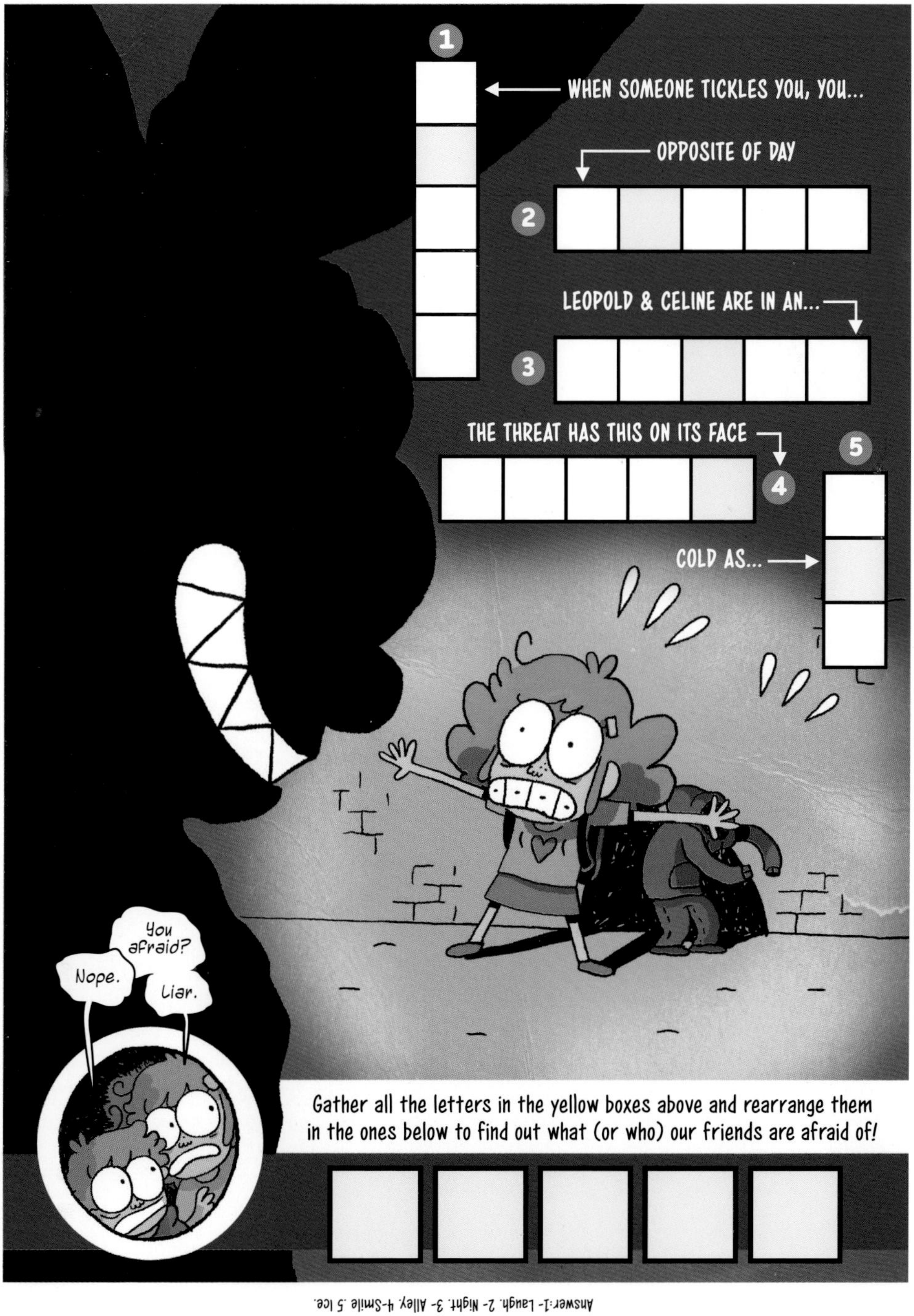
1
WHEN SOMEONE TICKLES YOU, YOU...
OPPOSITE OF DAY
2
LEOPOLD & CELINE ARE IN AN...
3
THE THREAT HAS THIS ON ITS FACE
4
5
COLD AS...
You afraid?
Nope.
Liar.
Gather all the letters in the yellow boxes above and rearrange them in the ones below to find out what (or who) our friends are afraid of!

Answer:1- Laugh. 2- Night. 3- Alley. 4-Smile. 5 Ice.

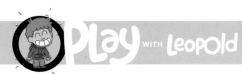

THE MISSING PIECE

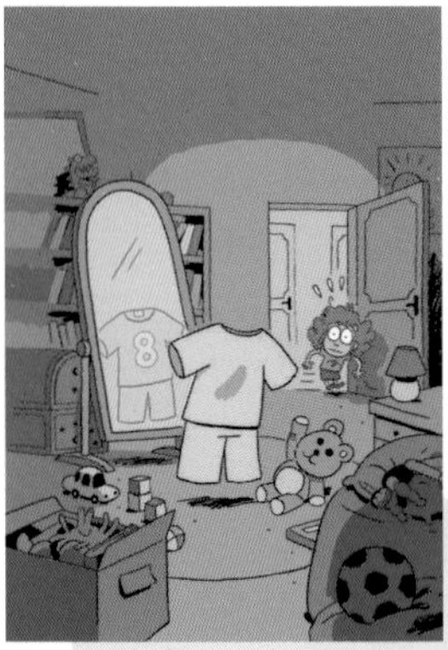

Leopold has cut up the cover to his own book! Celine has been trying to piece it back together but a piece is missing. Can you help her find which part of the image isn't there?

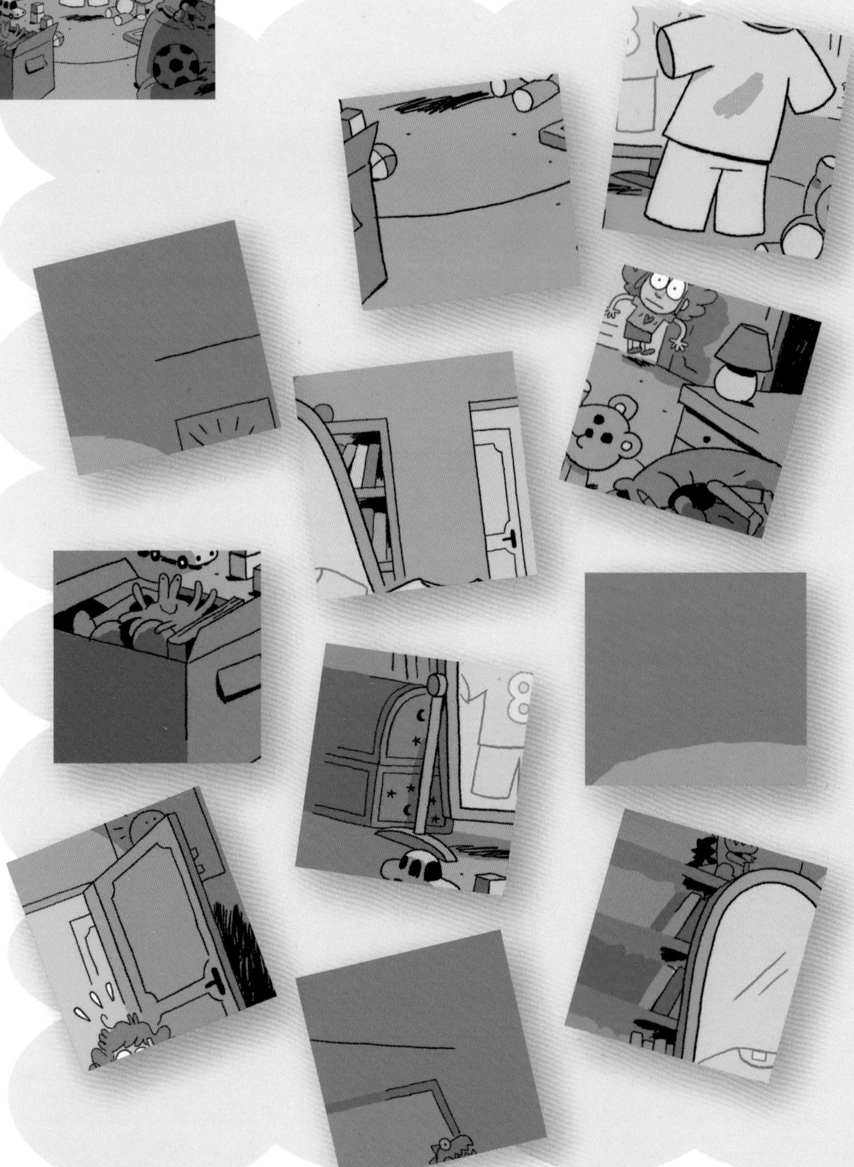

Answer: the part with the soccer ball.

INVISIBLE TROUBLE

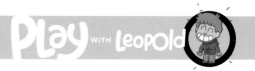

Uh-oh! Leopold has lost his invisibility powers and now someone else has inherited them. But Celine doesn't know who it is. Can you help her find out by connecting the dots by color?

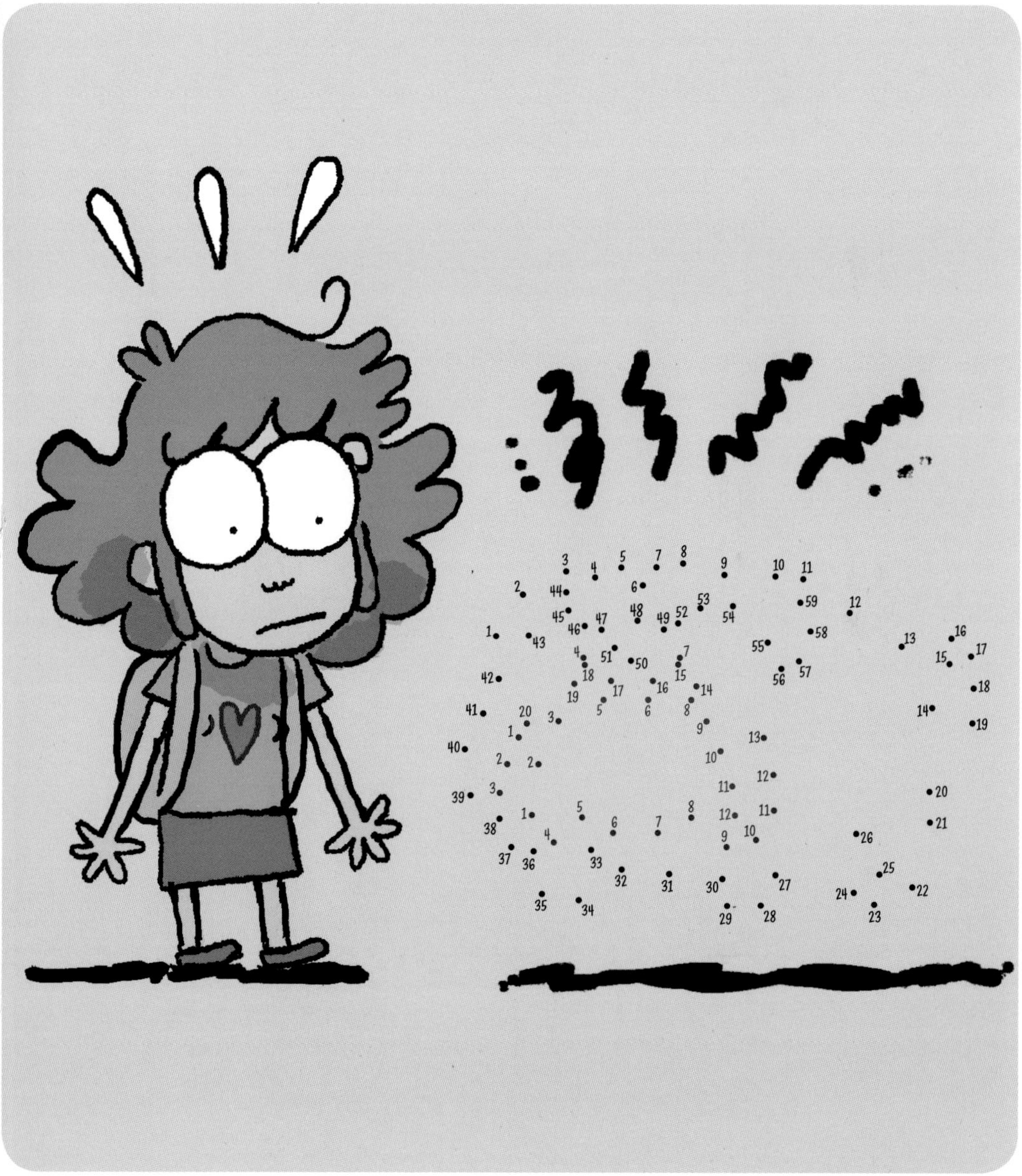

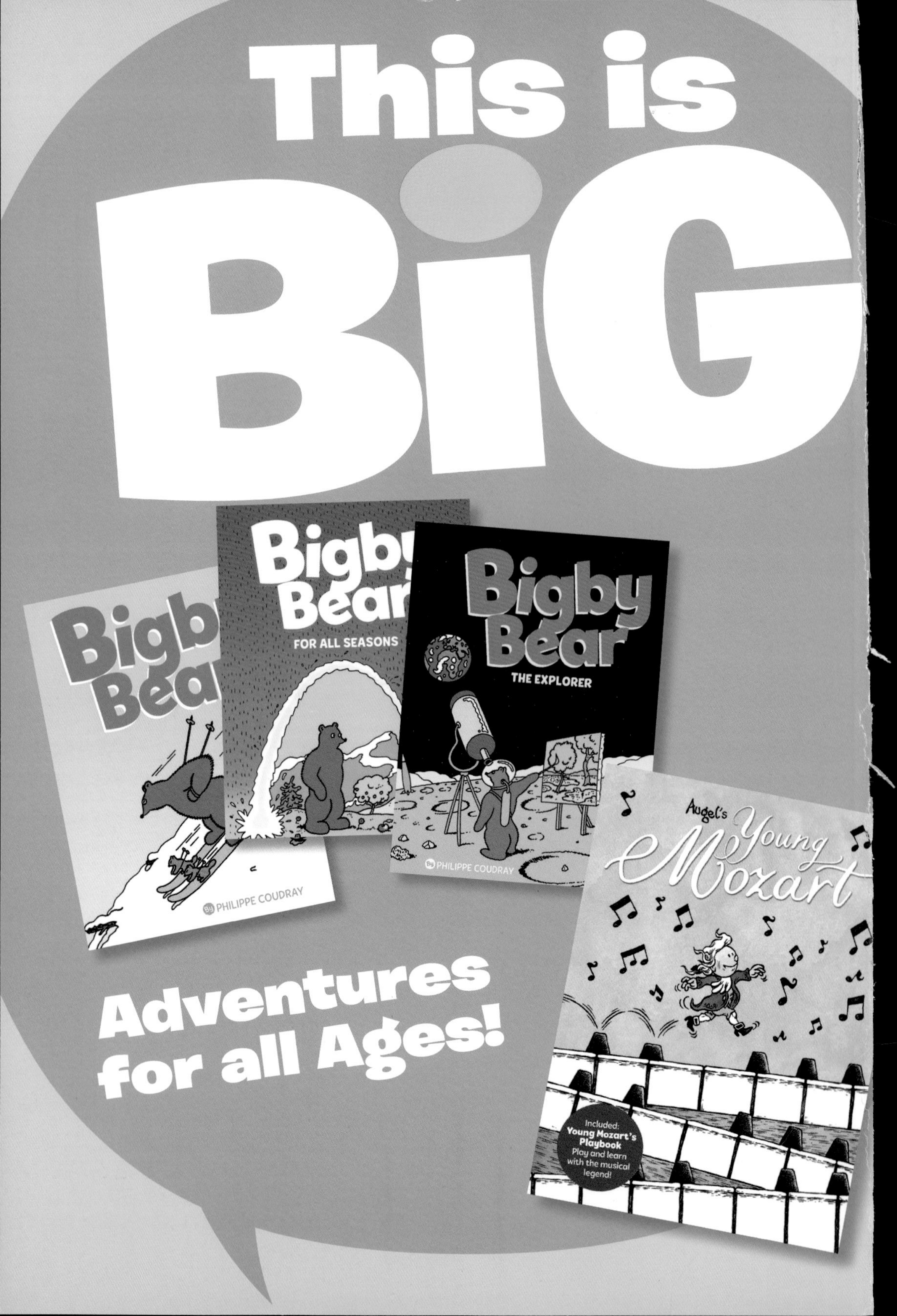
This is BiG
Bigby Bear
PHILIPPE COUDRAY
Bigby Bear
FOR ALL SEASONS
Bigby Bear
THE EXPLORER
PHILIPPE COUDRAY
Augel's Young Mozart
Included: Young Mozart's Playbook Play and learn with the musical legend!
Adventures for all Ages!